With mounting courage, he faced the dragon . . .

"Go away," he said. The dragon stood there, looking more and more frustrated and angry, its mean little eyes blinking rapidly, the sickly looking milky membrane covering and uncovering them, the fangs dripping drool. "It isn't listening," Miles told Cecily. "Oh God, it isn't listening." The dragon had them cornered.

"Foul monster, confront an armed knight!" Lancelot commanded, and drew it off, swinging his sword to get its attention. Arthur meanwhile scaled the cliffside to reach high ground and Guinevere. The dragon breathed on Lancelot, heating the armor to a red glow. Just like that. No strategy, no cunning. Just one blast of fire and Lancelot screamed and fell backwards into the stream . . .

—from "The Camelot Connection"
by Elizabeth Ann Scarborough

Invitation to Camelot

An Arthurian anthology of short stories

EDITED BY PARKE GODWIN

ACE BOOKS, NEW YORK

INVITATION TO CAMELOT

An Ace Book / published by arrangement with
the editor

PRINTING HISTORY
Ace edition / March 1988

ISBN: 0-441-37200-7

Ace Books are published by The Berkley Publishing Group,
200 Madison Avenue, New York, NY 10016.
The name ''Ace'' and the ''A'' logo
are trademarks belonging to Charter Communications, Inc.

PRINTED IN THE UNITED STATES OF AMERICA

10 9 8 7 6 5 4 3 2 1

CONTENTS

Foreword

As a dinner host, I try to invite the sort of people who can speak and charm for themselves, so I usually shut up and let them. For *Invitation to Camelot* I asked each of my guests to bring a story centered about or bearing on the Camelot Cycle in some way. They could adhere to Canon or wander afield as they liked. Surprisingly, almost every writer said, "Well, I *did* have an idea floating around, something I've been wanting to try." Or: "There was an idea that I couldn't get into my last book, but it really belongs there."

All I said was, "Come as you are."

The result is a gathering of tales not quite traditional but deeply imbued with an understanding of the Arthurian Canon and a willingness to explore neglected byways. Some are fascinatingly synthetic: well-known facets of the legends meet head on to create a third, not fleshed out until now.

There is a very good reason for JANE YOLEN's lovely lyric poem "The Storyteller" to preface these tales. It defines, far beyond my own abilities, what a storyteller does and has been doing since men gathered to listen to wonders about a fire. "Once there was/ and there was not,/ . . . It is all true./ It is not true./ . . . I am not paid to tell you the truth."

The storyteller does more than tell; he or she invokes.

I've brought eleven of them to join us. Welcome to Camelot.

Parke Godwin
January, 1986

The Storyteller

Jane Yolen

He unpacks his bag of tales
with fingers quick
as a weaver's
picking the weft threads,
threading the warp.
Watch his fingers.
Watch his lips
speaking the old, familiar words:

> "Once there was
> and there was not,
> oh, best beloved,
> when the world was filled with wishes
> the way the sea is filled with fishes . . ."

All those threads
pulling us back
to another world, another time
when goosegirls married well
and frogs could rhyme,

when maids spoke syllables of pearl
and stepmothers came to grief.

Belief is the warp
and the sharp-picked pattern
of motif
reminds us that Araby
is not so far;
that the pleasure dome
of a Baghdad caliph
sits side by side
with the rush-roofed home
of a Tattercoat or an animal bride.

Cinderella wears a shoe
first fitted in the East
where her prince—
no more a beast
than the usual run of royal son—
measures her nobility
by the lotus foot,
so many inches to the reign.
Then the slipper made glass
by a slip of ear and tongue.
All tales are mistakes
made true by the telling.

The watching eye takes in the hue,
the listening ear the word,
but all they comprehend is Art.
A story must be worn again
before the magic garment
fits the ready heart.

The storyteller is done.
He packs his bag.
But watch his fingers
and his lips.
It is the oldest feat

of prestidigitation.
What you saw,
what you heard,
was equal to a new Creation.

The colors blur,
time is now.
He speaks his final piece
before his final bow:

> "It is all true,
> it is not true.
> The more I tell you,
> The more I shall lie.
> What is story
> but jesting Pilate's cry.
> I am not paid to tell you the
> truth."

I know MORGAN LLYWELYN well enough to make one unassailable statement. Knock her down ten times, she'll get up eleven, and one extra just to show you you shouldn't have tried it in the first place. And maybe spit in your eye.

She is as indomitable as the Celts she writes about. I've always suspected Morgan should be a character in one of her own books.

After missing the U.S. Olympic horsemanship team by a heartbreaking fraction of a point, Morgan published her first historical novel, The Wind From Hastings, *in 1978, followed by the bestseller,* Lion of Ireland, The Horse Goddess, *and the beautiful symphony of a book,* Bard. *Her latest,* Grania, *the true story of the Irish pirate Grace O'Malley, was published by Crown in 1986.*

Morgan is usually on the run between her typewriter, Ireland, and New York, always with more to do than there's time for, which is one definition of success. The following story is completely within the bounds of Arthurian Canon, but still . . . not quite what you'd expect.

But neither is Morgan Llywelyn.

Their Son

by Morgan Llywelyn

Splendid and shining she was, my mother. I will always remember her as she was in my childhood, and none of the accusations I have since heard made against her can destroy that image.

The dark recesses of my memory are lit by sudden bright flashes of her. I see her leaning over the little carved bedbox where I slept, and she is smiling. Her hair, soft as rain, pours unbound over her shoulders, and her chuckle is warm when she bends to tickle me.

Even as a small lad I knew there was something different about her, of course—and something different about me, too, for I was her son. Others looked at her sidelong when they looked at her at all, and I heard caution in their voices. It was not the deference accorded to royalty, such as Arthur and his court, but the caution bred of fear. People feared my mother, my lissome, laughing mother, and I was obscurely proud of her for it. Until I began to suffer for it.

Other children who lived near the forest that was our home would not play with me. I was too young to know the meanings of the words when I first heard them call me by-blow, and woods-colt, and then something even darker, which made them snigger as they said it. Bastard they called me, shouting at me tauntingly from a safe distance when I approached, seeking playmates.

I asked my mother about it and there were tears of pain in my eyes, for I knew I had been insulted but did not understand why.

Her cheeks burned red with anger. "They are ignorant little scamps, forget about them," she said. "I will be your playfellow." And she sang to me and danced and devised a hundred different games, so I was content for a little while.

Then the longing for companionship came over me again, and I searched out other children only to be called bastard once more, by crueler voices. This time, when I begged her to explain, she told me, "It merely means you were not born from a priest-blessed union. In the Celtic way that does not matter, for every child is legitimate. How can it be otherwise? Yet the Christian priests have their own law and under it the innocent sometimes suffer."

"What union?" I demanded to know, putting grimy little fists on my hips and staring up into her face. I was growing older. "Who was my father, and why do we never see him?"

My mother's eyes were the color of smoke, and I swear they could see right through my head, to the very back of my skull. "Do not ask me to speak of your father," she whispered. I had never seen such pain as I saw in her face then, and I was frightened. So for a time the question was not asked again.

There were other things to stir my curiosity. My mother went into the heart of the forest alone, and there she performed rituals of great power which were so secret I did not even know their purpose. She left me alone in our cottage during these times, with an owl at the door to watch me and warn her if I tried to follow. I never doubted that she could speak to the owl, though I did not see her do it. But my mother could do many things that were beyond mere mortal ability; my splendid, shining mother.

When I was overcome with loneliness I sometimes begged her to take me with her, but she would just bite her lip and shake her head, and regard me with those slow, sweet eyes. It was useless to try to change her mind. She was a stubborn woman and nothing ever dissuaded her.

I began to think I hated her. Her reputation denied me the society of friends, and her secretiveness denied me any knowledge of my own heritage. In my loneliness I began to dream, as children will, of a secret parent more noble than any other child possessed. Perhaps I was hidden away in the forest because my sire was a great man who could, for some mysterious grownup reason, never acknowledge me. Perhaps —oh, surely!—the day would come when I would perform a deed so bold he would set aside his reserve and claim me as his son before the world, and I could walk away from my mother's lonely cottage into a shaft of brilliant light.

Such dreams I dreamed, in my childhood.

They were nurtured by the tales everyone repeated in those days, even the occasional tradesman who dared our pathway. So it was I heard of Arthur's knights and their quests, of their valor and daring and their women. Not all of them were married by Christian priests to the women with whom their names were linked. The older I grew, the more apparent that became, and I gave it a good deal of thought.

Perhaps one of Arthur's heroes was my father. In secret I whispered the famous names to myself: Gawain and Gareth, Geraint and Balin, Balan and . . . Lancelot. There was not one of them who did not know where she lived, my mother, for in one season or another every one of them had had some dealings with her.

A few were dealings they wished kept secret, occasions when one of their servants arrived at our door with hooded head and whispering voice, to beg a charm or philtre of which their own priests would not approve. But in the high bright days of summer Arthur's men came more openly into our territory.

My mother's principal support was an orchard she had planted at the edge of our forest. Each tree had been set out according to the phases of the moon and the lines of power radiating through the earth from the stones, mysteries my mother understood full well. Her trees yielded a richer harvest than any in the kingdom, and more than once I caught a glimpse, from my hiding place in the woods, of a knight on his caparisoned charger galloping among mother's trees, helping himself to a ripe pear hot with the sun.

I wondered about the mysteries, and the knights . . . I wondered so many things.

As soon as I was old enough to bestride a broom handle, I played at being a knight myself, galloping on my two legs and swinging a sword (a wooden cooking spoon) at dragons. But one cannot be a hero without an audience. So when the first stirrings of manhood touched me, I swaggered off to the nearest village to challenge the boys there—boys who had once ridiculed me.

They beat me half to death, of course.

They may have been afraid of my mother, but she was not with me. In my ignorance and bravado I must have made a very tempting target. Bruised and bloody, I crept home with one eye swollen shut. My mother met me halfway, as if she had expected me. No doubt she had; she always seemed to know what was going to happen.

"This is your fault!" I shouted at her in my humiliation. "I don't have any friends because of you. What have you done that is so terrible? Why do I have to suffer for it?"

She put her slim hand on my shoulder but I pulled away. "I did not want to see you hurt. . . ."

"Then make me stronger than everyone else, so I won't be hurt!" I demanded. "I know you can do it, you're a witch, aren't you? A sorceress? That's what they whisper about you. Give me some of your powers."

She looked alarmed. "You don't know what you're asking. You foolish child, would you run headlong down the same path to destruction that others have followed? I want better for you than that."

"And I want to be a warrior," I told her, slamming my fist against my palm for emphasis. "I want my own life, to live my own way. Send me to my father, whoever he is, let him train me to my station in life."

Her laugh was bitter. "Your station in life. Ah, yes, it would come to that, wouldn't it? Are those the first sprouts of a beard I see you starting?" She tried to touch my cheek but suddenly the feel of a woman's finger was unbearable to me and again I avoided her touch. I saw the hurt in her eyes but I did not care; I hurt, too.

"Some men are born to be warriors," my mother said, "and some have other gifts. You have your own talent, one that came to you in your blood. You must discover it for yourself and learn to use it. I will not cast some spell over you to make you invincible."

"Then at least tell me what blood is in my veins, so I can know what to expect of myself," I pleaded with her.

To my astonishment she burst into tears, a thing I had never seen her do before. She covered her face with her hands and bent double, wracked with sobs. I could hardly make out what she was saying, but her words seemed to be, "How much you look like him right now! Oh, it tears my heart beyond bearing!"

"His name!" I yelled at her. But she would not tell me. "You are too young for that burden," was all she said.

Nothing rankles like being told one is too young. Since the years cannot be speeded up, everything else must. I immediately began to attempt my own training as a warrior, devising weapons out of household tools and finally cutting off one toe in an abortive attempt to use a woodsman's axe for battle-axe practice. The sad truth was, I was inept. My mother knew it. I saw her watching me in silence, and that made me all the angrier.

Perhaps she wanted me angry. Perhaps she wanted to add fuel to my fires, so that in time I could be used for her own purposes. The thought occurred to me as I lay, sleepless and frustrated, in my bed, and one day when she was off in the forest I packed my possessions and abandoned the cottage, leaving the door agape to tell her what had happened.

I threw a rock at the owl as I passed him, and he hooted at me.

There were few roads in Arthur's kingdom. Here and there was a bit of old Roman highway, but the stones were frost-heaved and choked among weeds. For the most part people used roads pounded into dust or mud by generations of cattle being driven to market, or carved out through the woodlands by hunters. I traveled wherever whim took me, sleeping in caves or tree hollows or underneath the stars when the weather was good. My mother knew the patterns of those stars and what they meant, but she had never taught me.

For what purpose was I born?

When I had grown more, and proved myself in the world on my own terms, I meant to go back to her and show her what I had become.

But it is not an easy thing to prove yourself in the world. It is not even an easy thing to stay alive, to get enough to eat and a wrap to keep yourself warm in the wintertime. Having no training, I could not boast of having apprenticed to my father the carpenter or my father the bard. When I came to a settlement I encountered suspicion and sometimes open hostility. Everyone within five days' ride of Camelot seemed to know something of my mother, and my resemblance to her was enough to make them whisper and turn away from me.

But she had said I resembled someone else too. If only one person would say to me, "You remind me of your father, of Sir . . ."

No one did. And no one encouraged my friendship, so I could not ask. It seemed as if the whole world knew a terrible secret about me but I myself did not.

I ventured farther from Camelot, into regions of marsh and mountain where Arthur's name was still known but the details of his society were less familiar. I taught myself to hunt and fish, and in that way was able to keep some flesh on my bones. And as I grew I acquired enough muscle to be good for hard labor, if nothing else. A young man does not require either a name or a paternity to do hard labor.

In a remote corner of the land, a stonemason named Agglovale took me in and put me to minding his fire and sharpening his tools. He soon discovered that I had a talent for finding the fracture line on a stone, that place where it could most easily be broken. I was of some value, then; I could learn a trade, and live a peasant's life and be content.

But a peasant's life did not seem to suit me.

Sometimes in secret I tried to see if I had any of my mother's gift for sorcery. In spite of her efforts to conceal her womanly secrets, I had occasionally slept with one eye opened and watched as she brewed potions or made signs of power with her fingers. I had noted in particular the gestures with which she seemed able to stop the rain, and when a hard rain fell in the stonemason's region I undertook to stop it, without telling anyone.

I was no better at magic than I had been at swordplay.

The rain became a deluge that rotted the barley in the fields and gave us all terrible mud sores on our feet. The season turned into a disaster; there would be no fodder for the livestock to carry them through the winter, and everyone was sick with chills and fevers. And still it rained.

I felt miserable.

The stonemason had a daughter. I have since learned that many stonemasons have daughters, and many of them are as homely as Elyse was. But in my early manhood I did not think her so homely, because she was the only young female within my reach and she was nice to me. I suspect she might have been very nice to me indeed if her father had not kept such a strict watch on her, but she was his only daughter and the old man was something of a tyrant.

One day when she delivered our meal to the hut where we worked, Elyse lingered beside me. Old Agglovale had his back to us, he did not see the glances she was giving me from beneath her stubby lashes. "My father has no sons, you know," she said. "If some young man were to marry me, all this would be his someday."

She was not subtle, Elyse. And "all this" consisted of a hard, poor business in a hard, poor region. But the girl had down on her upper lip and round swellings in her bodice that tempted my hands, so I wanted to impress her. Without thinking, I said, "I might inherit much more than a mason's business. I come from noble stock."

The words were still wet on my tongue when Agglovale grabbed my elbow. He was old, but he was very strong. "That's what ye are, is it? Some knight's stripling lad, come here to dally with the daughter of an honest working man? Ye thought ye had me fooled, but I've known all along there was something false about yerself!" He had his heavy mallet in one hand and he raised it as he spoke, as if to crush my skull. "There've been enough of yer kind ridin' through the land of late!" he cried.

In that moment I envied Elyse, having a father so quick to jump to her defense. But in the same moment I realized he might well kill me, and his strength undoubtedly exceeded mine. Needles seemed to prickle through every inch of my skin with the rush of my fear.

And that same surge of emotion opened some kind of a door within me. I actually heard the click; I felt the release.

With an effort entirely of my mind, I caught Agglovale's upraised arm and held it immobile. I saw the shock on his face, for both my hands were still upraised in front of my face to defend myself. Yet he was surely held, and then, while he and I and Elyse all watched in astonishment, my mind made him twist the mallet and slam it down against his own thigh with such a forceful blow it knocked the leg from under him.

He fell on the floor, howling with pain, and the girl crouched over him. She cast me one furious look before bending to soothe him. "Sorcerer!" she accused.

I fled from the place. I knew Agglovale was not killed, there was nothing mortal about his injury. But I could have destroyed him. I could have turned his own strength against him and made him kill himself where he stood.

That was my gift. My talent. The one my mother had said I would find. I, who had so longed to be a hero, a warrior, a valorous and chivalrous knight, was no good with weapons but I could make a man destroy himself. Whoever my noble father had been, it was my mother's magic that tainted me.

Sickened, I ran from my knowledge. I did not even go back for my belongings, but ran through the pouring rain until my legs crumbled under me and I fell, exhausted, into a weedy ditch and a deep sleep.

In my sleep I saw my mother's face, watching me.

When I awoke the sun was shining but I had a terrible chill. I found a hiding place for myself in a dark glen no one visited but the wild things, and there I waited out the siege of fever. I slept each night in the hollow bole of a decayed oak tree, hugging my own knees because there was no other solace for me.

Birds' eggs and berries fed me, and because I was young at last I regained my strength and continued my senseless quest, looking for I knew not what. I worked in various ways and places, giving various names, and always moving on before my identity might catch up with me. During the day I watched for a face that could be the mirror of mine, praying I might find my father and the other half of the riddle that was me. At night, more often than not, it was my mother's face I saw in sleep, and knew she was watching me. Waiting to use me when the time was right.

So the seasons passed until I was a man full grown, as tall and strong as I would ever be. To the small education my mother had given me I added bits of knowledge about many things, so that I could talk on a wide range of subjects for at least a little while. I worked for a tailor long enough to acquire a decent set of clothing, and I worked as an hostler long enough to learn to ride a horse. I had some of the manners of the nobility, and I cherished them. If I ever found my father, he would not be ashamed of me.

Without being consciously aware of it, however, I had

let my wanderings take me in a large spiral that gradually narrowed again, drawing closer and closer to the great fortress of Camelot. And wherever I went, I tried to acquit myself decently, to let the good blood that must be in me outweigh the sorcerer's heritage. I raised my hand against no one; I fled from fights and let myself be called coward rather than take that final step and win the victory I always knew I could win. I did not want to find the flaw in any man and fracture him; make him destroy himself. It was a terrible gift and I hated it.

We Celts are a people of storytellers, of bards, and the nearer I came to Camelot the more stories I heard. Some were tales of courage and grand deeds, but others were disturbing. There were stories of betrayal that disgusted me, for I wanted to believe the king's band was pure and fine. I remember saying that over my ale in a tavern one night, and later when I slept I saw my mother's face in my dreams, and heard her laughing. "Pure and fine," she said, her eyes glittering.

My wandering ways became a great burden to me. I longed to have a wife and a home, to raise strong sons and comely daughters. I was in the full tide of my manhood and yet it seemed I was wasting my days, but unable to change. How could I offer marriage to a lady of noble birth, when I did not know my own heritage? How could I settle for an Elyse and a laborer's life, when my being cried out for something more?

The skin on the back of my neck prickled and I knew my mother's eyes were on me. She had given me freedom to roam and grow, though perhaps she could have pulled me back any time. Now at last I felt her summons, however; felt it unmistakably strong. As I had always suspected, she had a purpose for me.

When I found my feet following a familiar trail through Broceliande forest, I was not surprised. Long years had passed, but the cottage had not changed. Neither had my mother, when I saw her waiting for me in the doorway. She was still slender, with skin as gold as flax and as polished as satin. Nowhere in my travels had I seen a woman to compare with her and we both knew it.

She bade me enter and I did so; it was useless to try to resist her. Only as I passed her in the narrow doorway did I see the fine network of lines around her eyes, and the white threads in her hair. The sight hurt my heart, the heart I thought was steeled against her.

She gave me the best seat, next to the hearth, and a silver goblet brimming with the sweetest mead I ever tasted. The room filled with the fragrance of apples and honey. There was roasted venison piled high on a platter, and another plate of my favorite cakes. "This is a lot of food for one woman alone," I could not resist commenting.

"I have been expecting company," she said complacently.

"You knew I would come. I never had any choice, did I?"

She gave me a sorrowful look. "I would never again deny any man his freedom. You did not have to come back here. That door is as open as you left it when you ran away. Walk out it now, if you like. I will not stop you."

I bit into the venison and let the red juice run down my throat. "What kind of trick do you think to play on me, you sorceress?" I asked as coolly as I could. "In my travels I have heard your name mentioned, and though every time I heard it I ran away, so as not to be shamed by the memory of my connection with you, still I could not help learning that you once committed a disgraceful act with your magic. You tricked someone else, someone better than you by far. That much I know about you, and I wish I did not know it; it is a terrible thing to learn that one's own mother is deceitful and despised among decent men."

Her eyes narrowed and she ran her tongue between her lips, like the tiny darting tongue of an adder. "What else did you hear of me? Do you know what I am accused of?"

One of the cakes was a little burned around the edges. I crumbled off the blackened crust and flung it, bit by bit, into the fire, avoiding her eyes. "I did not want to hear anything about you. I only wanted to learn of my father."

"And have you?"

I shook my head. "The kindest thing I heard of you was that you were a whore, and shared your favors with many men. You flaunted yourself in Camelot, they say . . . I suppose my sire could be anyone."

"Oh, no," she replied, her voice very soft and far away. "Oh, no. Your sire was very special. . . ." Her eyes were starred with dreams. Indeed, she sat on a small stool at my feet, her hands clasping her knees like those of a worshipful girl, and some stranger looking through the window might have thought it a loving family scene.

"Camelot," my mother murmured. "Do you know how much I miss Camelot? I have been exiled for so long. . . ."

"And I!" I lashed out at her. "As your son, surely I deserved to grow up at court, too; to have all the advantages that were denied me because of you."

She bowed her head on its slender neck. "I regret that you suffered for my sake," she said. "But I have suffered, too, more than you know. I thought to escape punishment for what I had done, but all I accomplished was to make both you and me miserable. The time has come at last to put an end to it."

"You will tell me . . . ?"

"You will know his name," she said, looking at her laced fingers in her lap. "But first you must pay an old debt for me."

Wily she was, my mother. "I expected a trick from you," I said.

"This is no trick. I tell you there is a quest you must undertake that you alone can perform. And if you succeed at it, perhaps I will have balanced the scales a little." Her voice dropped and I swear I saw a tear in the corner of her eye. "Too little, and probably too late, but I must try." She swallowed hard and looked up at me. "What do you know of Arthur and Guinevere and . . . Lancelot?"

Of course I had heard the whispers, the innuendoes. The kind of court gossip circulating about the king, his queen, and his champion could not be contained within the walls of Camelot, but had overrun the countryside like a flood. It left a bad taste in my mouth and I had tried to avoid hearing it, as I had not wanted to listen to the tales about my mother. Still, I knew enough, and when I reluctantly repeated it to her, she nodded.

Then she told me what must be done. She looked into the future and saw how it would all play out, and not for the first time I wondered exactly how she had acquired that terrible ability—and at what price.

She had promised me answers when my deed was done. I did not want to do it, though; it ran counter to every image I had of myself. Yet she kept after me, wheedling, flattering, clinging to me, exerting those charms she had in such abundance. She could be warm and gay and witty, my mother. She could be irresistible; she had had practice.

I lingered in the cottage to watch her work her wiles. It was good to be in that old, known place, and the sound of the voice I had loved in my childhood fell sweetly upon my ears. I knew what she was doing but I confess I enjoyed watching her try. The world had never been as kind to me as she was being.

I cannot name the exact moment when I realized she had won. But she knew. She gave a great moan of relief, and before my eyes I saw age creep across her face as she relaxed.

She equipped me with a sword and a jerkin of boiled leather, though we both knew I did not need them. "Go and find him," she said, bidding me farewell. "Find the man I send you to and destroy him—that is the purpose for which you were born."

From a far distance, you can recognize the sound of a battlefield. There is the rattle of the drum and the skirling of pipes and the clang of metal on metal. Thud and scream are battlefield music. Birds and beasts flee such an area; I know, for I met them coming toward me when at last I neared my destination.

Topping a ridge, I saw tents set up before me with pennons hanging limp in the damp air. The day was dying, the sun was low and of a sullen red, like drying blood. As I went on, I saw where the knights had fought, for the

earth was mutilated by the hooves of many horses. The
battle was over by the time I got there. Only the final
victories remained to be won. Or lost.

A raven on the branch of a broken tree watched me
pass.

The air smelled of death and I hated it. This was what it
really meant to be a warrior, the glory and the trumpets led
to this grim field and the groans of the dying as they
begged for water, or shrieked their mothers' names.

Arthur's men were dying all around me. Men of both
sides, actually, for it had been an exceptionally vicious
fight and brother had slain brother. The dying all belong to
one family; they share a universal resemblance. Walking
among them, I looked down at the contorted faces of
heroes with all their heroism stripped away, and only the
pain remaining.

At the far edge of the battlefield I saw him. It could be
none other, for even terribly wounded he still wore the
look of eagles. He raised his head as I approached and his
hand still clutched the hilt of Excalibur. The setting sun
sparked fire from its jewels.

"Bedivere, is that you?" the king asked in a faint voice.

Before I could answer a knight shoved past me and fell
on his knees beside Arthur. He too was wounded, but he
ignored his injury to tend his sovereign with such loving
kindness I had to look away, feeling like an intruder.

This scene was not for me. The man who lay dying
upon the bloodied earth was not my answer.

On I went, seeking the other. He was also easy to
recognize when I found him. Hate and jealousy had twisted
his face into ugliness, but the bones of it were Arthur's
bones.

"Modred," I said.

He was wounded, as my mother had foreseen. Arthur's
final sword thrust would have killed any other man, and
surely everyone thought Modred dead of it. But when I
looked into his eyes I knew he would not die that easily. A
hatred beyond my understanding sustained him. He had
dragged himself into the lee of a boulder and torn his

clothing to make a tourniquet. Even as I watched, a little color began to come back into his face. If undisturbed he could hide there until he regained enough strength to escape altogether.

I stared at him. All that was chivalrous and noble, he had brought down. Like my poor mother, he had been unable to believe in purity and had tried to destroy what he could not understand. "It is in the worst of us, to try to destroy the best of us," my mother had told me. "I denied Arthur the wise councilor who might have saved him," she had said. "I cannot go back and undo what I did, but through you, perhaps I can prevent the forces of destruction from taking over his kingdom in the person of his son."

Modred looked up at me now. "Help me," he ordered. "Get me out of here and I will see that you have a knighthood." He raised himself onto one elbow and held out his hand, expecting me to take it.

When I did not he tossed his head to get the lank hair out of his eyes and peered at me more closely. "Who are you?"

I could not strike him with my sword; it was not in me to do that to any man. But with my mind I seized his own hand and lowered it so his fingers could grasp the tourniquet. I made him rip the cloth away from his wound. He glanced up at me in disbelief, then we both watched his life's blood leap out of him in a great, pulsing arc. He struggled desperately to regain control of his hands and shove the fabric back in place so it could staunch his wound, but I held him with my mind as surely as if I held him with chains.

Modred had thought he knew all the secrets and all the answers. He had learned, through his mother, every scandal and weakness in Arthur's court. He had loved gossip as I learned to hate it, loved conflict as I learned to avoid it. He had been a king's son—and thrown it all away.

I resolved then to tell no one that Modred's own hand had ended his life. Let the king have the credit. Arthur was a warrior, such credits were important to him. I had other, gentler needs.

As his eyes began to glaze, Modred coughed and asked me again in a hoarse whisper, "Who are you?"

I knew only one answer to give him. "Vivien's son," I said.

A dreadful fear leaped into his eyes, the expression of a man who meets an implacable enemy at the very last and realizes there is no hope at all. *"Merlin's son!"* the dying Modred cried.

For fantasy readers, TANITH LEE needs less introduction than Santa Claus, and everyone has a favorite Lee tale. Mine have been "When The Clock Strikes" and "Wolf-land" from Red as Blood. *But then there's "The Gorgon" and "Because Our Skins Are Finer"* . . . *and I really can't leave out "Draco, Draco" or "Three Days" or "Elle Est Trois (La Mort)."*

It's pretty tough to nail down one favorite.

New York's *Village Voice labeled Tanith Lee "Princess Royal of Heroic Fantasy"—an effusion that probably embarrasses her as much as the C-sharp minor Prelude did Rachmaninoff. Still, like him, she is an exquisite stylist in her slightest pieces and a master in her best. Her stories invite you in with a graceful bow and defy you to leave before finishing.*

In a Lee story, the sunlight sparkles even as the dark comes subtly on. You hardly notice the shadows moving across the floor.

But they do.

"The Minstrel's Tale" is just such a play of light and shadow.

The Minstrel's Tale

by Tanith Lee

It's true, I live by the making of songs, and of stories,
too. And sometimes by the making of a fine good lie. But
this is none of those, and so I swear, by any saint or angel
that was ever kind to me. It happened not long ago, a little
less than a year, and stays clear in my mind, though I'm
thinking it will stay clear as the rich glass in a lord's
church window, till my death day. Certainly, I'm a young
man, and a year younger then, a vagabond, a trickster,
though never yet, by god, a thief. But in the end, youth
and honesty and trade make small odds. Listen, and judge
for yourselves.

I'd sung a well-paid month in a town, for the castle folk
and the plump folk in the houses, and I'd had my stomach
full of that, and come walking away up into the heart of
the land, to sing in the villages and the inns, where you get
a pot of ale and a kiss for your work, and the sweeter for
that, sometimes. Here was a place I'd never journeyed
before, the country they call Dark Hills. And well named,
its deep curved shoulders sombre as old smoke at their
tops, brown and green as baked apple at their bases.
While, in the long shining gloaming of the North, each

19

peak and valley seems to swim away, growing ever farther off, like rings spreading in a pool after the flint is thrown in it, and I that flint.

In such a gloaming, between such hills, I passed a well. A may tree grew there, snowed with blossom, and below I saw the little stone cot with its stone-piled wall, and some tangled sheep sat cat fashion, with their legs tucked under, on the slope above.

Now it's a fact, no matter how long the twilight, it must end in a night. I had been thinking of a grass bed, and still thought of it, for not every wayside dwelling welcomes a fellow with a harp on his back. But I went to the door and knocked.

Vapour came from the chimney, which was not much more than a central hole, the old way, such as you find here. But being at home was no promise of admitting another. Then the door was opened, and a man stood before me.

I've heard it said: The shepherd resembles his flock, surely this one did. His face was dark and long, his eyes black, his long nose in the flattened Roman manner. His beard and hair might well have been a grizzled fleece. His hands and feet were tapering and miniature. To have him greet me on all fours would not have amazed me, nor to hear him go baaa. But instead he looked in my face, and he said to me:

"Aye?"

"God's evening to you," I replied. "My trade is harping and songs, but I lack shelter. Can we bargain on that, or shall I be off?"

He went on looking me over, and I looked at him in a way I've learned. Sometimes you must offer more than songs in the back hills, or seem to offer more.

At length he nodded. He put on a prideful foolish smile, and stood to one side, waving me to enter, which is an antique courtesy to the stranger. I thanked him, and ducked under the low lintel and went in.

It was dim inside, with smoke and dusk. There was the cooking place and the fire of peats, the black rafters, a

great chest with some tools laid by on it. A ladder went up
at one corner to a half room above. The bedchamber that
would be, for in winter the flock must cram in here with
the master. We sat down on sheepskins, and he indicated
the iron pot set to bubble over the peat.

"There's enough for all," he said. "When Rosemay
comes, she'll give us ale."

This did surprise me, I was not sure quite why, that he
should have a woman to tend him. Somehow he seemed a
solitary creature, and his house had a bachelor's air to it,
though tidy, no female thing scattered, and no carding
comb or spinning wheel, but they would be above, perhaps.

"Your wife's from home?" I said. It might, after all, be
a daughter; it was as well to know.

"My wife," he said. "Did you not spy her at the
well?"

I remembered the well and the snowy may tree growing
there. I had seen no one, or I would have offered to draw
the water for her, or carry the jar. By such ingratiating
ploys one sometimes earns one's lodging. But his tone was
humorous, as if this were some jest.

"No, I did not."

"Well, no grief. For here she is."

So I looked up, as he did, and through the opened door,
the earthen jar in her hand, stepped his wife, his Rosemay.

I have been about, and I've beheld a woman or two was
worth gazing at, and some indeed have been more than
sisters to me. But this one. No, I had seen none like her.

The grey-mauve sky was behind her, the dark fireglow
before, and she was a note of light between, tawny light,
like certain wines I've seen, or candleflame. Her gown
was yellow, a holy-day gown, too fine to fetch water or
cook supper in, yet she wore it. Her hair was paler yellow
than the gown, all loose, save for the two braids that held
the sidelocks off her face and bound them up on her crown
with a silk ribbon no different in colour than her hair. Her
face and throat and hands were kissed all over by the
summer sun. The lords' women keep themselves white,
like milk, but this maid was ivory and cream and rose.
Yes, a yellow rose she was, and with the beauty of a rose.

Then she stepped into the house, and darkened with its shadow to a rose of swarthy gold.

And here I was, about to be in his debt for a roof and a meal, and this his wife. As if to prove it to me, he said to her at once:

"We've a guest, Rosemay, a minstrel, no less. Fetch us ale, my lass, and hurry the food."

And she, to help the proof, Heaven forgive her, said to him in a voice lilting and pure as my harp itself:

"Yes, husband."

She said it with liking, too. With love, even, though that she should love him was beyond me. Me she never glanced at.

Well, I'm young. Flat-bellied, long-legged, strong and limber. I've good teeth, and women like my hair and my face, or so they tell me, and the rest, too, should we come to such dealings. My voice, I know, is better than most. So I spoke to her, I did, to the old sheepman's tawny Rose.

"Thanks for your generosity, lady."

But, "Be at ease," said she, and still she did not glance. Not even at the "lady" I'd gifted her, shepherd's wife that she was. Then she brought the ale in a skin, and two wooden cups. She poured his, firstly. The fire flared, showing me, as of a purpose, her young smooth skin. She was not more than sixteen, and he a world-bitten forty. Men will often die before they are forty in the South, but here they live longer. There's a strange still power in this land. The hills hold it, and men can take it to them if they will. So I've heard, and so I believe.

Well, next she came to pour for me, and as she put the cup in my hand, our fingers brushed, and as she leaned to fill the cup, the slope of her breast pressed against the bodice of her gown. And more than one cup was filled. I lusted for her, but it was more than that. The sight of her in the doorway, her voice, her sheen, her eyes—which now I saw were not blue, or brown, but the shade of that stone they mine for hereabouts, partly black and partly amber—all this thrilled me, deviled me. I had the feeling, more than to lie with her, to lift her up, to make her into music, like a new, bright bird-winged song.

As soon as she was finished pouring ale, she went over to the cooking place, and never once had she looked at me.

So it went on, then. We had supper, a tasty mutton stew and slabs of bread with the crust yet warm on them. She waited on us, not sitting to her own food till we were served, and she serving him always the first, smiling at him once, when he raised his shaggy brows, and never noticing me. I fancy, if another maid had been so circumspect, I might have guessed her shy or sly and begun to hope. But this one's way was not like that, but rather as if I were invisible—like that absent guest they will lay a place for at the table and serve with food, though neither he nor anyone sits there. During the meal there was no conversation, for this was no castle board; one thing came at a time. When we had had our fill—I asking an extra portion, a thing I rarely do in a poor house, but to get her attention, and not getting it—she took the bowls out to cleanse them. The shepherd meanwhile fished a hunk of meat from the stew, and moved just outside the door with it, whistling his dog. I'd thought it odd not to have seen a dog before, and odder yet when, through the doorway, I saw one come skulking down the hillside by the sheep, as if it had done something bad. I followed the man, and stood leaning on the doorpost. The gloaming was fading at last, but I could see Rosemay, walking over the turf with the bowls. The dog, as it sidled towards the cot, slunk by her and ran to the man, snatched the meat from his grasp, and made off at once, back up the hill with it. The shepherd turned, and with a grunt went by me into his house. I, amused a little at the dog, which treated the woman somewhat as she had treated me, strolled forward in the gloom to intercept her.

"The dog does not like you, it's plain. Silly, witless dog."

"It is my husband's dog," was all she would say, and was gone by me again, into the house to her elderly mate.

I went in after them with a silent oath, leaving the great landscape of Dark Hills to wind itself away on the spindle of night. Now I'd play for them, for a bargain is a bargain. I'd play, and see what that would do. I have had women weep, even swoon at my songs, or they pretended they did.

He, when I took up my harp and let it from its cover, gave off that slight unfathomable noise the audience, large or small, will generally give, settling itself. Naturally, I squinted, too, over my tuning, to see how she did. But she sat motionless beyond the fire, though she had taken up no piece of women's work to mask her idleness. It seemed she would listen. Well, then.

I sang some songs, I forget now which they were, the usual sort with which one begins, catching the mood, or making it. The shepherd relaxed, smiling and nodding, sometimes drumming his fingers in time. But my tawny rose, she sat as if a bee were buzzing in the room. So I came to the song I wanted. It was an old romance, old as the Dark Hills themselves, maybe, and it travels under many names and manier guises. But the gist of it is this: A young minstrel-knight falls deep in love with the woman of his liege lord, so deep in love he forgets battle and loyalty and honour for her sake, though he tells her nothing of the affair. And this I sang, and when I came to the tally of the woman's virtues, I made them hers, her hair, and particolour eyes, her honey skin. Even the royal lady's gown was saffron, in my song. It was a fly thing to be doing, you'll say, but I reckoned him too unparticular to rouse at it. He seemed half asleep as it was. And she. What would she do?

She sat with her chin on her hand, and her eyes downcast, but she was very still now, so still I could not see her breathe, and in the shadow beyond the fire, she seemed scarcely to be there.

Then I struck the chords, and told how the minstrel-knight, who loved so unrequitedly and so well, resolved to redeem his honour, and died in the war of his master, died with twenty-seven wounds in his young body, and not one of these at his back. And when he lay with his fair noble face lit by the sky, the very clouds wept for pity. And his men took him to the castle, and the royal woman grew pale when she was told, and went to visit his corpse. As she bent over him, one single tear she could not restrain fell on his lips, at which they parted and his soul spoke to her from within the cadaver: *Lady, this is not death to me, for I died long ago when first I looked on you. I ask your prayers who never did ask your love.*

I sang dulcetly. I had something at stake. The song, which is a worthy one, and not easy to play, came sweetly, and moved me. It is a tale warranted to overthrow a maid, but I admit there were tears in my own eyes, when I looked for hers.

But she did not sit crying. For a moment I believed I had cast my glove at the moon, as they say, and wasted the effort. And then her gaze came up like two jewels in the shadow. She stared full at me, and such a stare it was I felt burned to my very marrow, as if I had been shot with fire. And I own I trembled, too. For these eyes said, sharp and plain as swords: Oh, *I* would give you more than tears.

The shepherd was slumped, aware in a daze the music was over. As he bestirred himself, she got to her feet, his Rosemay, and without a word she drifted to the ladder like a blowing leaf, and up it went. And he, the big dull ram, shambled after her, grumbling some phrase of approbation at me I was too fey, by now, to understand. On the mid-rung of the ladder, however, he bent on me a weird grin that did alarm me for an instant, as if he knew it all, and other things that I did not. But then he was gone, and I took it for imagining.

Alone, I sat, and I vow I waited.

The dusk was gone, night come, and the peats on the fire slumbered and went out. The very night slumbered, and those broad shoulders of land outside the door, if ever they do sleep, were sleeping too. For him, I heard him snore after a while. Then my pulse ran, to be sure. I sat, and I waited, in the fireless dark, to hear the soft sole of her foot on the rungs of the ladder, whispering like grass, or the rustle her hair might make.

Once, some tiny night beast, having got in under the door or by the chimney, flew against my cheek, and the blood tumbled in me, for I mistook it for her fingers.

Then I lapsed somewhat, and lay down; I was tired enough for that, though not to sleep, I thought, in my fever. A man, having seen her eyes in that one gaze, could not have slept.

Strung tense as a bowstring, I reclined there. Presently the moon rose, and slid in at the cracks in the door and between the stones of the wall, and finally through the chimney hole overhead. Then I told how late it had got, and that she had not come to me. Well, she might linger to be sure of him. Next, the moon went down. Supposing she was virtuous? But what had this to do with virtue? I had wooed her—wooed, mark, not thieved—wooed and won her. This night she was rightfully mine. Yet the night would soon be done.

I dozed, and I dreamed she stepped from the ladder and leaned over me and kissed my forehead, but I woke and it was the morning breeze fluttering from the chimney. The shaft of light was nearly blue, and when I opened the door to look out, the sky was like a plate of silver behind the black foldings of the hills. It had a comely scent, the morning, but stale and vile to me. It seemed she had dallied with me, made a mock of me after all. She cleaved to her old shepherd, and would have none of me, be I young as day and strong and handsome as a hero. So. Her loss, not mine.

I walked from the cot, my harp on my shoulders, sour and heavy, cursing both of them, and under all strangely puzzled, strangely ill-at-ease. For night long I had heard him shift about above, but never a sound from her. And when I glanced back from the brow of the ridge beyond the cot, I saw the whiteness of the may tree, and I remembered the well and how I had not come on her there; and later I remembered, too, how the dog had avoided her. A witch, perhaps, was golden Rosemay, and I ensorcelled one whole night, writhing, with her flame on me she had not deigned to quench.

Now you may suppose that is all my tale, and be wondering why I puffed it up as such a curiosity, and laugh at me, reckoning I was only astonished, being vainglorious, that a woman said no to me. But indeed, there's something more to be told. If you'll be patient, you shall have it.

Three mornings after I walked from the cot, I reached a village under the hills. It was of stone, as they are in these parts, a prospering place, and busy, for it was market day. No harper in his right wits will pass a market by, and accordingly I chose my spot and conjured my songs and collected some coin—when they could hear me for the bleating of their goats. At noon, I paused for ale, and as I was drinking it, I heard one man say to another: "Mad Rose is about again."

That name, of course, stayed me. I turned my head, and a second man spoke up.

"Aye, and there's the harper listening."

"Who is mad, then?" said I.

"I'll tell you," said the gossip, "for it'd likely make a fine song." At that, I must buy him ale, which I did. Sometimes, in this way, you do get a yarn worth refashioning with music. He supped his drink a minute, then he began. "It's simply told. One market day a young man drove five of his sheep to our village, and on the street he met with our Rose. Now Rose was beautiful, and her hair was done up with ribbon, and she in her yellow dress, for you know how a maid is at market. But Rose was worse than most. A minx, Rose was, spoiling for every man, looking at him with her eyes till he thought he might do as he pleased, and then she'd run off, or set him at some other man's throat. There was near-murder done now and then, and Rose at the edge of it. She had no father, do you see, only a sickly mother could not keep rein on her. Then the young shepherd drove in his five ewes, and he saw Rose, and she danced for him like the rest, first not looking at him, as if he were invisible, and then darting a stare at him fit to have him catch alight. Now he was a honest lad, this shepherd. Before the evening came on, he went to the mother, and offered to have Rose wed him. The mother, be sure, would have been glad to give her daughter away, but Rose, why she laughed and she made sport of him, and when he only stood in her mother's house, hanging his head for shame, Rose took up a pitcher of slops and emptied them over his crown. Now when she did that, his mildness left him, and they say he bellowed like a bull with rage. While outside, his sheep dog, that had lain quietly by the door, began to bark and howl as if it had the madness.''

The gossip hesitated, his ale drunk down, to see if I would replenish it. But my heart was striking me in the side. I made no move and, good-natured enough, he went on.

''Well then, they say that he said this to our Rose: 'I will have you, whether you will or not. And you will be true to me and obedient to me, and fetch the water, and cook my food and pour my ale, and lie by me in my bed all night. And that bold barren look you flaunt shall be only for those others I let see it, and you will be hid from those I wish not to behold you. But on me you'll smile and fawn and be always with me, and that I swear.' And this said, he called the snarling dog, and they went off along the hills, leaving Rose cawing with mirth like a crow.''

The man looked at his ale pot again, less a reminder now than a perusal, feeling for the next words, for he was good at his storytelling, was the gossip.

''Now who knows but that the shepherd might have returned and carried her off, but he did not. There was fever about that spring, he took it, and he died, and the dog lay down on his feet and died too, and was buried with him under the may tree by the well, for the priest would not put this shepherd in the safe earth beside the church. The priest pronounced him a waerlog, and there may be something in that. For I've met those say they've spoken with a shepherd at dusk, near that well, and he grizzled by his forty-first summer, which he would have been, had he lived. As for Rose, she went lunatic on the night he died. Mad as the moon, and no help for it. They keep her indoors when they can, but sometimes she'll get loose and mope about. A sight it's a pity to see. But the notion is she's no more mad than you or I, but has only lost her soul. For the shepherd took it, and keeps it by him to do all he said, in her exact likeness as she was that day, sixteen and a rose, when he first set eyes on her.''

I peered at him as if I, too, were crazed. I shook from head to heel. And then the other man touched my wrist and pointed behind me, and a silence fell on the inn.

I turned, what else? And turning I saw her, as before, coming in at a doorway. And yet not as before. Mad Rose. Truly, she was a pitiful sight as he'd said, her elf locks wizened to grey, yet still weeded by a girl's yellow ribbon, her maid's yellow gown, once moulded on a slender ripeness, now slack, raddled and grimed by more than twenty years' soiling. She was forty, and a hag; old as the earth she looked, her brown skin loose on her bones as the gown was loose on the frame of her. Her eyes were filmed and colourless and darted all about, but here and there they fixed on a man with a fierce and intimate stare.

I went chill to my blood. I was faint, and put my head down on the table, so I did not see them coax her away, though dimly I heard her screaming. Nor did she go quite away, for she stays in my mind, in either shape, eldritch or maiden, madwoman or rose soul.

I told you, the Dark Hills are enduring, and men can draw power from them. When once I leave, I shall not come here again.

PHYLLIS ANN KARR can write gritty-tough when she wants to, as followers of her woman warrior, Thorn, know very well. She also displays a delightfully dry and sardonic touch in such works as Idylls of the Queen.

Her present story draws on the Camelot created for Idylls *and peoples it with familiar and new faces.*

I like "Two Bits of Embroidery" for what it says about love and hero worship, how two very different men react to it—and how each of them, in his own way, is exactly equal to just what is served him.

Two Bits of Embroidery

by Phyllis Ann Karr

Both Sir Lancelot and Sir Kay went late to the great Assumption Day tournament at Camelot. Neither had planned to go at all. The Queen, pleading poor health, was remaining behind in London. The court gossips found Kay's decision more surprising but less meaty than Lancelot's—the love of the churlish seneschal for his foster-brother's wife was and had always been, perforce, virtuous.

Then, a few hours after the King's departure with most of his knights, Guenevere sent for Sir Lancelot by daylight and remained alone with him for only a few moments. After supper she played chess with Sir Kay, sitting in sight of a few favorite attendants at their needlework. In the morning Kay began delegating his stewardly duties while Lancelot quietly disappeared from court.

Some gossips said that Lancelot and the Queen had quarreled again. They were not entirely right. Others said that Guenevere had finally persuaded her lover to wear her token in the tournament. They were entirely wrong.

Elaine of Astolat trailed the visiting knight into the garden and approached him when he thought he was alone.

31

Her stomach (she thought it was her heart) churning with hope, she half knelt, half sat on the path before his bench. "Fair sir," she began, "will you wear my token?"

He looked at her with the same kind of smile her father used when telling her it would not be time to think of marriage until she could no longer have worn her brother's breastplate without discomfort. "Fairest damsel," the visiting knight replied, "I have never worn the token of any lady, matron or maid."

She flushed, realizing he still thought of her as a child. But she had put her dolls and knucklebones away at the beginning of the summer, turning to the pursuits of a grown woman—embroidering a tapestry during the day and something more important during the intimate evening hours. "Sir, my brothers were knighted on St. Magdalen's Day, and if I had been a boy, I would have been esquired to one of them. I am old enough."

"I do not doubt it, fair child," said he. "But have you ever bestowed your precious token before now?"

"Only to my brother Lavaine, sir. And only in sport, before he was made knight. To no one else."

"Then bestow it on your brother again, and wait for a worthier knight than I, my dear, before you bestow it outside your own family."

Elaine shook her head. All her family knew, from the way their guest gently withheld his name and the way he avoided King Arthur's encampment in the meadow below, that he was one of the King's own knights, traveling on to fight incognito at Camelot. Knights, even of the Round Table, had visited sometimes in Astolat Manor before now. Sir Gawaine himself had been their guest in the spring, before Elaine had put her toys away. She knew there was only one knight in all Britain greater than Sir Gawaine, and she thought it must surely be this tall man with the nobly scarred cheek who sat smiling down on her. Already she had guessed the stranger to be Sir Lancelot.

"You are taking my brother Tirre's shield to Camelot, sir," she said, "and you're taking my brother Lavaine himself to be your man. Am I alone to be left behind?"

"Your good father knows what is best for you, my dear. There is blood spilled at tournaments, and often death as well."

"But I don't ask to go myself, sir—although I can look at blood. Didn't I help bind up Tirre's wound when Lavaine pierced him through in their first joust as knights? But don't keep me away completely, sir—take something of mine with you, too."

"Send your token with Sir Lavaine," he repeated. "Your brother will be proud to keep it safe for you."

"Not with him, fair sir. With you." When the King and his company had encamped yesterday evening in the meadow below the manor, to await their own last, straggling knights and the company of their ally, the King of Scots, Elaine thought Love was about to come at last; and when the stranger who must be Sir Lancelot arrived, traveling in secret, and asked for the loan of a virgin white shield, she knew that Love was before her and it was time to take her part in such a tale as she had often read to her old nurse from her two treasured books.

The visiting knight plucked a rose from the arbor above him, bent forward, and carefully twined the flower in her golden hair. "What difference does it make, sweet damsel, who carries your token, so that it graces the lists at Camelot?"

Elaine had not been pampered, for her father was poor—she knew this by comparing what they had with what the noblefolk had in her books, and so she had never asked for what he could not give her. But neither had she ever been denied anything for which she did ask; at worst, she had been promised it not now, but later. So she would not be denied now. This time she would not even accept a promise of "later." But she understood that she was being tested. As the ladies in the romances were witty, so Elaine knew she must be witty if she was to win her knight's love. "My brother Lavaine, sir, may find another dame," she said. "Must he not remain free to carry her token?"

"And should I not be free, sweet child, to carry the token of no dame, however fair?"

She drew a deep breath. "So by your own confession, my lord, your heart is free and you may wear my token if you choose."

His hand, still lingering in her hair, moved down and gently touched her cheek. So this, she thought, was the first touch of a lover, the beginning of the caresses she had read and dreamed of . . . and it was lovelier than her dreams.

He sighed. "Very well, then, child. Show me your token."

On that same afternoon, some miles away, a young scullery maid was furtively watching a practice joust with blunted lances and wooden swords in the tiltyard of London castle.

Tilda might have been a year younger than Elaine; no one knew the exact month of the kitchen foundling's birth. Once she had a wooden doll with jointed arms, and she had liked to think her unknown father made it for her, but it was painful to remember the doll after Nap Knucklebone threw it on the fire one afternoon while Tilda was learning to baste a pig. Now her only toys were kittens from the time the mother cat let them be fondled to the time they were grown-up mousers.

Tilda did not know how to read and had looked inside a book only three times, when old Father Amustans showed her the pictures of God and the Saints in his Book of Hours. All that the kitchen maid knew of the ways of knights and ladies was what she glimpsed briefly of the court life that went on above her and what the other servants said of it. But she knew exactly, without guessing, which knight she watched now at his practice. He was the knight who often came down into the kitchens to make sure all his workers were at their work and to scold or punish them if they were not. He frightened most of them, even old Tychus Flaptongue the second cook, but he also knew them all by name, and whenever he found any of the older scullions teasing Tilda or threatening her kittens, he always came to her rescue. On the afternoon when Nap had burned her doll, Goodwoman Chloda, the chief cook, rapped the scullion's head with a ladle and rubbed Tilda's fingers with grease while scolding her for trying to snatch her toy from the coals, and Tychus Flaptongue had said Nap's deed was just as well, since if ever the seneschal had found Tilda shirking her duties to play with a doll, he would have thrown it into the fire himself. But Tilda secretly believed, no matter what they said, that if Sir Kay had visited the kitchen that afternoon, she would still possess the only thing that might have come to her from her parents.

This afternoon she had arrived, panting, near the end of the practice joust. It was very hard trying to follow Sir Kay's movements all day through rumors and gossip, watching her chance and meanwhile keeping her plan secret and working feverishly to get everything done so she could beg a few moments' rest when the chance came. But she was not sorry for the trouble, because her heart beat less quickly when she was hurrying about her tasks than when she had to wait doing nothing, and she thought that had she been a lady in truth, with little to do all day, she might never have had the courage at all.

But if a lady, she would not have needed so much. She tried to borrow bravery by watching how the knight she thought the greatest of all got up again after being unhorsed and finally splintered his opponent's weapon and beat him to his knees.

The defeated opponent, wiping his face and unlacing his padded tunic, left the tiltyard first. Tilda huddled on the other side of the stairs as he passed, and he did not notice her. The seneschal lingered awhile, giving his helmet and shield to a squire and speaking to the grooms who were taking the horses. For a few moments Tilda feared he would go on with them to the stables, but at last he turned back and came toward the hall. The kitchen maid took her stand not quite in his way, but where he must notice her.

He reached her, stopped, and looked down. "Isn't it about time to be cooking supper, Tilda?"

For the space of a heartbeat she wondered if he would

have thrown her doll into the fire, after all. "I worked very hard all day, sir. I even helped make the pasties today. Old Rozennik said I could have an hour to rest— they don't need me right now, sir, with the court so thinned and all."

He grunted. "So is the staff thinned. Why we didn't all just progress to Camelot in a body as usual and be done with it . . . Well, so you came to waste your hour watching a practice fight." He glanced around the tiltyard, empty now except for two squires still practicing at the far end. "It seems you're the only person in London who thought blunt lances and wooden swords might be interesting to watch."

He started to walk on. Quickly, before she lost her chance, Tilda held up her precious kerchief, folded in a bit of clean rag to keep it from any accidental soot or sweat.

Elaine's token was a sleeve of scarlet samite, sewn with seven large pearls, each one surrounded by flowers, leaves, and birds embroidered in brightly-colored silken thread. Although none of the embroidery was crude, an improvement could be traced between those designs that had clearly been stitched earliest and those done last. Between the pearls, wide expanses of cloth remained undecorated; it was apparent that the Damsel of Astolat had been working this token little by little, not knowing when she would bring it forth for her knight, and trying to keep it ready to produce at any moment, while continuing to fill in more patterns as she waited through the months.

"But these pearls are too precious, sweet lady, to be risked in battle," said Sir Lancelot. "Do you know how much one of them would purchase for you and your family in London or Camelot?"

"They were my mother's, sir. They would never be sold. The cloth and the colored silks were hers, too."

"And does your good father know that you would give them away, my lady?"

The maiden shook her head. "But they were in my mother's chest, my lord, that my father said must come to me, and I know my mother would approve."

"Your mother was a most gracious and most beautiful lady," said Sir Lancelot. "I see her live again in her daughter." He had never known Sir Bernard's wife, never having visited Astolat before today; but he must speak both courteously and delicately to Elaine of her mother.

"She fell from her horse when I was scarcely two years old, sir," said Elaine, "but I've felt her hand guiding mine every night when I stitched these patterns."

"And you would give so much richness and so much labor to a strange knight on the first day of meeting?"

"A stranger only to my eyes, sir, not to my heart." Elaine drew another deep breath. "My heart knew you the first moment my eyes beheld you. Sir, all unknown, I love you."

Sir Kay was tired, hot, not overly satisfied with his own performance in the practice bout, and feeling pressed by the details he still had to attend to before he left in the morning for Camelot. None of this improved his temper, which was not of the gentlest in the best of times. His first impulse was to thrust the packet back at the kitchen maid and stride on. But Tilda was a hard worker, one of his favorites (though he tried to show no favoritism), so he paused to unwrap the rag and examine what it contained.

He found a linen headkerchief, one of the kind given every Easter to all the women servants. It had been embroidered over every inch with birds, flowers, and beasts, crudely executed and stitched with linen and woolen threads of various thicknesses, many of them still crinkled from having been originally woven into cloth. The colors were browns, russets, greens, and muddy golds, the common, readily available dyes used by the common folk. The needle must have been too large and thick for the cloth, since in several places the linen was snagged. Still, all in all, it was a remarkable piece of work to be given by a scullery wench who had probably not yet entered her second decade of life.

"Tilda," he said, "who embroidered this?"

"I did, sir," she replied timidly. His voice must have been harsher than he had for once intended, because she sounded more as if she were confessing than bragging. "You're—you're not angry, sir?"

"Angry? Why should I be angry? Who taught you to do work like this?"

"No one, sir."

"No one?"

"I . . . looked at the tapestries, sir. Whenever I was abovestairs . . . you're not angry?"

"Not yet, but I may be very soon. Why in God's Name should I be angry if you looked at the tapestries? They were made to be looked at, weren't they?"

"But I should have been at my work, sir," she said in a very small voice.

"Well? You always finished your work when you got back to the kitchen, I hope?"

"Not . . . not always. Not that . . . that day last spring, and not on St. John's Day before that . . . but I never worked on the token unless my work was done, sir."

He laughed. Then, looking down again at her little face, frightened but strangely eager, he sat on the stairs and motioned for her to sit beside him. She did not sit, however, until he told her aloud, "Sit down, girl. Now then," he went on, "I'm going to tell you a secret, but I'll whip your bare back if you ever tell anyone I said it. Do you want to hear it?"

She nodded eagerly. "I would never, never repeat it, sir."

"All right. Most people are lazy clods who will take every chance they can to shirk their duties. If we told them all they could go around gawking at tapestries, or clouds, or rabbits, they'd never do anything else. But there is no reason on God's green earth why someone like you, Tilda, who does her work without a scolding every other day, shouldn't take a few moments to look at tapestries whenever the chance comes. And for the love of our Lady, don't worry about St. John's Day. You'd be a saint yourself and work miracles if you could get everything done every day of Christmas."

The child nodded and timidly sat an inch closer to him.

He began to unfold her scarf on his knee, thinking of the hours she must have put into it, wondering where she had borrowed the needle and begged the threads. So this, he thought, was why she had continued to wear her old kerchief and refused to name anyone when he questioned her, fearing some of the young scullery devils had stolen her new one.

"So you looked at the tapestries and embroidered this," he said, turning it over to examine the reverse side and nodding. Bumpy, but probably not much more so than the stuff done by the Queen's own handmaids at Tilda's age. "Why the secrecy about it, girl?"

"I wanted . . . to surprise you, sir."

He unfolded the kerchief the rest of the way, spread it out, and stared at an embroidered key in the center, not unlike the device he wore on his own shield. "Well, you succeeded. Now, why did you want to surprise me?"

Blushing crimson, she gazed down fixedly at something on the step below her. "I . . . I hoped . . . you might use it for . . . for your token in the great tournament, sir." Then, in a rush, "I love you, Sir Kay!"

Sir Lancelot accepted Elaine's declaration with the aplomb born of years of hearing or sensing similar declarations from half the dames and damsels of his acquaintance. Only one, Elaine of Carbonek, had ever tricked his body away from that of his own queenly leman, and that had been when he was still young and green. Another, the fair Dame Amable, had dedicated her virginity to him as other ladies dedicated theirs to Christ; flattered, but not surprised, that she should make such a choice, he had repaid her with whatever virtuous service lay in his power. For the rest, he had lost count of them, but, having refused the blandishments of the great Queen Morgan le Fay herself, and of more than one lesser enchantress, he could accept the adulation of any mortal woman without feeling his loyalty to Guenevere threatened.

He was old enough to have been Elaine of Astolat's father, but since such an age difference was no bar to a

man's or woman's hopes for love and wedlock, he did not
mention the fact. He had not asked this child to love him,
and she, like most of the others, would get over him—
sufficiently, at least, to find another knight of her own.
Meanwhile, her affection was flattering. It added but a
drop to the fame and affection he already enjoyed on every
side, but that drop was all the more precious in that she
offered her admiration without knowing who he was. She
proved to him that it was still his person, not merely his
fame, that drew the ladies' love.

More to the point, when he had agreed, at Guenevere's
insistence, to leave the Queen in London and go to the
Camelot tourney after all, he had vowed to fight incognito
on the side against the King. It mattered not at all when
the Queen pointed out that this would cut in half the whole
reason for his going, which was to avoid further scandal
by making it clear that she and Lancelot were not, after
all, in the same city together while Arthur was elsewhere.
And when Guenevere had further pointed out that by
fighting unknown against his own kinsmen and comrades,
many of whom were men of might, he would put himself
in a modicum of needless danger, he was actually angered
at her fears. Cheated of several nights abed with her, he
insisted on the compromise of fighting as a nameless
knight with a virgin white shield, proclaiming that he
"would take the adventure God sent him," and aware that
the added dangers of fighting unknown would once again,
as often before, increase the glory of his victory.

It was no longer so easy, however, to remain incognito
in tournament or private tilt. His size and style of riding
and fighting were too well known. But he had never, in all
his long career, worn the token of any lady, not even of
the Queen. Lack of a lady's token was as much a mark of
Lancelot as his size and style. So now, if he suddenly
appeared with a token on his helmet, especially a token
that could not easily be traced to any one dame, his
incognito would be all the better preserved.

Moreover, it would hardly be just or courteous to refuse
the poor little maiden the small favor of accepting a token

on which she had labored so lovingly and which she now proffered so eagerly. Nor could any harm befall Elaine through it, for who would suspect such pearls of having come from the comparatively poor manor of Astolat? And, even if the truth were discovered, it could only be to the poor girl's honor to be known as the first who had succeeded in pressing her token on the great Sir Lancelot du Lac—for all Lancelot's protests of unworthiness were merely courteous pretenses; he was well aware of his own glory. Elaine's innocent relation with him might even be considered as part of her dowry, bringing her a higher husband than she could otherwise have won for all her budding prettiness. And how proud and happy she herself would be when she learned to whom she had given her first real token!

"Fairest damsel," said Sir Lancelot, "I do for you what I have never done for any maid, matron, nor widow in my life before now. I make you my vow to wear your token into tournament, thus winning honor for you and myself both. And in return pledge, here I entrust my own shield into your keeping, to hold for me until I return."

He took her face between his hands and kissed her tenderly on the forehead. When she fell forward a little, as if she were half fainting with the pleasure, he held her, fatherly, in his arms until she recovered. Sir Lancelot was well pleased with his kindness and courtesy that afternoon.

For a moment Sir Kay was dumbfounded at Tilda's declaration. Like Elaine of Astolat, the old seneschal knew more of romantic relations from books than from experience; unable, and usually unwilling, to curb his tongue, he considered himself fortunate to find a few ladies who would scold him back like sisters. Nor would he have wanted more than friendship from any dame except one, and from her he must, perforce, be contented with friendship alone. All he could find to say now was, "You have an unusual taste in men, Tilda."

The child peeked up at him, then quickly looked down again, shaking her head.

"Haven't they told you I'm a cruel ogre who eats naughty scullions for breakfast?"

Tilda giggled a little before falling back into silence, but she did not withdraw her statement.

"Besides, I'm old enough to be your grandfather."

"I know I'm not a lady," said Tilda, almost in a whisper, "but I only hoped, maybe, just this once . . ."

For all anyone knew of Tilda's birth, she might as easily be the bastard of gentlefolk as of peasants. True, she had been wrapped in rags when old, one-eyed Rozennik found her; but some rascal could have stolen a rich blanket from around the baby before leaving her in the kitchen. Nevertheless, even baffled as he was by the situation, the seneschal realized that trying to comfort Tilda by telling her she might be of noble birth could lead to further trouble by discontenting her with her place in life.

"No, Tilda," he said, without taking time to choose his words more carefully, "I'm not going to wear your token." He dropped it back into her lap.

She touched it and bowed her head a little further. "It's all right. I understand. I only thought, sir . . ."

He tried, after the fact, to soften the blow. "What would Nap or Scarhand say if they knew about it, eh? Or old Flaptongue?"

"I only thought . . . nobody would have to know, sir. They woudn't have to know it wasn't a real lady's. . . ." She touched the token again. "But it . . . it doesn't look like a lady's, does it, sir? Not fine . . . I'm sorry, sir!"

Snatching it up, she jumped to her feet as if to run away. He caught her arm. Almost immediately he regretted the impulse. "Don't go back to the kitchen without washing your face," he ordered her, looking for something to say.

"No, sir." She shook her head, starting to wipe her eyes with the ill-fated token.

He took it back from her before she thought of blowing her nose into it. "I'm not going to wear your token, Tilda," he said, "but I'm going to give it to another lady. It's a very good piece of work. I think she'll like it. Do you mind?"

"Oh, no—no, sir!" Tilda looked up with a crooked half
smile, then looked down again, using her sleeve instead of
her token to wipe her eyes. He could not tell whether she
was a little solaced or not, but as yet he did not want to
say more about his plans for her embroidery. "Remember
to wash your face," he told her, and watched her run
across the tiltyard to the well beside the far archway.

Needlecraft was one mystery Sir Kay did not know
except by results, which he could only judge as they
pleased or did not please him. He thought, however, that
Tilda's handiwork was remarkable for a child her age with
no one's teaching but her own. He had not told her that the
lady to whom he meant to give her token was the Queen,
lest it frighten the child or raise her hopes prematurely
high. But if boys like Beaumains, Tor, and Percivale de
Galis could come to court in the guise of peasant bump-
kins, demanding and receiving knighthood on the strength
of their desire without reference to their birth, then, thought
Kay, by the Holy Virgin, a hard-working little wench like
Tilda, whatever her birth, deserved her chance to have
something else than a life in the kitchen, too!

Three months later, not many days after Martinmas, a
mute oarsman steered a black barge down the Thames to
Westminster. In the barge lay the body of Elaine of Astolat,
the fingers of her right hand curved loosely around a letter
that told the end of her tale. It did not tell the beginning
nor the middle, for Elaine herself could not have put that
part into words.

Growing up in a manor that was already half hermitage,
raised by a father who assumed that whatever girls did not
instinctively know of life and love they were taught by
their husbands when the time came and by a nurse of
peasant stock who assumed that ways of love among the
gentlefolk were really as in the tales her nursling read to
her, watching two older brothers preparing for their roles
in a knighthood that seemed exactly like that in the books,
Elaine had spent a happy childhood waiting for the Love
that must inevitably come to her, also.

Then Love had come, kissed her, embraced her, worn her first true token and left his shield in her safekeeping. When she learned he had been wounded in the tournament, she had traveled through the woods until she searched him out and helped nurse him back to health. Then, in the end, he had refused her.

She could understand his refusal to wed her. Her guess was correct: he was Sir Lancelot, far above her. But that he should refuse even her offer of love without marriage— that she could not understand. Had not another Elaine borne him a son?

Moreover, when he refused her—the only man she could as yet conceive she would ever love—it was as if all mankind had rejected her as unworthy. She did not think of herself as a child, but as a ripe and eager woman; and his offer to dower her with a thousand pounds yearly at her marriage to some other good knight had seemed to her a bribe she would need to attract the husband who would not otherwise want her and whom she could not believe she would ever want.

Had the blow fallen at once in warm August, and not in November, Elaine might have begun to eat and sleep again before the chill struck her weakened body and killed her. But perhaps Elaine herself would have called it as well that early death gave her the chance to leave the world with a gesture of the romance that had failed her in life, and, after refusing Sir Lancelot's thousand pounds yearly, beg of him only one Mass-penny for her soul.

Lancelot was shocked to see her body, but he quickly calmed his conscience. When her last letter, bidding him farewell by name and asking his Mass-penny, was read aloud to the court, he told how he had done for her all that, in honor, he could. His greatest concern was that Guenevere might consider him guilty of more than had actually passed between him and the child, and so he explained to the Queen, as clearly as he could in the hearing of the court, that he had had no choice but to deny Elaine her wish, "For I love not to be constrained to love, madam," he finished, standing over Elaine's bier, "for

love must arise of the heart, and not by any constraint.'' It
did not occur to him that, by his courtesy and his actions
that first August afternoon, he had constrained to himself
the love that had arisen in Elaine's heart.

Lancelot had been gravely wounded in the Assumption
Day tournament because, as the Queen had feared, his
own kinsmen, not knowing him, had attacked him all
together during the melee. Otherwise, his ruse with the
blank shield and the lightly worn token had been entirely
successful, enabling him to cover himself with fresh glory.
Sir Kay had won no glory at all in that tournament, but
neither had he been seriously wounded. When Elaine's
black barge came to Westminster in November, Kay was
chiefest of the knights who helped draw it in to shore.

From one of the castle's upper windows, the Queen's
youngest handmaiden had watched Sir Kay and the others
draw in the barge. She was the Damsel Evaine, once the
scullery maid Tilda, whose name had been changed with
her station.

Her hands were no longer red and in need of rubbing
with goose fat every night. She was learning to read and
write, but she preferred weaving, embroidery, and chess.
As she saw the younger knights and older squires more
closely, she had begun to think it quite possible she would
someday fall in love with a young man of about her own
age; but she would always remain grateful to Sir Kay. She
was now embroidering another scarf for him, this time
using silk and sewing with a fine, thin needle, not the
blunt, thick one old Rozennik had lent her in the kitchen.
Working by good daylight, she hoped to have the new
token finished in time for the jousts at Christmas. This
time, he had promised to wear it.

Nevertheless, she laid her own work aside willingly for
a day in order to join the Queen and her other handmaidens
in making a new samite pall for Elaine of Astolat.

ELIZABETH ANN SCARBOROUGH served four years with the Army Nurse Corps, including a tour in Viet Nam. She spends her time writing, ". . . playing and listening to folk music, weaving, cat-admiring."

Her humorous fantasy novels are well known to fans: Song of Sorcery, Bronwyn's Bane, The Harem of Aman Akbar, *and* The Drastic Dragon of Draco, Texas.

It may be that the only serious things in life are death and taxes; of the two, I'm only sure about taxes, and Ms. Scarborough may agree. She's rarely serious about anything for very long, which may be the direct result of looking at real horror in Nam, and any legend, icon or shibboleth is the healthier for an honest horselaugh now and then. Hamlet *was marvelously served by Stoppard's* Rosencrantz & Guildenstern Are Dead, *the New Testament by* Jesus Christ Superstar *and* Godspell. *Someday even* Oedipus *may get its turn. ("Look here, aren't you coming on a bit strong over an honest mistake? You weren't to know. So you like older women. Push on, old boy.")*

"The Camelot Connection" is what happens when two trendy therapists try to set a classic problem to rights. Ms. Scarborough says she "read entirely too many self-help books in between fantasy stories, which resulted in the following hybridization."

The Camelot Connection

by Elizabeth Ann Scarborough

"Of course not. This isn't anything like possession," Miles argued. Cecily knew him well enough to recognize that he was arguing, even though he kept his voice calm, well-modulated, and soothing. "Not in the hocus-pocus demonic sense you mean, anyway. We're not demons, after all. I am a scientist—a therapist. And these are very sick people we're discussing here. Very sick."

"Miles, that's Merlin the *Magician* you're talking about," Cecily said, pointing to the image on the screen of the Chronological Retrotransport Astral Projections System monitor. "*The* Merlin the Magician. You can't just use his body like a—like a hotel room. And the others—King Arthur, Lancelot, Guinevere, I mean, they're *royalty*."

"Cecily, you sound like an adulating adolescent. I'm perfectly aware that these people were royalty. Otherwise they couldn't have possibly made such a mess out of Western civilization with their neurotic hangups. You're letting your illusions get in the way of your objectivity. We aren't going to harm our host. We aren't even going to interfere with his daily routine. Look at him! He's already succumbed to Nimue's blandishments and in his own time has already been inactive for a period of months. He's essentially comatose. We will simply resurrect his body and reanimate it in order to help those he would help if he were able. Darling, how do you think it makes me feel watching you cry every time you reread *The Once and Future King* or listen to the soundtrack from *Camelot* when I know that thanks to current technological and theoretical advances in therapy and the development of my CRAPS design, we have the wherewithal to abort that sad situation, so that you need never cry about it again?''

His velvety brown eyes pleaded with her like those of a dog who wanted only to be her friend. Of course, Miles had been much more than a friend for several months and he *was* a brilliant therapist, as all of his viewers, readers, and listeners would gratefully affirm. And it was sweet of him to take an interest in her favorite story. Silly of her to imagine he'd been jealous of her preoccupation with Arthurian lore. Why, he had even gone so far as to read the novelization of the latest remake of *Camelot the Movie*. She had just never expected him to put her interest and his together like this. She didn't know if she liked the idea.

''Cecily, it's your decision. But I think we're dealing with some genuine pathology here. Do you want to participate in this or not?''

''Well, sure, but I don't see why we have to come in right at the saddest part, right when Lancelot and Guinevere fall in love and Arthur knows and they know he knows and he knows they know he knows. . . .''

''Because, darling, that's when the crisis requires intervention. But if it's too traumatic for you, you needn't participate. It's your choice. I want you to be clear on this now.''

''Okay.''

''You're sure?''

She nodded tentatively. She'd figured on rubbing elbows with stars when she started going with Miles Standish, *the* Miles Standish of *Miles to Go*, the smash success quick-fix self-help TV talk show. But she had never imagined she'd meet crowned heads—especially *those* crowned heads.

"I want you to be absolutely certain," he was saying. "*Are* you?"

"Absolutely . . . I—I think," she said. She was disgusted with herself for not being more definite, for doubting Miles. Why was it that as soon as she started sleeping with a smart guy like that she lost respect for him? Miles was not only a charismatic TV personality, he was a genius. Everybody knew that. Long before men started purposely streaking their hair gray in imitation of his, before his chocolately eyes sent thrills of trusting lust through his patients-by-proxy, he had been a brilliant researcher, an innovative engineer.

The controversial but effective REALLY device that helped people *really* see what their therapists had to offer and changed lives almost instantly was his invention. Inexpensive and simple to manufacture, the device could be used with any therapeutic regime. Before the devices had hit the market Miles had been too busy developing them to do any therapeutic theorizing of his own, and afterwards he started lecturing, writing best-selling books, and going on promotional tours.

He kept up with all the latest popular treatment modalities by playing tapes of the other self-help docs to himself while he slept. It made sleeping with him really weird sometimes, but interesting. Fortunately, he never took any of what he heard personally enough to wonder why he was only seriously attracted to much younger women. Cecily was profoundly grateful for that. Romantic that she was, she didn't begin to fool herself that she was in any way a match for Miles but he did seem to like having her around. Around the clock and for all time, apparently.

Time travel, huh? Well, for sure no football hero her own age could get her a box seat at Camelot. She wondered if CRAPS would give her a hellacious case of jet-lag. "Sure," she said. "I think the whole idea is really neat, Miles. I guess I'm just a little dense sometimes."

"I'm very pleased at your decision, dear. I didn't want to pressure you with the magnitude of the social implications before you had made your choice but whether you realize it or not, we have before us the unique opportunity to change one of the biggest tragedies in history. Camelot was the crucible of Western civilization as we know it. Once the rulers became stressed out by emotional problems, their society degenerated into free-floating aggression, and it was downhill for the world from there. But we can fix that, you and I. Do you realize that when we return here, to our own bodies, it may be to a safer, saner world, one without the threat of global and interstellar warfare— all because we are going to nip world hostilities in the bud by setting some key people straight about human relationships?''

''But what about all those laws about interfering with time? In the old *Star Trek* episodes—''

''Even if they weren't fiction to begin with, dear girl, those laws would be made obsolete by my methods. The only thing that's really critical about time travel is the danger of meeting yourself coming and going. With CRAPS that's impossible. We never leave our bodies, merely transfer our consciousnesses to a body existing in the time we wish to enter.''

She looked dubiously at Merlin sleeping away up on the monitor screen. Funny to realize it wasn't just some guy's idea of what Merlin looked like but the real, actual Merlin, scientifically located and validated. And she and Miles were going to occupy his body. ''Isn't it going to be a little crowded in there? With both of us, I mean?'' she asked.

''How much space do you imagine consciousness requires, darling?'' Miles asked, indulgent and amused. ''I weigh—what? One eighty, and I'm a good foot taller than you—are you admitting that I am therefore more conscious? Now, you know I would never dream of squelching your questing intelligence, but we are a bit limited as to our entry time. I have to be at the studio for makeup at five A.M. tomorrow, you know, so we have to locate our subjects, provide therapy for them, and be back in the cave in time for the transfer, or I'll miss the show. So why don't you just lie back now and stare into the screen?''

She plopped down on one of the army cots positioned underneath the tilted screen. Miles could have afforded nicer, but it wouldn't have looked as serious when the people who gave grant money came around. Abruptly, she sat up again. "What if something goes wrong?" she asked.

"Like what?"

"Like the central computer goes down or a power outage—"

"My dear girl," he said kindly, taking her shoulders and shaking them gently. "It's all right to be afraid, but believe me, nothing can go wrong. Do you think I'd risk taking you, someone completely outside the project, if I thought there was any danger? I just felt that since no camera equipment or other tangible paraphernalia can be transferred yet, which means I need an observer to verify my data, that observer should be you. Your compassion for these people inspired the project, after all. And you've studied the period—I feel your insight will be invaluable in presenting our findings. Also, I'll admit, I thought you might be helpful with the Queen. I gathered from the book that she and Merlin never developed much rapport."

She sighed and lay down again, concentrating on the picture of Merlin. Slowly, it began throbbing, alternating auras of color expanding and contracting. Miles lay beside her, a tranquil smile on his face. She didn't see it. She just knew it was there.

Merlin kept throbbing. And sometime later, in an undesignated cavern not so far from the castle at Camelot as once believed, the great mage sat up, stretched, swung his legs over the edge of the stone platform he'd been lying on, and jogged around the cavern several times to get the circulation going. Then he went looking for the King.

"How do you intend to find him?" Cecily asked Miles inside Merlin's head.

"How many castles can there be in the neighborhood?" he replied.

"Gosh, that's right. And I guess Merlin's body probably knows the way too, huh? Do you suppose it might just sort of 'poof' us there?"

"Perhaps. But I'd think you might have had enough poofing for one day."

In Merlin's towertop laboratory at Camelot Morgan La Fey gazed deeply into a crystal ball not unlike an enlarged version of Miles's REALLY seeing device. "Where the hell does that old fart think he's going?" she asked. "I'm surrounded by incompetents!" She smacked the ball angrily and sent it spinning on its base "Nimue!" she snapped into the ball. "Nimue! Get yourself hither at once!" That order issued she stood clicking her long hennaed nails against the ball. "Now then," she wondered aloud, "where can that nephew of mine be?"

The King sat at his desk with maps spread around his crooked elbows, which supported his palms, which supported his head. His Majesty had another migraine.

He brightened, however, when he looked up and saw his old teacher. "Merlin!" he said, "You've come back."

"Hi there," Miles said.

"Hi there, Your Majesty," Cecily whispered within Merlin's mind. Her sense of fitness was well-developed. "He is the King, you know. Poor dear, he looks like he could use a neck rub."

"Since we're operating here within my area of expertise, let's handle this my way, please, darling," Miles replied, asserting his authority. Really, Cecily had such an unrealistic fairy-tale orientation to life. His primary reason for including her in this rather critical experiment was to try to help her overcome it, to see life as it really was, even once upon a time. The man before him looked like any of his other poor disgruntled marriage counselees.

"Old friend, I feared you had abandoned us for good. How glad I am to see someone I can confide in. I'm at wits' end for what to do about this. First my son appears— why didn't you warn me about him? Then there's this business with Lance and Jenny. And all at once. I have never needed your advice so badly. Be a good chap and give my shoulders a rub, would you?"

With an inner hmph at Miles Cecily took charge of Merlin's old hands. They looked so strange to her, with their wrinkles and liver spots, but they were so much stronger than her own that when she applied moderate pressure Arthur winced. She modified it and His Majesty grunted with pleasure.

"Do you seek my advice, King Arthur, or my approval?" Miles asked.

"Eh? Approval? Don't believe so. I don't believe so. I'm the King, as you keep telling me, and don't need anyone's approval, but your advice would be most welcome. This thing's getting out of hand. The business with Lance and Jenny, I mean. I'm sure it's all perfectly innocent, but nasty rumors have started. I have a position to maintain and this is damned awkward. How will I explain it to my people? Have I been such a poor husband? Such a poor friend and King?"

"Mmmm," Miles said wisely. Cecily thought her heart would break. Right now Arthur didn't look as if he could pull a sword out of butter, much less stone. He looked a lot different than she had imagined. He had crooked teeth, jug ears, and freckles, and his wild red hair was in no way tamed by the circlet he kept disarranging as he ran his fists up and down his head. The empty wineglass beside him bespoke the way he was handling this problem. Despite his battle-hardened thews, or she guessed those were thews, poking out of his robe, sort of bony and veiny and muscular, he had a wistful, wimpy look about him that appealed to Cecily, who would have taken in stray cats and dogs if her landlord allowed her to.

"It's okay, Your Majesty," she said, and instantly felt Miles's disapproval.

"It is *not* okay, Cecily, okay? King Arthur has to work through this. He's asking us to validate him but he'll never be helped until validation comes from within himself. The man's a flaming neurotic—I mean, the Queen cheats on him with his best friend and *he* assumes responsibility for their actions *and* the opinion of all England, for pity's sake."

"Oh."

"The man needs to learn better coping mechanisms. Do you understand?"

"I guess so." She didn't. She was touched by Arthur's pain. God, maybe being neurotic was catching.

"Good, now then." The old magician spoke to Arthur in Miles's low, reassuring tones. "How do you feel about Lancelot's and Guinevere's affair, Arthur? Is it really okay with *Arthur*? It's bound to have caused you a lot of hurt in *there*." He thumped Merlin's chest with his fist. "You must be having a lot of conflict over this. Aren't you mad?"

"*Rah*ther."

"Then show it, man. Let it out."

"I can't. Lance can beat me at any joust. Besides, I don't want to."

"You don't want to what? Joust? Or lose their love? That's really it, isn't it?"

"Well, yes."

"But you don't want to lose your people's love and respect either."

"Of course not."

"Do you think you're a *good* King, Arthur? Would you call yourself a tyrant?"

"That's mean, Miles," Cecily hissed. "Arthur was the best king England ever had. How can you say—"

"Shh . . . Well, Arthur?"

"I try not to be a tyrant."

"Don't you feel it's a little tyrannical to try to dictate to your people how they should feel about you?"

"I—Merlin, what is this? *You're* the one who taught me to try to understand how others feel so I can be a better ruler."

"Under*stand*, yes, but not dictate. And if you're always behaving in such a way as to manipulate people into feeling the way you think they should, that's the same thing, isn't it?"

"No, I mean, yes, I mean, I don't know. Merlin, this whole thing has me so confused, I think I must be going mad!"

"Calm yourself, Majesty. I'm here to help you. . . . Keep massaging," Miles added in an aside to Cecily. "Now then, Arthur, tell me about Lancelot. How long have you been attracted to him?"

It took Miles several delicate tries to be specific enough that the King understood him. After all, the King's sword still lay beside him on the table. Miles detested violence and the sight of even a normal sword would have made him edgy. A magic sword like Excalibur must have been even worse for him, Cecily thought.

Once Arthur understood the question, he laughed. "Well, naturally—I was trained in the Roman soldiering tradition, you know. But that sort of thing is for long campaigns, not for my bedchamber, old fellow, where I have had, thus far, a perfectly good wife."

"Aha! But now we *are* getting somewhere. Arthur, I need to retire to my laboratory. I have something there that will be of great assistance to you."

Arthur's weary eyes lit slightly. "Magic again, old friend? After all these years?"

"Of a sort. But I must speak to Lancelot and Guinevere as well. Individually, and then I'll want a group therapy session to wrap things up. So, if you'll summon the other pa—uh, Lancelot and Guinevere so that I may speak with them, I'll just run along and, er, clean up a few details."

"Do yourself while you're at it, old man," the King said, clapping him on the back. Arthur looked more cheerful, though no less confused, after their talk. "I'll have the servants take fresh things to the baths for you."

"Baths?" Miles queried.

"Roman baths," Cecily said, "like in Dr. Newman's book. Oh, come on, Miles, let's. I never thought Merlin might have fleas, but this beard is sure itchy."

Camelot's decor was not much different from that of the castles in coffee-table books—ornamentation was sparse, and the servants had to scurry around a lot to keep everything from smelling bad. Well, so what? There had to be several hundred people living here and it was before Lysol. Cecily had always sort of dreamed of Camelot as being more like a fairy-tale castle than real ones—open and light and comfortable instead of dark, dank, and drafty. Even the giant tapestries were dark with dust, and big as they were, they weren't a patch on the vast acres of blank stone wall. She saw a woman spinning by an arrow slit and wanted to go talk to her. She had this friend in Berkeley who spun. Miles hustled her onward.

"We must find Merlin's lab," he said. "It's been so long since I've had to handle a client without using the REALLY device that I'd forgotten how time consuming and tedious it is. Merlin should have the ingredients though. Fortunately, they're fairly common and the devices are easy enough to make."

Once more she felt a rush of pride in his ingenuity. He demonstrated it again almost at once as they approached a sulky-looking boy who bore a strange resemblance to that classic old movie star, John Travolta.

"Having a nice day?" Miles asked the boy. "Look, I'll give you . . ." Stumped by the currency problem and Merlin's lack of pockets, Miles paused. "Uh, I'll pay you well if you'll come with me to my workshop and—"

The boy smiled with delight. "Lost, Merlin? Find Nimue's spell disorienting, do we? Or is it just senility? No, no. No thunderbolts please. Just joking. Right this way . . ."

The boy kept looking behind him and smirking. When he opened the door to the workshop and swept the floor with his cap as he bowed mockingly low, the reason for his amusement was clear. "See what I've brought you, Auntie," he said to the lady who glared triumphantly at them as she emerged from the lavender, ochre, and lime-colored smoke trailing out of various bubbling beakers. Her hair stood out in a black frizz and from her eyes Cecily wondered if she was on drugs.

"Paranoid schizophrenic if ever I saw one," Miles said.

"Auntie, aren't you going to tell me how clever I am? I've only brought you Merlin himself, come to reclaim his laboratory. I knew you wouldn't mind company."

"How very perceptive of you, Mordred darling. But I told you to get your ass up here an hour and a half ago."

He shrugged. "Probably fate prevented it, Auntie," he said with ponderous solemnity.

"Fate? Was that her name? Never mind."

"It's Morgan La Fey," Cecily hissed to Miles. She'd known the witch at once. Who else would wear black macramé over bare skin and gold-gilt eye shadow in the middle of the day? "The evil sorceress."

"Of course it is," Miles said. "I knew it at once. Delusions of omnipotence, persecution complex, sees visions, hears voices—oh yes, it could hardly be anyone else. But evil? Cecily, my dear, it's unlike you to be so insensitive. The poor woman is the product of a fearful and superstitious background. Why, didn't it say that she was traumatized by witnessing the rape of her mother at an early age? That sort of thing is bound to engender some aberrations, poor dear." To Morgan he said with great empathetic warmth and kindness, "Good to see you, Ms. La Fey. Really good to see you."

"*Is* it?" the enchantress asked, undulating towards the old man's body and producing a physical reaction in the anatomy that made Cecily want to make Merlin giggle.

"What's the matter with you?" Miles asked sharply, not very pleased to be distracted from Morgan.

"Nothing. I think I suddenly understand all that stuff about penis envy is all."

"What are you going to do, Merlin?" Morgan asked. "Create some new potion? Unleash some new powers? Weave a mighty spell?"

"Something like that," Miles said. "Actually, it's simply an ingenious adaptation of microelectronics for use in a pre-electronic age, if you catch my drift. Ah, what have we here?" he muttered, pawing through objects on the tables and shelves and selecting some. "Uh-huh—silicon-based crystal, good. Looks here like the makings of a dry-cell battery, excellent. And the other things, for the ultrasonics, umm-*hmm*. Yes, yes, everything is here. Won't take but a sec to whip these up. My dear lady," he said absently to Morgan, "I don't wish to seem rejecting but you *are* in my light and are eliciting an unsolicited erotic response totally at odds with my present need for urgency and also with my commitment to my primary relationship. Also, I must confess, I've never been partial to brunettes."

He then concentrated Merlin's focus so totally on constructing the REALLY devices that the spell Morgan was weaving went unnoticed until he finished. Cecily had felt a creepy sensation at their back but had been unable to tear their eyes away from Miles's work long enough to investigate.

"You don't fancy brunettes, eh?" the thwarted witch cried, producing a wall of flames within which she and Mordred stood untouched. Cecily thought flames were pretty old hat, a crude way to handle someone with Merlin's clout. Then she realized the flames were just a kind of symbolic hors d'oeuvre, when the naked nonbrunette nymph slithered forth from the fire. Her hair blended with the fire, red and gold as autumn leaves, her eyes a flashing yellow-green. She also had big boobs. That struck more fear into Cecily than the fire. Miles had a thing for big boobs.

"My love," the girl sighed effectively, "why have you left our bower of passion?" A tear trickled down one bright eye along the peachy length of her neck and onto the nearest ripe curve, where it sizzled.

But Miles was a brick. A prince. A hero. He actually managed to look into her eyes. "Nimue, right? Ah, ah. None of that sort of body language out of you, my dear. Let's see if we can't talk about what's *really* going on with you, shall we?"

He held up the newborn REALLY seeing device. A prismatic crystal powered with the same throbbing emanations as the computer simulation of Merlin, the device was appropriately attractive and nonthreatening. Though she tried to ignore it, the nymph, like many anxious and defensive clients, was drawn to it, first examining it curiously, then being soothed by it, her mind opened to perception and insight by its benign radiations. Her green-gold eyes turned dreamy and friendlier than Cecily was, strictly speaking, glad to see.

"Nimue," Miles said. "What *are* we doing with this torch-singer's entrance, dear? Why do you feel compelled to power trip poor old Mer—me? You're a lovely, talented woman who shouldn't have to lock up mature magicians to be happy in life."

"Yes, I do," the nymph replied, "or Morgan will turn me into a tree frog."

"That's a cop-out, Nimue," Miles scoffed in a sincere yet jocular manner. "The choice is yours—you're the one who decides what Nimue does. And *you*, not Morgan or Mordred or Merlin, are the only one who can turn yourself into a toad—that will only happen if you don't believe in yourself. Do you see?" He gently tapped the side of the REALLY seeing device.

"Morgan," Nimue said. "Morgan, it isn't my fault and you can't blame me if your schemes fail. I'm tired of playing these games. I think I'm going to go back to the woods and have some alone time now—"

"Dammit, Nimue, don't you *dare* fail me!" Morgan growled. "What the hell kind of a nymph are you if you can't enchant an occasional dirty old man when I ask you to?"

"I don't care," Nimue replied, protruding a petulant lower lip, "I'd just rather not. Merlin used to be kind of sweet but now, well, he's just *weird*."

"*You'd* rather not? You'd rather *not*?" Morgan demanded. "Well, then, I take it that what you *would* rather is to be that tree frog after all. How many warts would you like? I'll make sure to turn you an unbecomingly bilious shade of green."

Nimue tossed her fiery locks and kept staring into the REALLY device. "You can't do it. He said so. And I think, weird or not, he's more powerful than ever now." With that she stepped from the flames and paraded across the room and out the door as if she were wearing a train instead of her birthday suit.

Morgan fumed and gestured but it was to the nymph's back, which turned only a little verdant around the edges.

"Miles, that was *wonderful*," Cecily said. "You've stood up to Morgan La Fey's magic."

"Not quite yet," he said, as the sorceress turned her glittering eyes on Merlin. She had to look at the device to look at him, however, since Miles had plastered it to Merlin's forehead. "You don't really want to toy with *me* do you, Morgan?" he asked sadly. "You know, manipulating a young girl to harm another person is quite a different thing from facing your fear of that person yourself—but then, direct confrontation isn't exactly your style, is it? Morgan, by not being open about these needs of yours, you're hurting nobody but yourself. Work with me on this and we can make a healthier, happier witch out of you, one who can rise in her career through her own merits and won't have to envy anybody. . . ."

Morgan warily watched the REALLY device with her gilt eyes, and briefly, Cecily thought the device might be working—the glitter in the enchantress's eyes seemed wet. Then the sorceress drew herself up and flung the black-mesh sleeves of her gown open like wings. "How *dare* you presume to lecture me, you addlepated old power monger!" she thundered in a voice that sounded like Boris Karloff talking through a rock band's sound equipment. "See if I ever pander to *your* perverted tastes again, preposterous old poop!"

Then, flinging the sleeves above her head, shielding her face, she disappeared.

Mordred clapped happily and turned back to Merlin as if waiting for the next trick. Eyes lowered so that he addressed the area somewhat to the left of Merlin's right shoulder, he avoided looking at the device. "Your little bauble certainly got the wind up dear Auntie, Merlin," he said. "Jolly clever of you. I can think of the most fascinating applications. May I examine it more closely?"

"Certainly," Miles said, tapping Merlin's forehead. "Just look right up here—"

"Oh, but I'm a very tactile person," Mordred said, his eyes widening with naive innocence that was extremely shifty. "Auntie is forever saying that I need to have my finger in every pie. I need to handle it to really appreciate it."

Cecily clapped Merlin's hand over the device. "Afraid not," she said.

"You wouldn't derive full benefit from it that way," Miles added soothingly, prying Merlin's fingers loose from his scalp. "I think it would be much better if you just examined it from there while we talk about your feelings of self-hate because your father rejected you. . . ."

"I don't agree," Mordred said. "I think talking is quite useless. I will like myself much better once I have that thing that enhances your power, great mage, you who never needed so much as a wand before. Now give it here like a nice old fart or I shall have to confiscate it forcibly. If I refrain from looking at it until it is mine, I doubt you'll be able to stop me."

Cecily doubted it too. Without the magician inside of Merlin, there was no way to defend the aged body. She plucked the device from the mage's forehead and thrust it forward as Miles protested, "You mustn't allow a disadvantaged childhood to ruin the rest of your life."

"Disadvantaged? Hah! Hardly. I could do anything I wished, have anyone I wished, and I intend to keep on doing and having. Starting with what you have there. Now *give*—" and he lunged across the worktable, smashing beakers and other precious equipment.

"Security!" Miles cried authoritatively. "Send a security officer at once!"

"Heelpp!" Cecily screamed, her mode of expression being somewhat less acculturated. "Save us!"

The door flung open. "Hullo, there you are," said the handsomest man she had ever seen in her life, his beauty doubly reflected in his shining armor. "Mon Dieu, but it is smoky in here. Milord Mordred, I believe your fencing master awaits you. And Merlin, *mon vieux*, the King suggested we might walk together to the baths. I have just returned from an invigorating ride over two hundred miles of rough terrain, rescuing damsels and single-handedly conquering five neighboring kingdoms in the name of Our Lord and King Arthur. His Majesty says a dash of cologne will not suffice."

"And what does *Her* Majesty say?" Mordred asked. But it was his parting shot. Faced with armed might instead of doddering age, he beat a hasty retreat.

"What a nasty crack!" Cecily said. "I don't believe a word of it. Just look at those clear blue eyes and those angelic curls and cute little dimples. The man has the face of a saint. I think Mordred made it all up."

"Hmph," Miles said. "Not to mention the broad shoulders and small waist and that enormous tin jockstrap, eh? Saint indeed. If you'll recall, the guy was a religious maniac who transferred his addictive obsession to the Queen when he decided angels weren't allowed to be horny."

"Miles! That sounds judgmental to me," she said.

"Merely confronting reality, my dear. It's part of our mission, in case you've forgotten. And please stop batting our grizzled gray lashes at him. It conveys the wrong sort of message." To Lancelot he said, "As a matter of fact, Sir Lancelot, what *does* Her Majesty think about all of this?"

"Ah, Merlin, like His Majesty, I too am delighted to have you back. You are always so refreshing, so direct. Do you know that although you are of a deplorably pagan religious persuasion you remind me of the chaplain at Palais du Lac, my beloved old Frère Jules, in whom I could always confide."

Frankly, from the time the knight peeled off his shining armor and stepped into the warm Roman bath with them, the conversation was a blur to Cecily. She was too preoccupied processing more compelling data to take note of the therapeutic chitchat passing between Miles and Lancelot. It was no problem for the therapist, however, to keep Merlin's old eyes wide and receptive while the well-sculpted Lancelot poured his heart out. And it was no problem for the noble client, with the help of the device, to really see the wisdom offered him by the ancient magician. Lancelot saw it as clearly as if it was the Grail itself, and gratefully accepted it, understood it, and was transformed by it, much to Miles's delight.

"*Merci, mon ami,*" Lancelot said, and with dripping

hand shook dripping hand as he emerged from the bath. "I do see now that it is enough to be a person, one of God's creations, and a person alone, than to have to all the time be worrying what my liege will think of this or that that I do, to look to him as my God on earth, as though he were my father, and to sinfully wish to take unto myself his wife, as I might wish to take my mother, were I so far debauched. I feel cleansed of this passion for good now that it is all clear to me—"

"That isn't *exactly*—" Miles began.

"Yes, yes, I know, it is not exactly what you wish, that I thank you, but I must, and again I say *merci, merci, merci*. I go now to clothe myself in fine raiment, to eat a good meal, to take a long nap, and to find a fair maiden who will indulge me by teaching me the art of tapestry making, something I have always wished to learn but have never had the time for and have felt was unbefitting a knight's station. Now I know that such arbitrary distinctions are unimportant. *Merci*, again, *mon vieux*, and adieu."

"He's still a bit mixed up but over all I think we've made definite progress with that lad," Miles said, as the knight gathered up his armor and clanked away.

Not everyone was so pleased.

From beyond the doors came the murmur of voices and then a woman's, raised in protest, "But Lance, it's been *months*."

"Madame, I commend to you your husband," Lancelot's voice said, and the clanking receded down the hall.

Merlin's aged hands had barely had time to pull his robes decently over his creaking joints when the Queen, oblivious to the protests of her attendants, flew into the room, her cheeks flushed to a becoming mauve which handily matched her gown. Her golden hair flowed loose beneath her circlet and shot off sparks of light and static electricity. "What have you told Lancelot about me, you old blasphemer?" she demanded. "What have you said to my lord and husband?"

"Your Majesty!" Cecily exclaimed, and tried to drop Merlin into a curtsey.

Miles, unaccustomed to having clients cross his boundaries by invading his bath, was nevertheless cool. He whipped forth the REALLY device and held it up, saying, "Queen Guinevere, isn't it? Nice to meet you. I seem to hear you saying that you feel I've told Sir Lancelot something about you—maybe something derogatory, and that you also are worried that I've been speaking to your husband, the King. Is that correct?"

The Queen, her anger and anxiety reflected back to her as inappropriate in a reigning monarch, sank to the floor of the bath chamber, a bit of her hem gradually soaking up water from a puddled footprint. Her eyes filled with tears but did not leave the device.

Before she had finished crying so that they could proceed with the therapy, King Arthur barged through the doors. "God's bones," he said, "I had forgotten how you seem to stir things up around here, Merlin. The servants came to tell me Guinevere had joined you and Sir Lancelot in the bath and I thought I perhaps ought to investigate. Oh, there you are, my dear. Whatever are you doing down there? You'll catch your death sitting in a puddle like that."

"Actually, Sir Lancelot couldn't stay but the Queen and I were about to have a little chat," Miles said smoothly, raising the device so that Arthur could see it.

Guinevere turned guiltily to Arthur, "Your forgiveness, sire. I've caused you embarrassment again, haven't I?"

"Not really my dear, though I must say if you wished to talk to Merlin, that *is* what we have studies and drawing rooms and that sort of thing for."

"Yes, milord," she said meekly.

"Does it bother you that we're talking beside this pool, Arthur?" Miles asked. "Is it a threat to the kingdom that the King himself must see to—"

"Well, no, of course not, it's just that in view of the delicacy of the current situation, I thought—"

"You thought or one of Guinevere's servants thought? You still feel you must be in control of what everyone *thinks*, don't you, Arthur?"

Arthur stared into the device. "I—I suppose I do. Yes, I do. And it's a bloody nuisance, if you must know. I can't get a single thing done without three other things intruding and my private life, as you can see, is a long way from private."

"Does that make you feel important?"

"Miles, come on," Cecily said. "He's the King. How much more important does he have to be?"

"One is not always realistic about these things, dear. Believe me. I'm an expert," Miles answered.

"No," Arthur was saying. "No, it doesn't. It annoys me. But I let it happen anyway. And I needn't, need I? I am the King, after all. No one has a right to pry. Do you know how long it's been since I've been fishing? It's been this campaign and that treaty and this dragon and that grail since I started. I'm good and sick of it is what. Now they're trying to turn my own wife against me."

"You see how it goes then?" Miles said. "You do see that all of the problems that people give you are not your problems. Lancelot's problems are his. Guinevere's are hers, mine are mine. Get it?"

"I do," Arthur said, nodding his wild red hair vigorously. "Jenny, you're Queen. Run the kingdom for a while while I go fishing, won't you?"

"Uh, yes, sire, I suppose . . . ," she said, looking at him as if he had suddenly taken up swallowing flies.

He bent to drop a kiss on her nose. "Good. There's a dear. Well, so long then. I'm off."

"Well how do you like that?" she asked, when he had gone. "Lancelot is gone for months and comes back and snubs me and now Arthur leaves on the spur of the moment and just dumps the country in my lap. I ought to have gone to the nunnery like I wanted to while I still had the chance. He never tells me anything about what's going on or takes my side in disputes, he's so bloody careful of his precious reputation and laws. You know, my parents were both Roman citizens. We had a modicum of sophistication in our household, far from court as it was. You'd think when a person got to be Queen she'd get a little respect but no. My slutty sisters-in-law have bedded half of Britain, including my husband, and the first time I show the slightest sign of having a little crush on someone everybody cries "Burn the bitch!" You have to be a witch to get anyone to pay attention to you around here. Trying to be a decent Christian queen is most unrewarding. I'm treated with no more regard than a peasant child until *he* decides he wants to go fishing! And now Lancelot—"

"Lancelot doesn't want to play with you either, is that it, Guinevere?" Miles said, back in control of the dialogue again with the REALLY device held firmly before the Queen's eyes. "Don't you suppose it might have something to do with the fact that you, a grown woman, a sophisticated woman by your own estimation, treat your husband as if he were your father, calling him 'sire' all the time, and expecting him to administer the kingdom without your help? Do you think maybe the reason you've sought solace outside your primary relationship is that your concept of your husband as a father-figure interferes not only with you attaining the respect you think a queen should have but also keeps you from having a satisfying sex life with him? Do you think"—Miles hunkered Merlin down until he was eyeball to eyeball with the Queen, the device held up between them—"that maybe your attraction for Lancelot, the most uptight, moralistic, religiously conservative square in the whole Round Table, might have less to do with his sexiness than with punishing yourself by being with someone who is guaranteed to keep you feeling guilty for not being your 'sire's' good little girl? If you want to be a queen, be a queen, Guinevere. Take this opportunity to exercise your authority. You seem to feel you can rule as well as your husband and yet you haven't bothered to press him for details of running the kingdom. Assert yourself, woman. Show your capabilities. Would *you* respect a royal freeloader?"

"No," she said, rising. "No, I certainly wouldn't. You're absolutely right, Merlin. I see that now. I've been clinging to Lancelot because being in Arthur's shadow has made me feel so helpless and inadequate, but I don't really need either of them. As for learning about the country, I shall set out this very afternoon on a tour of the countryside, assessing the tax base, as it were and, er, seeing what wrongs need righting. And you, trusted advisor, shall ride beside me.''

"But I, uh . . .'' Miles began. He needed to have Merlin back in Nimue's chamber in time to be retransported for five A.M. makeup.

"I command it,'' Guinevere said, and swept from the room, her damp hem trailing a wet swathe on the tile floor behind her.

Morgan gazed gleefully into the crystal ball. "Mordred, darling, why on earth did you ever think we needed to rid ourselves of that dear old man? He's doing a much better job of ruining Arthur's life than either of us could possibly manage.''

Mordred shook his head disparagingly. "Auntie Morgan, when will you ever learn not to be so easily distracted by what amuses you? Ruining my beloved pater's life is not the point—at least not all of it. Acquiring control of the kingdom is the point, remember? And where that is concerned, nothing essentially is changed.''

"How very shortsighted of you, darling. Of course something has changed. For all our maneuvering, the three of them were previously unified—oh, miserable, true, but unified—behind the glorious image of Camelot. It could have gone on for years like that, while people were deluded by Arthur's tiresome ideas about chivalry, honor, charity, protecting the weak, and all of those other unprofitable enterprises. Why, even with the scheme to discredit Guinevere and Lancelot, we stand to make a martyr of somebody. This way, if we allow Merlin to continue, the kingdom will probably fall into ruin as Arthur abdicates responsibility while he rests on his laurels and lets Guinevere mismanage everything. Lancelot will weave inept tapestries while leaving the championship of the throne to those less able—making easy pickings for us.''

"But I don't want the kingdom after it's been ruined by

mismanagement," Mordred said sulkily. "I want it *now*. And I don't want to take the chance on what Merlin might do. That device he has is far too powerful. Can't we sort of help things along?"

Her eyes flashed for a moment and then she smiled slowly, playfully, and patted his cheek before turning back to the crystal. "Darling boy, you know I can't refuse you anything. What do you think? Shall we introduce a new factor in this little drama? Something in green, I think, rather large, and very, very hot."

"Brother Ignatius," Guinevere said, "take a note please. I don't think our peasants should continue this strip-and-burn method of agriculture any longer. There must be more efficient and attractive ways to farm. It's dangerous too—look there, they've burnt down the village while they were at it."

"Yes, Madame."

"I wish she'd finish this so we could return to the castle," Miles said, as Merlin coughed at the smoke still rising from the fields. "I really can't miss that makeup call. And I am dying to start the documentary on this event. Oh, for a video camera."

"You have to admire her though," Cecily said. "She's really good at this queen business. Really concerned with the poor people. Look how quick she picks up on what's happening. . . ."

The guards stiffened to attention as a dark figure appeared against the distant hills. They relaxed somewhat when they observed that the figure was wobbling on its feet as unsteadily as any newborn lamb—a black newborn lamb. "Your Majesty, Your Majesty, oh, thanks be to God you've come," said the burned-and-ash-smeared peasant as he collapsed as near to the Queen's horse as the guards would allow him to totter. "A dragon attacked us just after midday meal," he gasped, "destroyed our village, burned our crops, killed everyone in sight. I know not if there be other survivors."

"A dragon?" the Queen said. "In this day and age? I thought Arthur and the knights had rid the kingdom of such vermin long ago. Oh, why are men never thorough? And—oh my, it just came to me. This is July, is it not?"

"Yes, Madame," Lady Elaine murmured.

"No wonder it seemed wrong to me for the fields to be black. The dragon has come at a most inopportune time, burning everything before harvest. This is going to *seriously* affect the tax base. The King will not be pleased. He'd hoped to build a navy this winter. Well, the dragon will simply have to be stopped. Sir Lionel?"

"Yes, mum," said the aged knight at her right hand, his post more one of honor than utility since he was even more elderly and infirm than Merlin.

"Who is the greatest dragon-slayer in Britain?"

"King Arthur, mum," Sir Lionel replied, immediately providing the politically correct response.

"No, no, not him. I realize His Majesty has been responsible for the demise of many dragons, but it was strictly in an administrative capacity and I'm handling that right now. I mean, who is actually the best actual sword-wielding *slayer* of dragons?"

"Oh, that. Sir Lancelot, then, mum," the old knight said without hesitation.

"I'd, er, I'd rather not use Sir Lancelot right now. How about the others? We had a great many knights who went up against dragons, I recall. What about them?"

"Retired for service-incurred disabilities, mum, or deceased," Sir Lionel said. "Turrible things, dragons."

"You see there, Cecily," Miles said sadly. "*There* is your romantic Camelot, filled with ignorance and superstition. Dragons, for pity's sake! Undoubtedly government propaganda to explain bandits or Vikings or rival armies or—"

"Or maybe big birds like that one over there with the kind of spiny things on its back and the sun shining on its mouth so that it looks like fire?" Cecily asked, and turned Merlin's face toward it. Miles pointed Merlin's arm and let out a strangled cry.

After that, the situation deteriorated rapidly. It wasn't that everybody chickened out, exactly. Cecily firmly believed the guards would have gladly stayed to defend the Queen, if only the horses had cooperated. But Sir Lionel's reared and fell on him, the Queen's reared and threw her, and the other horses, riders and all, beat a fast retreat for the forest. Merlin's horse took off so fast it sort of dropped him in the process—leaving Merlin's body on the ground, staring.

Guinevere, meanwhile, had apparently decided that if being Queen meant she had to slay dragons, she would slay dragons. She tugged at Sir Lionel's sword but when it finally came loose, the release of tension sent her reeling and she staggered backwards under the sword's weight. Cecily got Merlin to the Queen at the same time the dragon reached her. The beast's piggy little eyes reflected its flame for what seemed an eternity. Then Miles, possibly acting automatically, shot Merlin's hand in the air, bearing the REALLY device and the dragon hovered for a moment, then covered Guinevere, Merlin, device, and all with its great claws and flew away with them. For once Cecily and Miles were in accord. Merlin fainted.

The great thump of their landing wakened them, accompanied by a shriek from Guinevere and a sharp intake of breath, followed by a sort of whimpering pant. Sharp things bit into Merlin's old flesh. "Ouch," Cecily said.

"OoawAW," Guinevere said.

The dragon settled down with a sound like a train putting on the brakes.

"Merlin, Merlin, while it's eating me, save yourself and go find Arthur. Tell him I—aahah*ah*!"

"What's the matter, Your Majesty?" Cecily asked.

"I seem to have broken my leg. Or to be more precise, I think the dragon did. Even if it goes to sleep I can't run and I've lost the bloody sword."

Merlin's old eyes adjusted to the dark and the Queen's pale face gradually appeared. The dragon was thrashing about trying to get turned so it could see them.

"Merlin, have you some spell that might save us?" the Queen asked.

"Uh-no, not on me—"

"As I thought," the Queen gasped. "Your spells never were convenient. Very well, then, you must sneak away and find Lancelot and Arthur while the dragon is devouring me. Hurry."

"But we—I—can't just leave you," Cecily said. "I mean, you can't just die like that. It's . . ." She tried to think what Miles would say, if he were saying anything, and wished he'd pull himself together enough to do so. "It's defeatist, is what it is. And, uh, not being nice to yourself. And being a martyr too. Yeah. You can't do that. It isn't healthy." The Queen was looking down at Merlin's hands and nodding, and Cecily noticed through a sort of daze that Merlin was still holding the device. The dragon had liked that device.

Now the great monster's tail thrashed as it righted itself so that its face was in the cave, its mouth, smelling of burned blood, turned towards them.

Suddenly Cecily realized that now was not the time for argument. The Queen had been making good sense when she suggested that Merlin, who had two sound legs, should run for help while the dragon was distracted with the Queen as an appetizer. But she just couldn't leave her that way. "Hi, dragon," she said, holding the device up so that the beady little eyes caught the glitter. She had no way of knowing it, but this particular dragon was more than commonly fond of glitter. "Listen, I think you ought to know, the latest studies show that a high protein diet is definitely the pits for your liver. Vegetarianism is not only much more humane, but the fiber content keeps you regular, you know? And there are lots of really yummy veggie dishes you can try. Not to mention breads. Uh, Her Majesty knows a whole lot about all kinds of great meatless quiches and megavitamin drinks and things that will take that green tinge right out of your scales in no time, right, Your Maj?"

"What?" Guinevere asked.

"I did come up with one little spell after all. Just go along with it and talk about nonmeat products till I get back."

And Merlin's fingers pressed the device into Guinevere's. Fortunately, cooking was something of a hobby of the Queen's and she launched into a discourse on the joys of herbal seasonings at once, keeping the dragon's tiny eyes fastened on the glittering, throbbing device while Cecily slipped Merlin around the tail and out the front of the cave.

The cave bored into the side of a cliff, fronting a tumultuous stream. Cecily pointed Merlin upstream. She sorely missed her own fit young body when she tried to push his elderly one into a jog and ran out of breath within two minutes. She also missed Miles, who seemed to have conked out again. She had begun to despair of ever making it back to the castle in time to save the Queen, who surely couldn't know *that* many recipes, when she heard a horse whicker anxiously, no doubt aroused by the dragon smell still lingering on Merlin's robes.

King Arthur, a fishing pole extending between his knees and the stream, awoke suddenly and lunged for his sword. Even when he saw that the intruder was Merlin, he looked no gladder to see him than the horse had.

"Your Majesty, am I ever glad I found you!" Cecily cried, sinking Merlin's aching body onto the turf beside the King. "There's a dragon ravaging the countryside," she announced, feeling pretty proud of herself for remembering that ravaging was what dragons did to countrysides and that was the way Merlin would say it.

"I wish you'd be consistent," Arthur complained. "First you tell me to take a rest, then you come and bother me with reports of dragons. I left the Queen in charge, you know."

"That's just the problem. The Queen's broken her leg. She's about to get eaten."

"It goes with the territory," Arthur said. "If you're all that concerned, why didn't you use your magic to save her?"

"I did, sort of, but I used all I had to stall the dragon till you get there. . . . Miles, explain it to him," she nudged. "Miles, what has *happened* to you?" and this time she felt a stirring.

"Ahh," Miles said. "I thought it had to be all a dream. Fire-breathing dragons indeed! Anyone knows they're just symbols of inner conflict."

"Miles, that symbol of inner conflict is going to barbecue the Queen unless you convince King Arthur to go save her."

"How sexist of you, Cecily, to assume that the husband has to do such a thing, presuming there *is* such a thing."

"Sorry," she said, "but I couldn't think of anybody else close by who knows how to slay dragons. And you know very well there is a dragon because you saw it yourself, uh, in a manner of speaking."

"If I do as you ask, it will set King Arthur back in his therapy and I don't think that's very ethical. However, I realize this experiment has been a shock to you—"

"*I'm* not the one who passed out."

"So I'll give it a go. Where's the device?"

"Queen Guinevere is holding off the dragon with it."

"But it hasn't been tested on dragons yet! My dear girl, to put the device in the hands of a layperson to use untherapeutically on an untested species is extremely irresponsible! We must retrieve it at once."

"Talk to the King about it, Miles," she said. "I don't think Merlin can climb back up there."

"That was very manipulative of you, my dear," he said sadly, but spoke to Arthur.

"And I was just getting over being anxious about how the kingdom was going," the King said. "I mean, I finally felt like I was making progress and now you want me to go back in again and slay more dragons."

"You do have a contract with the people, sire, and the damage to their property was very bad."

"Yes, and I'm sure I'll hear all about it at tax time. Why don't peasants ever take care of themselves, for heaven sakes? Or wives, for that matter. I'm not at all prepared for dragons right now. I haven't my armor or anything with me, just my sword. Fighting things is really Lancelot's department. I'll do what I can until you can fetch him and the proper equipment, but I'm really not supposed to be getting my hands sooty these days. I'm management.''

Mordred, mounted and resplendent in designer armor with matching horse accessories, trotted across the drawbridge from the castle. He looked mildly astonished when a bedraggled Merlin heading the opposite direction flagged him down.

''Prince Mordred, there's a dragon abroad in the countryside and Sir Lancelot's services are urgently required. Have you any idea where he is?''

''I do indeed. But it won't do you any good. The other victims already told him about the dragon and he's not at all interested, thanks to you. He's far more concerned with tangling skeins and being charming, causing all the ladies to prick their fingers. He's in the west tower. Ta, now. I must be off. *Someone* has to take charge in the kingdom, you know.''

''Don't you even want to know where the dragon is?'' Miles called after him.

''Oh, I know.''

''I'll bet he does,'' Cecily said. ''And I bet his idea of helping is to cut Guinevere and King Arthur into bite-size pieces for the dragon so it doesn't have to strain its jaws.''

Whatever Mordred's motives, Lancelot could hardly care less.

''Madame and Monsieur Pendragon may fight their own battles,'' Lancelot said. ''As for me, it is better for my immortal soul if I take no part in them, n'est-ce-pas? I shall always be fond of Guinevere and consider her a friend, but I now know, thanks to your wisdom, *mon ami*, that there will be other women, that I am strong enough to forge other, healthier relationships and do not need this so sick addiction to my friend's wife. I also know that it is not fitting that I subjugate my life to my friend. For how can true friendship grow if it is always I who give and he who takes, he who commands and I who acquiesce? Therefore, *non*, not this time. I have somewhat outgrown those relationships, though I bear no hard feelings.''

"The dragon does though," Cecily could not help putting in, "and don't try passing the buck to me because I've already done what I can. That dragon needs a sword, not magic. It is going to cream your outgrown friends if you don't help, Sir Lancelot."

"Cecily, don't whine," Miles said. "It sounds like you've been doing a lot of thinking, Sir Lancelot. I'm glad to hear it, because I'm sure you'll have a lot of time to rethink your priorities when Prince Mordred ascends to the throne, which ought to be sometime tomorrow from the way the dragon was carrying on when I dropped King Arthur off at the cave."

"Prince Mordred? That *cochon*? That snake in the bushes? *He* will never sit on the throne of Britain—"

"I wouldn't be too sure," Miles said calmly. "He was heading for the dragon's cave as I rode up. Probably will see to a decent burial for the royal remains, that sort of stuff."

"But don't worry," Cecily told him. "You guys will get along just fine now, now that you don't care about duty or honor or chivalry or undying love anymore. He never did go for that stuff."

"That— Merlin, you speak more and more strangely but I think I cannot deal with that just now. I think right now I choose to don my armor and sally forth. Adieu."

"Adieu," Miles said, "and good luck. Give us a hug good-bye now," and Cecily knew this was because both parts of Merlin were sagging with relief. Lancelot gave them a cold kiss on each cheek and strode off down the stairs. "Now then," Miles said. "I guess now that our mission is accomplished we'd better get Merlin back down to the chamber. I'm missing my makeup call right now."

"What do you mean our mission is accomplished?" Cecily asked. "Everybody is more mixed-up than ever! Mordred may be King tomorrow, thanks to us being here."

"That isn't our responsibility. . . ."

"Then whose is it? And whose will it be if he uses that little doohickey of yours on everybody in the kingdom so that they're all like him? What were you going to do about that?"

"Cecily, you are becoming hysterical. Now that you remind me about the device, of course, we must accompany Sir Lancelot. I cannot leave the REALLY seeing device here to fall into untrained hands, and psychotherapy isn't going to be invented for centuries yet."

Hit-and-run dragon bashing was no cinch, even for a legendary king armed with a magic sword. King Arthur had hidden behind a rock when he called out the dragon, who was by then glad of the distraction from the Queen's spells of zucchini ragout and strawberries with custard sauce.

Possibly the dragon's dim little brain wouldn't have grasped the idea that it was the target of guerilla warfare. It might have vacillated the rest of the afternoon between turning its fire ineffectually on the boulder shielding the King and getting smote while the Queen, who had dragged herself to the cave entrance when the dragon slithered out to confront the King, dazzled it with the magic jewel and songs of apples roasted in herb butter. But Mordred arrived to take matters in hand. He wanted the jewel and he was not particular about how much damage any of the others, including the dragon, incurred while he acquired it.

When Lancelot arrived with Merlin in tow, the Queen was occupied with fending off Mordred, who had climbed up the cliff to the cave and was trying to wrest the device from her. The dragon was not so stupid that it did not realize it couldn't hurt the rock that was between it and the King and had set about removing the impediment, first by tugging with its claws, then by turning and whopping the boulder with its tail. King Arthur, without the benefit of armor, was caught between a rock and the cliff face and had only the strength of his thews and the lever of Excaliber to save him from being crushed.

Sir Lancelot dismounted before his horse could throw him, and Merlin hastily followed suit. The dragon roared. Sir Lancelot waded manfully into the stream, bold as a fireman on the six o'clock news, risking rusted knee joints and wet socks as well as instant immolation. The dragon, its face turned away from the cliff as it whopped at the rock with its tail, belched fire at the new challenger, but Lancelot was still out of range. The tail whopped again and the dragon bellowed again. Lancelot rattled his sword.

Guinevere screamed and Mordred laughed. "Sorry if I seem to have stepped on your sore leg, Madame, but you were being awfully stubborn." He held up the REALLY device and it continued to glitter, despite the growing gloom of oncoming evening. "Now then, everybody, pay attention. Especially you, wretched beast."

"Prince Mordred, there is no need," Lancelot said from where he had stopped in midstream. "I will slay the beast now."

"Are you sure you really want to do that, Lancelot? I mean, think how painful it will be cooking inside that hot metal and for what? To save your king so he can try you for treason for doing whatever it is you're doing with his wife? Good God, man, you can't be serious."

The dragon gave the boulder a somewhat tentative additional whop, and Sir Lancelot shifted from one foot to the other, almost losing his footing in the ripples.

"Lancelot," Cecily said. "Go on and slay the dragon. Prince Mordred won't do anything with all of us watching but if he lets the dragon eat us, he can have everything. What are you waiting for?"

"What am I waiting for? I am thinking it over, that's what. He is perfectly right, you know. There is no guarantee I will slay the dragon. It might slay me. This is something one should consider with much graveness."

"He's right, Cecily," Miles said judiciously. "The man has a right to examine his motives and be in touch with his feelings about all of this before he acts."

"Phooey," Cecily said to Miles, and to Sir Lancelot she said, "Look, Lancelot, I don't mean to nag or anything but don't you think all this thinking it over stuff is maybe what was covered in your knight's oaths? I mean, maybe you took the oath because you thought it over ahead of time so you wouldn't have to bother with thinking it over at times like these and—"

"And just when did we become such an idealistic old dear, mage of mages?" Mordred said. "Could it be about the same time we lost all our other powers, or perhaps invested them in this handy little gem? I think I'll have it made into a ring. A ring of power. I like that." The Prince looked suddenly stricken. "Oh, I say, you haven't made more have you? You really mustn't make more—you mustn't be *able* to make more. Great Worm," he addressed the dragon, which had been getting bored and was about to go back to whopping. "Great dragon I think you should dis—" and he fell forward in a great clattering heap, while the jewel bounced to the ground ahead of him. The Queen leaned over the edge, brushing her hands and glaring triumphantly down at him.

"The device!" Miles said, and sprinted Merlin across the stream, past the dragon, and along the cliff wall to where the jewel beckoned. The fall down the cliff face had not been a long one and Mordred righted himself with surprising agility. A mail-clad gauntlet closed on Merlin's arthritic fist.

"You must not have this," Miles said. "You are not authorized to use it."

"Aren't I?" the prince asked, and squeezed. The gem popped out of the old man's hand and into the Prince's.

But the dragon had seen it and lumbered over, saving its fire for fear of losing its prize. Its claw covered both men to the shoulders and lifted their arms, threatening to tear them off to gain the device pulsating so alluringly from within Mordred's hand. "Now see what you've done!" Mordred spat. "Father! Sir Lancelot! We're about to be dismembered here! Save us!"

Lancelot and a very shaken Arthur dodged around the periphery but Cecily could tell they were afraid to do anything for fear of making the dragon breathe fire and kill them after all. Cecily, for one, certainly appreciated their caution. The dragon was only using three of its claws, daintily, to hold Merlin and Mordred. It most wanted the REALLY device in one piece. The thought also occurred to her that maybe it was recalling her nutritional advice against eating meat too, but that wouldn't rule out the possibility of it killing them just for the fun of it.

"Mordred, you little sneak!" snarled a familiar husky voice and Cecily raised Merlin's eyes to behold Morgan La Fey, draped across the dragon's forehead. "Thought you'd steal a march on me, eh? Give it here."

"I can't. We're somewhat encumbered, as you would realize, Auntie dear, if you'd but look."

She said an incomprehensible word to the dragon, who reluctantly removed its claws. Mordred, device and all, stood clear for a moment.

"Now then, dear, I think you've had quite enough entertainment for one day. Come along," the witch said. But just as the Prince was starting to dematerialize, Cecily karate-chopped his wrist, almost dematerializing her hand with him. He dropped the device, swearing, but continued to disappear, as Morgan had already done. The dragon looked more and more confused and unhappy.

"This works on that—that prehistoric monster?" Miles asked.

"Uh-huh, more or less, I think," Cecily said.

"Okay," and he aimed the device at the by now very bewildered dragon. "Go away," he said. The dragon stood there, looking more and more frustrated and angry, its mean little eyes blinking rapidly, the sickly looking milky membrane covering and uncovering them, the fangs dripping drool. "It isn't listening," Miles told Cecily. "Oh God, it isn't listening." The dragon had them cornered.

"Foul monster, confront an armed knight!" Lancelot commanded, and drew it off, swinging his sword to get its attention. Arthur meanwhile scaled the cliffside to reach high ground and Guinevere. The dragon breathed on Lancelot, heating the armor to a red glow. Just like that. No strategy, no cunning. Just one blast of fire and Lancelot screamed and fell backwards into the stream. Guinevere shrieked and the dragon rounded, mouth open, and Arthur threw Excaliber at the open craw. The magic sword sang through the air, its blade catching the red rays of the setting sun, and twanged past the dragon to plunge into the ground beside it. The beast closed its mouth and took a deep breath. Cecily hoisted the device again. "Look, pretty, shiny!" she said. The dragon was not taken in by that ruse again however and swiped at Merlin's hand.

"*That's* about enough of that!" Miles commanded, his inner voice booming so hard it nearly blew Cecily out Merlin's ear. "Don't you have enough sense to know when you're being rejected, you overaggressive, adolescent, fire-fixated aberration? Now I want you to go somewhere else and channel this intense energy of yours constructively, or a more controlled environment—say an asbestos-lined zoo—is definitely indicated. If you persist in acting out in this fashion, I refuse to even be concerned about the carcinogenic effects of asbestos. Now, uh, *begone!*"

The dragon, never losing its belligerent look, opened its mouth. Miles opened Merlin's too, howling, "Okay, if that's how you're going to be. You want this, *take* it!" and flung the device into the dragon's maw. Whether because it now had the device or because Lancelot had risen dripping from the stream and Arthur had retrieved his sword, the dragon flapped its wings with a bellowslike effect that knocked them all over again, and took off.

"Miles, that was the bravest thing I ever saw," Cecily whispered to him as they rigged a litter for Guinevere and prepared to ride back to the castle. "That was, it was—"

"*Valorieux*, Merlin, *tres valorieux*," Sir Lancelot said, clapping him on the back. "That spell with which you drove away the dragon was the most truly magnificently valiant piece of magic I have ever seen you or any other sorcerer perform."

The left side of Merlin's face blushed. "Uh, merci, guy. Merci a lot."

"Told you he was the best teacher there ever was, didn't I?" Arthur said, clapping Merlin's other frail shoulder. "Why, I'm half inclined to think he magicked up the whole scheme, just as he did when I was a boy, to illustrate his meaning to us. Knew you had us confused with all that fishing and tapestry business, eh, Merlin? So you had to provide a little example—''

"Not at—'' Miles began, but Cecily stopped him.

"Don't confuse them anymore or, if you're right about this being the time that decides about nuclear war, we may not have a home to go back to,'' she said.

"Why, Cecily, dear, how incisively intellectual of you,'' he said, and she felt his discomfort at the idea. Aloud he said, "Not at first, of course, but when I saw that you didn't understand that I meant one has to use judgment— there are, of course, times to be valiant and honorable and to, er, fulfill one's oaths and lay down one's life for one's comrades and beloveds and that sort of thing and then there are, er, times to go fishing and make tapestries. You just have to learn not to get carried away, you see?''

They both looked agreeable but still slightly baffled, and nodded, and shifted the litter to its place between the horses. The jostling hurt the injured Queen, and her hand tightened slightly—on Lancelot's. He looked down at her with an expression that said that if only he could take her pain as well as his own burns and bruises, he would bear it gladly.

"Ah well,'' Miles said, "personal growth *is* a gradual process. But all in all, I think my original point is well borne out. These people are normal, healthy people behaving in a fashion that, however inappropriate for our time, is necessary to their development in theirs.''

Cecily sprawled across the bed and thumbed through her *Camelot* coffee-table book as Miles greeted his television audience. She was glad to be back again. Glad to be in her own body, in her own bed, with her own stuffed animals around her and a fresh bowl of popcorn nearby. She paused in the book at the picture of Guinevere and Lancelot, not looking at all like themselves, holding hands.

"We'll be talking a little later about this evening's topic—interdependence and the concept of honor as a self-enhancer—but right now I'd like to talk to our first caller.'' He turned, and the camera focused on a successful-looking young executive whose tan was presently waxy yellow.

"Hullo, Dr. Standish, this is Emory Peters from Dallas? I called in yesterday?"

"Excuse me, but you couldn't have. I mean, I wasn't—" Miles started to say.

"And I would just like to ask you one thing, sir. That infusion of bats' wings you prescribed for my fear of heights did do a wonderful job, and I was able to fly to Cleveland without even gettin' nervous. But it gave me a terrible case of the runs—do you know of any reason it should do that?"

"Bats' wings?" Miles's smooth voice roughened just a little. "I'm sorry, Emory, but you must be mistaken. I missed the show yesterday. I was . . ."

Cecily flipped the page to a picture of Merlin the Magician lying peacefully on the stone slab in Nimue's cave, a small bemused smile on his face. She gazed at the picture for a moment, smiling back at it, then closed the book before she got to the sad part, and turned off the television.

While writing Firelord *I was concerned that a pivotal character like Modred could be allowed so little time onstage and almost none for a development of his own viewpoint. This was impossible in a novel where Arthur was the first-person voice, and to drag it in by the heels so late in the book would have warped structure and arc.*

After finishing The Last Rainbow *five years later, I knew a great deal more about the Prydn (Faerie) of northern Britain. Modred's voice still haunted the outskirts of imagination, and there was a word I'd often described but never spelled out, the Prydn word for love. Uallannach.*

Like love itself, the word holds a world of meanings.

Uallannach

by Parke Godwin

I don't know what I expected of Modred. Something more
human, a little glad of life, but when all your life has been
running and fighting, perhaps glad has no meaning. For
this I yearned so many years? . . . This cold, purposeful,
malignant, girl-pretty serpent of a son who'd cut my throat
and walk away whistling.

—Arthur of Britain, *Firelord*

Be Modred Belrix, son of Gern-y-fhain Morgana of Reindeer fhain, most beautiful of all Prydn women, whose
presence was greater than that of all other gerns.

No—I must use your Briton-speech for tale-speaking.
Must say *I* and *you* and *mine* and *yours*. Tallfolk need such
words, lacking the closeness and sharing of my people, the
Prydn. You call us "Faerie"—a poor sound like all your
words, so weak you must use five to make one of our
meanings that come from the first days of the world. Like
Dronnarron. If I tell you it means "the good green time
that was," you know it only as the blind man who puts his
hand to a stone and thinks he knows the mountain.

Like *uallannach*, which means love to endure forever.

Shape it with care on your lips. For that love and hate come from the same heart and hurt, the same word bitten off like the end of a thread or a life means hatred to last as long. My mother's search was for *Dronnarron*, mine for *uallannach*. To find one, to satisfy the other.

I was always soft clay to the shaping hand of Morgana, molt bronze in her sure mold. Every drop of me set in the lines of her purpose, but one betrayed Morgana in seeing beyond her vision to the folly and hopelessness of it all. Following Morgana, our Prydn had become a power north of the Roman Wall, rich in gold, flocks and child-wealth. Now Morgana would go to her third husband, Artos, my father, who led all of Britain-fhain. She would ask of him a gift of land to be ours forever. I knew it was madness and years too late.

Briton-men have always thought my father—their great Arthur—was got on a Cornish woman by Uther. Like most of their beliefs, only half true. Uther was his father, his mother the wife of a Cornish lord but of Prydn birth, born to a woman of Reindeer fhain in a year of famine and placed as changeling in a Roman cradle. When Artos came into manhood, Morgana put a binding spell on him to make him love her. But magic can turn in the hand of the fool. My mother it was who lost her heart, loved Artos all her life. As I loved her and hated him.

Artos comes for the end now. I see the dust his horses raise as they follow the bait I laid for them, a trail of Orkney blood from far south of the Wall to this place Britons call Camlann. The end will be soon, so I will speak of beginnings.

This Samhain past I saw Artos Belrix for the first time, since he left Morgana before I was born. First sight, but ai! did I not know him all my life? Was not his shadow, as hers, over me from the first? Did beg Morgana not to rade south into Britain-land. She promised only caution, even when Artos said she might come only with her own family. There were five of us: Morgana, myself, her husbands Cunedag and Urgus, and my young uncle, Drost. We were brought by Artos' trusted companions, Bedwyr and Gareth.

They showed respect to Morgana, but I did not trust them overmuch.

I first beheld Artos in his great rath at Camelot. Mother had eyes only for him, so I let mine be everywhere. This Camelot might only seem less of an enemy than Pictland. The tallfolk lords in the hall wore clothes of fine wool and rich linen, worked in fashions and colors I would not have thought possible, but the men carried swords and even the women little knives in their girdles. Were not so different from Picts, then, only cleaner.

Artos and his *adhaltrach* Gwenhwyfar sat on raised chairs at the end of the great hall. He left her and came down to Morgana. Now my eyes were all for him, as she had stuffed my ears with him, him, *him* since the day I left her body.

I tried to read him like the land before me, for threat and places to hide, and could see at first no danger in him. A big man, even for tallfolk, with hair like the light of Lugh-Sun at midsummer. Nothing of Prydn about him except the marks of Reindeer on his cheeks. I felt a strength in him. Will not take that from Artos before I kill him. A strength and a spirit like that of my uncle Drost, of gentleness and laughter. That could be false, as Prydn can crouch still on open moor and look like stone. Agrivaine's Orkneymen are learning that before they die.

Belrix put his hands in respect to my mother's belly, and all I could think was: *did leave her.* He spoke in our tongue. Morgana, whose presence was always a robe of dignity about her, in the blink of an eye became a child, hurling her arms about Artos's neck while he swung her up like a child before she remembered that dignity and presented me to my father.

"Greet thy wealth, husband."

I hated him. Did leave her.

Not only the sign of Reindeer cut on his cheeks, but his eyes. They were Prydn; not blue or brown like tallfolk, but the gray of ours, and set *so* in his face. Truly he was born of a Prydn mother, she who was left in a Roman cradle in a hungry year.

But did leave my mother. *Do not search for thyself in my face, Artos. Be not there.*

Morgana bade me speak to him. "Father," I managed, though the warmth did not come with the word. He searched my face and drew aside my sheepskin vest to study the scars on my chest.

"Thee's fought," said the great, golden Belrix. "Who scarred thee?"

This one was my blood, then. This one made me. "Venicones," I answered. "Dead ones."

I saw in his eyes something that hoped and was disappointed because I turned it away. There is softness in you, I thought, but none in me. We have turned on the hunters and hunt them now. We have burned them, killed their flocks, taken their child-wealth to grow as Prydn. They call us demons, which is Roman-tongue for "small gods." That pleases me, for we were in this island since Mabh and the Time of the Ice. Bow to a small god, Artos Belrix.

"Now greet the second wife of Belrix," Morgana commanded me. I obeyed, thinking she gave too much presence to tallfolk. Mother had changed much in her last seasons, but her word was rule. I approached Gwenhwyfar, seeing the fear and disgust she tried to conceal. She wore the sign of the Christ-man, a cross of iron. She is of the Parisii who believe Prydn are reborn spirits of the evil dead who cannot look on or touch iron. Although she knows many ways and tongues, Gwenhwyfar cannot blot this lie from her mind. I speak her fair, little as I know of Briton-tongue, and read what can be seen in her white face.

Yes, there is courage and strength in Gwenhwyfar, and a hate strong as mine. Yet, like Belrix, she seems to be searching me for something she wishes to find. Only a flicker, a flash of color like the finch swooping low over heather, then gone.

"You are unclean," that look tells me.

I stretch my hands to her stomach—she shrinks back

from me—and say, "May *adhaltrach** have many years and child-wealth."

I think of that as the Orkney horsemen draw closer across the moor. They have killed their own kind in treachery. How neatly their hot blood will work with the cold in mine, the uallannach. Morgana is murdered. For that murder, I rade south of the Wall as she never would. No longer do I take children to raise as she did but leave them hacked where they fall. Like wielding a sword in gorse, will hew a space about me, will kill all I can find.

These Orkney lords are the men of Prince Agrivaine and a gift to me. We were stalking Agrivaine's brother Gawain, who rested carelessly on the open moor. I planned to kill them while they slept (as my mother was slaughtered in Camelot) but Agrivaine came and did our killing for us even as we watched. He trampled his own brother and all with him. Prydn do not kill each other like this. Do have no word for it, only wonder that *we* are called devils.

One of Gawain's men was not killed. After the murderers left, he staggered up, dragged the great body of Gawain to horse, and moved off toward the south. *Then* I saw my vengeance for Morgana. Artos was not far away, still at his peace meeting with Gwenhwyfar and the Parisii. Do not wonder that I know this; wherever Prydn ride, we take pains to know who else is there and why. This helps to keep us alive.

Gawain was oath-brother to Artos. When some of my Prdyn wanted to finish the one survivor, I said no. "He will take this deed to Artos, who will follow Agrivaine with all his *combrogi*-men after him. Agrivaine is our bait. The game comes to us."

---

*The Prydn language was pre-Celtic but had borrowed many Gaelic and Brythonic words from Picts, Britons, and early Scots. Modred and Morgana used "adhaltrach" in its original sense, merely a second wife. To the Christianized southern Britons, the word had come to mean an adultress. In Gwenhwyfar's case, the unintended accuracy was fatal to Morgana—Ed.

When Agrivaine's band pauses to rest, the horses spent, we wait the night through. Before the moon goes down, one of the Orkney shakes off his cloak and rises to make water. My arrow takes him in the heart, and he falls without a sound. When the others find him, they know they are stalked. Time is precious. They must leave the dead to the ravens and ride on.

It is easy to hide from tallfolk. You do not know the meaning of stillness or how to look and really see. When we take two more of Agrivaine's men in daylight, he dashes here and there about the moor to find us. Fool: we are in plain sight, but he cannot see. Artos will; must find a different plan for Artos.

Yes . . . he is following. Will drop more bait for the Bear of Britain, kill him and spit on him as he dies. I swear this by all Morgana was to me. Follow, Father. Greet for the last time your child-wealth out of her body.

I wait. The ravens wheel in the sky.

She was the first and one enduring love I ever knew. My earliest memory was the sound of her voice and the sweet warmth of her breast against my mouth. My first remembered sight should have been a firelit rath and fhain gathered about the firepit. Not so, a different fire, a burning Votadini village and Morgana lifting me to horse, Prydn folk shouting to each other, amazed by their victory. Someone screaming. My mother splashed with tallfolk blood. No Prydn child born in the same winter as me can recall a season when we were not killing and running, or when the summer raths were not full of tallfolk children growing up as our own. Nor a time when we were hungry. Because of Morgana, there was always plenty.

Life was not always so for us. As I grew, Cunedag and Urgus told me of the old life. We lived in a shameful peace with tallfolk and took that miserable portion they left with us. Taixali, Venicones and Votadini had the good lowland pastures and left us the rocky hills. My mother changed that. Never was change so needed.

"Artos knew truth," she told me many times. "Prydn must find a new path."

Morgana's meaning will not be easy for you to understand, but if there be one picture to show the difference between Prydn and tallfolk, it is in how we see and touch the earth. Each tallfolk tribe claims to own so much of the land. To us, the word for earth is "Mother." There is no word for owning in our tongue. Prydn were the first in Britain. Mabh herself, greatest of all gerns before Morgana, cut Britain from the larger lands to the east to make it an island, but no Prydn has ever taken one piece of Mother over another and called it his. The tale-speaking of Mabh is given each Lughnassadh by the gerns to their folk before moving on to winter pasture. Twice in each round of seasons, Prydn moved with their flocks, scornful of the way the later, bigger people rooted in one place and scratched at the earth to coax food from it. Until all the places were "owned" by tallfolk and there were more of them than Prydn because, somehow, more of their child-wealth lived through their first year. This was so tens of seasons before my birth. Artos and Morgana were the first among Prydn to see how we were losing, that we could die out of the land unless there was change.

Change needs youth and strength. First daughters became gerns, but Morgana's elder sister Dorelei was a spirit of love and peace, more concerned with children than change. The spirit of prickly gorse and fire was Morgana. She could not forget that tallfolk killed her first husband, Melga. That her first child died before it ever walked, too weak from hunger to stave off the evil that covered the poor bairn with sores. That there was no "future" for us.

I must use the Roman word. Since the beginning of the world, time has been a circle for us, while you tallfolk see it as a straight line like the marks you make with your plows. What part of a circle is greater than the rest, what season more important than others when each has its place and unchanging tasks for us? For Prydn, there is now. Where you say years, we say tens of seasons, how many being no great matter. Nevertheless, Morgana bent her circle to a straight line. When Artos came, she knew she touched the future, as one grasps a knife in the dark, unseen but sure in the hand.

Dorelei's second child died at birth, a hard blow to fhain. On the same day, Artos left Morgana for his Briton-home and old life. Left her with myself not born yet. Treachery, but would Morgana turn on him for that? No, never against Artos Belrix. In the first days when I was young, when none of her shining black hair had yet dulled to ash, when she rode like a small god to burn tallfolk villages in sight of the Wall, Morgana would never cross into the Briton-fhain of her husband. "Husband" she called him ever until the day Britons murdered her. That firm it was in her mind. That foolish.

Then sweet Dorelei herself was killed by Votadini cattle herders for nothing except hatred. Our sheep had wandered down into a glen where the Votadini herd was grazing. Dorelei went to cull them out. The Votadini made a great noise and flapping of arms to frighten and mill the stupid cattle. Dorelei was trampled under them.

For more sport, the herders left her body on the hill below our rath. Her husbands, Nectan and Bredei, were sick with grief and the blind need to kill. Only Morgana knew what to do. As they placed Dorelei's broken body in the barrow, my mother saw how future and change must and would come to be. Born in the waning of the moon, Morgana always knew she could bring evil when she wished. If she wished it then, Artos Belrix, if she washed sacred pebbles in the blood from her own flow and offered them in the stone circle on nights of no moon with dark prayers and no sound else but wolves and wind—whose the blame? Dorelei was not the whole of her rage, only the final blow.

See another picture: a man walks the same path every day and always stubs his toe on a certain stone. Tens of seasons he walks and stumbles and curses the stone for being there but never thinks to clear it from the path.

Then comes a day when nothing goes well for him. He stubs his toe too hard and knows it will be the last time.

With all his anger in his hands, he claws out the stone and flings it shattering against a greater one. So with Morgana. She tried to live in peace with tallfolk as her mother Cradda did, but saw the folly of it when Dorelei died.

"Be nae peace atwixt fire and water," she told me many times.

"Ai, what did thee then?" I would urge, most eager listener.

"Did go among the other fhains and speak before them. I was Gern-y-fhain now since first daughter died and Cradda was old and sick and without heart for war."

Mother was only twenty Bel-teins old then. She took me as a swaddled bairn and urged the other fhains to make war with her. The choice was plain, she told them, quick war or slow death. Since Morgana was of the blood of Mabh, the others gerns gave respect to her presence but remained cautious. They spoke of Salmon fhain in seasons past who turned from Prydn ways to follow the Jesu-Christ. They tried friendship and sharing with tallfolk and were spat upon. They also tried war—and where was Salmon now?

"Where any of us next season?" Morgana answered them. "Salmon struck with no plan, but they knew change must come. Must change to live. Who will rade with me against the Votadini? One village at first, then more and more until they fly before us or pay gold to be spared."

If my mother had much courage, there was much folly in the mix. Far away, where the farthest hill met sky, Morgana saw her aim, her *Dronnarron*. When that Prydn folk grew strong enough, she would take me to Artos in his Camelot. He would greet her like a true queen, give us land and help protect it.

"May husband do less for first wife?" Morgana reasoned.

A few fhains joined her, enough to start. One morning, before Lugh-Sun rose, they struck the Votadini village whose men had murdered Dorelei. They were burning and dying before they woke. I remember the flame and stain of smoke against sky, and Morgana pointed with a reddened knife. . . .

"As Mabh marked the stones in the first days," she cried to her victory-stunned folk, "so we put our sign on Lugh's own sky."

But quickly: must speed away before more tallfolk came, burdened with treasure, flocks and bawling Votadini children. You think it strange to take children? Ask the great King Artos how precious children are and how many, like his own mother, were left in tallfolk cradles only that they might not starve. I have two bairn myself. This will not happen to them.

"Have left enough child-wealth," Morgana vowed, and for once I agreed with her. "Will take back now."

So we ran out of Votadini land with fat sheep, gold and squalling bairn. So it began as other fhains came to join us. Asking was done. Now we took.

Can fool a man's eye but not a horse's nose. Their horses feed on oats, ours on open graze. Horses can smell the difference, so must keep downwind of them as we stalk Agrivaine and take pieces of him. Artos knows fhain-smell. I want him to know I have done this. When Agrivaine sends two men ahead to nose us out, we are not there but behind them. The Orkney column hurries on, Artos' dust clear to our sight in chase. Come not too swiftly, Father, nor too late. Agrivaine will cross Wall today. We will be waiting for him, but first a little more bait to keep you coming on.

The Orkneymen are alert, eyes everywhere. Those in the rear see a single Prydn rider on a low hill. As they watch, the rider dashes for what little cover the hill can give, but they see his horse go down. The rider stumbles to his feet, but they can see the man is hurt.

They argue among themselves, eager for revenge. After him, then? No time. But we *have* him. Aye, and how many more waiting? No matter there, the thrust-out arms tell us: small Faerie horse cannot outrun ours. We want vengeance.

Three of them wheel out of the line and bolt toward the rise as the others press on. When they top the hill, there is the hurt Faerie not far beyond, trying to mount his horse near a patch of gorse and dark rocks. They come down swiftly, swords swinging, separating to hit him from both sides—

The gorse rustles, the rocks move.

When we have dragged the bodies together, I take one of their long swords and cut Reindeer marks in the earth to either side of them. Artos will know it a greeting and challenge. As I cut the signs, I think of him and my mother, how she talked always of him, made his looked-for approval the measure of our success when we were already beyond hope.

"Do rade toward a new day," she told me proudly before we journeyed to Camelot. *But I knew, Mother. No day we neared, only rode deeper into night. Why would you, wise in all other things, never see the truth?*

Uallannach.

"Must ride, Modred," my war-brothers urge me now. "Artos Belrix comes."

I look off to the north. "And Agrivaine?"

He will cross Wall at the nearest possible place, near Camlann. We will cross west of that where soldiers are fewer. Like Morgana, I let my men see only my strength. I speak of "tomorrow" as she always did, though for tens of seasons, I have seen only falling night and tasted the bitter truth that my mother always placed my need for her behind her love for Artos.

This is what comes of leaving the magic of our own circles for the straight lines of tallfolk, to think in the shape of "yesterday" and "tomorrow" and "next year." After Camelot there were only yesterdays. I could have told Morgana. I *tried* to tell her. . . .

I grew toward the day when fhain scars were cut in my cheeks, not in quiet crannog or rath but running with Morgana's warband that swelled with each season. Must always move swiftly. The sick and weak were left behind now, a thing unthinkable before. By my tenth Bel-tein,

Morgana had fought and defeated villages of every tribe north of Wall. Our raths were not scattered or hidden but clustered thick where we pleased, our flocks grazed where the grass led them. Even Taixali moved their herds aside and came with gold to be left alone.

"Tens and tens of Prydn," Mother boasted to me by the fire. "As I did tell Artos I would do. Was a braw man, Modred. Let me tell thee of his coming and the magic I made then. . . ."

As if I needed to hear it yet once more. *Always* Artos in her heart, where I would be. We grew rich with gold and still she would not cross Wall to take one sheep or bit of gold from fat Parisii or Brigantes, because they were *his* folk. When I had seen my sixteenth Bel-tein, I was first husband to Eddaina, a woman of Wolf fhain, but all followed after Reindeer now, old custom forgotten. Instead of my going to Eddaina's fhain, she and our own child-wealth rode with Morgana.

As she grew older, Mother seemed cooler and more cautious, more given to mulling a thing in her mind than acting in the same breath that bore it. Many of the older gerns went back to their own raths, sick at heart from years of war. Those who stayed frowned on the younger of us for whom killing was the way of life, most so the tallfolk changelings ever quick to prove themselves all Prydn in their hearts.

I must say it: did always love Morgana more than my wife, looked to *her* to be proud of my deeds. Came to her with my wounds, counted for her the tallfolk dead by my hand. Honed myself like knife on stone to an anger and determination like hers. Became a bronze mirror where she could see herself in me. Did this make her love me as I needed or turn her gaze by so much as a hair from that other mirror? Let me tell you, tallfolk.

There are some things that men share apart from women, and be times when no man will be ruled by any woman, not even a mother. When my first child was born, I wanted to shout to earth and sky how well I did. Five of us young men were riding near Wall and drinking strong *uisge*. I would bring Eddaina and my son a gift of Briton-gold, and Morgana would not stop me. I was drunk and reckless. Gifts were not all of my thought then. Somehow I needed to take something from Artos. We slipped across Wall into Cair Ligualid and out again with a few trinkets from this house or that, but harmed no one. That far against Morgana's rule I would not dare.

Was far too much anyway. My mother heard of it, came cursing into my rath and pulled me from the sheepskin where I lay with my wife. Eddaina made to touch Morgana's belly in respect, but my mother only thrust her aside and dragged me by the hair from the rath to cry my shame to all Prydn.

"This fool, this worthless son of my body would ruin all we have labored for. Has *stolen*"—she used the dirty tallfolk word—"in the land of my husband, Artos Belrix. For this, he will nae ride at my side but like a child at the rear until he learns to heed gern-law."

Then, before all the people, Morgana struck me across the face. Not the blow that stung but the injustice, the wrong of it. When Morgana was angry, the gray of her eyes went dark as the smoke from the fires of all our slaughters, and her face seemed cut from stone.

"Be nae man like thy father but a child, Modred. A killing child!"

And who did teach me to kill?

"*Thee* the wealth I shall show thy father and these thy gifts to him?"

"Not my father!" I stormed back at her. "I will nae call him that."

"But thee will," Morgana said, as always with no thought to any wish but her own. "I see more now than when we started."

Do you so? I raged in my heart. Do you see what is before you as I do? You love this Artos who lay with you a few seasons, but do you see me? Why so much of your love to him? Have I not ridden with you since the cold Brigid-feast of my birth? Was it Artos who burned and killed for thee, brought you his wounds to heal and deeds to praise, helped make your name a fear among Picts? Who has honored thee before his own wife? Look at *me*, Morgana. I am the one who loves thee, not him who left even before I came from your body.

So I thought but dared not say it. From that moment, cold even for my long cold life as second to *him* in her eyes, I stood apart from Morgana. Loving her no less, I saw her girl-sick with foolish love for something that never was or could be. Raging in silence, I could not lie with Eddaina for days or take pleasure in anything but hate. Love is pain, but did say *uallannach* has a tangle of meanings.

More seasons passed. Morgana began to speak of an end to running and fighting and of her nearing vision. She was now the strongest gern among Prydn, with hundreds behind her, most of our people yet alive in Pictland, and no one tallfolk tribe could muster as many to fight as we could to crush them. Before last Samhain—and it was truly my mother's last—she called to her all the loyal gerns and their wisest men and women, and told of her vision.

"Now we are a power in the land and a pride," Morgana said. "We will go into Britain and meet with third husband Artos at Camelot rath. Will show him his wealth, Modred, and ask him as Britain-gern to give us back *Dronnarron*."

Oh, Mother, I despaired. Where is there such a place for us? Only my love keeps me from running from your folly as I have run all my life at your word. I cannot leave you any more than hand can leave arm, but heart can war against head. You are a fool.

That day she wore her richest torc and the blue cloak taken from a slain chief of the Vacomagii. She sat with her back straight and legs crossed on her stone in the position of gern-speaking, that we knew her words were law.

"I go as wife to husband, gern to gern, with respect. Let all hear that. With respect. Nae one village, man or woman, sheep, cow, rath or smallest coin will thee touch while we rade to Camelot. Gerns, tell it to thy young men and women. Do love my people, but whosoever breaks my word to Artos will die. Die and nae be barrowed but left for raven and wolf, their names forgotten in rath and crannog.''

Speaking so, Morgana turned her graying head slowly about, holding every eye that met hers, lingering on me that I know she would not set me above this rule.

''We will go.''

Seeing clear truth, I was sick with fear for my mother who could not. Morgana had grown too used to winning to think she could lose. She saw only Artos, not how far from the hills she would lead us, or that, even if Artos still loved her, he would be the only one in Britain. Twenty years we have made fires of tallfolk houses and rivers of their blood. Could not look for them to love us for it or give us place among them.

Yet, mad as it was, Morgana's dream had the strength of *uisge* in the mind. Drinking, one could forget the *uisge* could leave the head aching and the belly poisoned.

''Could such a thing be for us?'' Eddaina pondered when we sat alone by our fire, and the wealth asleep. ''Do thee believe?''

I had only cold truth for answer. ''Have made war all my life.''

''And I, husband.''

''Truly. Cunedag and Urgus tell me of the old days, but what do any of us know of peace?''

Eddaina looked into the fire. I could not read her thoughts then. ''This Britain-rade be madness. Do want to believe, but. . .''

Eddaina spoke for many Prydn who had no more heart for this new thing than I did. They wanted to believe but could not. The elders said little about the rade, more resigned to it than promised. Yet I could hear in what they did not say the lingering wish for the dream to come true. Young mothers like Eddaina thought first of their child-wealth, trusted no tallfolk, but yearned toward such a place, a *Dronnarron* where their wealth could prosper without the wound-scars and halt legs from broken bones most of us carried. Hanging between belief and doubt, none would speak of their uncertainty to my mother but let me know in one way or another that I should.

I went to Morgana's rath. Entering, I knew that I would only be shouting into the wind. All her gold and finery were laid out to be chosen from. Her newest sheepskin vest shone from brushing, and she was driving the brush over her long blue cloak. The rath smelt not of mutton fat or goat's milk, but a sick-sweetness that wrinkled my nose in disgust. A small chest stood open by the firepit. Mother had tried more than one of the scents it held. I remembered the Taixali woman she took it from, who smelled of this when we killed her. I tried not to breathe deeply. Morgana had even reddened her cheeks with this tallfolk folly.

A girl, I thought. A foolish girl gauding herself for first night with a husband. For *him*. She never needed this weak magic before. Such a thing was beneath Prydn women. But for him, for Artos, nothing was too much. Would go to him with the moon about her neck could she fix it on a chain.

She greeted me in an absent manner. For Morgana, I was hardly there. She folded the brushed cloak and, taking a handful of her hair, began to brush it out.

I put my hands to her belly. "My mother be greatest gern since Mabh of the first days. Will hear thy son?"

She nodded assent but went on brushing. A strange, soft mood was on my mother that night. Morgana was far away from me. I squatted by her firepit.

"Mother, this rade thee speak of. I do not trust tallfolk."

"Nor I," said Morgana.

"Then why go among them?"

As often, she treated me now as a child too slow to learn the simplest things. "To see thy father."

"Thee would go to Artos Belrix out of love, out of *uallannach*. Out of the same—would stay for me?"

"Modred?" Her hand paused with the brush. A shadow of concern: "Speak so?"

"I must, Mother. Would nae speak against the Britain-

king, but do beg thee. In all my life have never begged
one thing of thee." *Only love, and that was never said.*
"Forget this rade. Will only harm us."

Morgana only laughed at me. "Fool boy, have spoken
as gern."

I tried not to scream at her. "I am a Prydn man. Did
follow at thy side when thee bade and in shame at the rear
at thy same bidding. That well did thy son learn obedi-
ence, but I am no fool. Dost think that magic alone kept us
safe all these seasons? Was shrewdness, Gern-y-fhain.
Was the truth of swift horses, few Picts and always distant
hills where they dare nae come after us. But in Artos'
land, tallfolk are thick as flies on dung. One treachery
there—just one—and all thee's made would be undone."

"Oh, son," said my mother with a tired shaking of her
head. "Thee ken so little of kings and queens. Artos is my
husband."

"With another wife," I dared, desperate now. "And
thy foolish wealth is thinking indeed of kings and queens
before all else."

Did speak with respect then, but with truth as well.
Artos' second wife Gwenhwyfar was Parisi, sister to their
prince, and both would kill anything north of Wall quicker
than deal with them as equals. Did not Gwenhwyfar's
father kill Morgana's first husband, Melga? Even if my
mother could speak for Artos' heart, what of his new
wife? What of the others about him? Bold we had always
been, but never attacked without knowing a clear way out.
Deep in Britain-land, the door would be barred behind us.
If there were treachery, we would all die there, and if
Morgana died, what gern with enough presence to hold so
many fhains together? All would be finished; could not my
mother, so wise in all other things, see the truth of that?

No, she could not, only picked up her brush again,
spreading the long strands of black hair to frown at the
gray. She seemed to see it for the first time. "This plan
was in thy father's heart and mine from the first days. Will
be his gift to me. We have changed much. Will change yet
more when do have our own land."

"Mother, please." I knelt beside her, grasping her hand. "Do I use the word 'beg' so lightly? Leave this thing."

"No, Modred."

"*Leave* it. What is there in Britain we cannot take for ourselves here?"

"The new day," Morgana said, calm as stone. "Thy father will refuse me nothing."

"Think, Mother. Tens of seasons he has been apart from you."

"In tallfolk counting, little in ours. Artos has not forgotten me. He could not."

I had not noticed until now how gray her hair had become, or how deep the lines under her watchful eyes. She had the look of a hunting wolf like all of us, but in the last two seasons I had seen the small ills she hid from others. Winter and rain stayed longer in her bones. She rode less than before and always with a double sheepskin for saddle. Speaking as gern pained her back which must be held straight while seated cross-legged on the gern stone.

An old wolf who now hoped to kennel with the hounds.

"Modred Belrix." My mother made a picture of the words, dreamed with them. "Thee were made when thy father was chosen lord of summer. Belrix: the Firelord. So be thee named, and to my purpose."

In that purpose I heard the end of Prydn, though Morgana thought it a beginning. Tallfolk drew pictures of the land in different colors that the shape of what they owned was known under one name, like Britain. Within that Britain would be a smaller shape but as clear. Morgana and Artos Belrix would cause the makers of such pictures to give our land a new color that would be forever a kingdom of our own.

"You are young yet," Morgana said with the scant softness left her. "Will see. Artos will love you as he does me."

I was helpless, miserable. She must not come to harm but would not let me stay her from it. So Morgana scented herself and dreamed of Artos and went to her death.

*New day, Mother? Was night already and the false light
in your eyes only him.*

Men have always said that Artos had a magic to bind
their will to his purpose. For all my caution, his manner
softened my hate: strong yet gentle as Drost. In his every
look to my mother, each touching of her hand, the way he
spoke of their few shared memories, there was respect for
her presence, love for the woman. In the rath prepared for
us, Artos gave place to Morgana and sat in the second
place about the fire, one of us. Yet I saw how Morgana
warmed to him, glowed under his regard and the sound of
his voice. She was like to a dew-fresh girl again.

Artos joked with fhain brothers and listened to their
words. He remembered small things about each that they'd
forgot, made me remember the small god who was my
mother. Will say it before I kill him: *uallannach*. Love or
hate. I was filled with him. To stay free of that spell, I
studied the tallfolk house we were given, saw how every
line of it departed from those we knew—doors, tables,
stools, the many gifts to us, more straight than curved, all
Roman. Nae, was mad to think Prydn could live so.

And yet I would . . .

When my fhain brothers grew weary and Morgana kissed
Artos good night one last time out of tens and went to rest,
I spoke alone to him, sterner than I felt, fighting with
every breath against the magic that came from him. Losing. I spoke my true doubts of Morgana's dream. With
contempt, to *show* this tallfolk that my love was harder
won than hers. That he dealt with an equal, perhaps his
better. It seemed I labored too far to prove I could hurt
him, to let him see only the hardness in me.

And was rewarded with success. That was all Artos
saw. He turned back from it. "I want to love you, Modred,"
my father said, and I could hear that the desire was hardly
satisfied. "I will do all I can for fhain."

Losing myself. Lost. I gazed into his face and saw
myself in it, and part of me reached out to my father-self.
Was evil that magic, stealing through my veins to find a

weariness I never guessed until that moment. Listening to Artos's voice, I saw a picture of Eddaina and our wealth driving the flocks to a safe byre that would be ours by right. Sleeping in peace, never more having to rade for new pasture among folk whose respect for us was only that they gave to the wolf pack. *Ours.* I tasted the owning-word and it was good. All my life I killed for Morgana and savored it as salt to my food. Now, under this new magic, I turned away for the small space of one moment from killing, not sickened but gorged, done with it.

I believed his lulling song to a tired mind. When he went to bed with my mother, I lingered awake by the firepit, drinking the gift-wine slowly. Then I lay down by the curtain before the bower they shared, pondering before sleep took me away.

Could it be? Out of my mother's strength, out of my faith that never wavered from that strength, and Artos' magic—could we at last make dream into waking?

The smell of the air and sounds of the night were different here. I closed my eyes with one hand on my knife. Lying so, farthest from any opening, I saved my life, if such could be called a saving.

As always in sleep, I did not know when my spirit left its body to walk. One moment I was thinking of Eddaina and our children sitting outside our own new safe rath, and then did see them there. Running to my wife, my spirit begged with a passion I could never speak in waking.

"Could it be, wife? Could make this place ours?"

"No."

Then it was not Eddaina's face but Belrix's before me. Denying, laughing at me, all the magic ended.

"Thy life's done, Modred."

Not alone Morgana's death cry that woke me but truth like cold water dashed over my closed eyes, opening them. In the barest moment before my mother cried out, I woke and knew it all a lie and saw the tallfolk men coming through the door with swords.

"Mother!"

I tore aside the bower curtain, better able than Belrix to

see in the dark. There he was, the sword in his hand, the shape of another man writhing on the floor by the casement.

"*Mother!*"

And there was Belrix striving to say this was none of his doing, even as I lifted Morgana's shoulders from the dark-stained bed and her head lolled back. I hissed one word at Artos before I struck at him, my flesh hot with Morgana's blood.

"Liar!"

Would have killed him then but for the fox-wariness of a lifetime. *Wait,* it stayed me. *Might kill him but these others will finish thee with no vengeance done. Wait and take many with him.*

I dove through the casement onto the earth, hearing the shouts in the rath behind me, ran to the murderers' horses, leaped one full running. The brute was frightened, already smelling blood; it sprang forward with me flat along its neck, grabbing for the rein. Did use the horse's fear for speed, ran it through dark and sunrise into day, then took another from the byre of a Coritani chieftain. Hid by day, rode by dark and lamed three mounts in all before crossing Wall to the hill where Morgana's folk waited.

Her blood was still on my arms. Would not wash it off until the wind picked it, dried drop by drop, from my flesh. I showed the dark smudges to our people and told them the end of Morgana's dream.

"Will go to Britain as Morgana said." I lunged back and forth before the people, hungry to be at it even then. "But in no peace. Here, on my arms, is what my mother's peace brought her. Will take tens of them for every drop."

When the older gerns hesitated, I knew that Morgana had driven a spear forever between the old way and the new. To fight Picts was one thing, the gerns argued, all Britain another. Winter was coming; there were flocks and child-wealth to think of. If such a war against Artos were wise, would be as wise in spring when Prydn could live off the land they raded through.

"War be *now*," I commanded. "What gern among you can lead Prydn as my mother could or myself now?"

No, the gerns would not be persuaded. My mother was always too rash, they said, took too much decision to herself. Wolf Gern said what her sister gerns felt.

"Thy mother's dream rested on *uallannach*. Her love for one man. The bravest she was but not most wise. Wolf fhain will rade north among the Atecotti where we can rest the winter in safe crannogs."

But the Prydn young and the fierce changelings scorned this. Born running and fighting like me, they knew or wanted nothing else. They would follow Modred Belrix, the Firelord. The gerns disowned me, but when they were done, full seventy young men and women crossed to my side of the stone circle. The rest rode north.

To my faithful I gave my first speaking as gern. "Let those women whose flow be on them, mix their blood with the strongest of poison root and flower. Let the sacred moonstones be boiled in this. When the moon is dark, we will make a killing spell for Artos of Britain and take it to him."

"And shall we take wealth from the cradles as thy mother did?" Eddaina's anxious face showed a troubled spirit. She loved children and used the tallfolk word "future" more than the other women did.

"No," I ruled. "Wealth will slow us when must ride more swiftly than ever."

"And what then for the days to come?" Eddaina argued. "I have no wealth in me, few of these others do."

I could not say she was foolish. I thought only of Morgana who made her very life into a sword: did she not die of one flaw in that blade? One moment in Camelot when even I softened—and came alone out of that place of treachery, all my dearest dead. I could thank Artos for that small mercy, allowing so few of us to Camelot, that my wife and children were not sent to the slaughtering like sheep.

"Thee may take from any cradle what will not weigh thee down," I told Eddaina and the others. "An arm or an ear."

The changelings grinned at this, but Eddaina turned away from me. When we were alone, she spoke to me like an unloved stranger. "Thy own mother said it, Modred. A killing fool."

Lugh-Sun was high over the stone circle when she said it. When Lugh moved the shadows of the stones only a little to the east, Eddaina had taken our children and ridden after Wolf fhain. That was her right. Child-wealth descends through a mother. They belong to her and she to her own fhain. Watching her go, I knew she was not ever the closest thing in my life, nor were the children. Were other women, would be more child-wealth. I could not feel much grief then. My heart was barrowed with Morgana and mourned that love in darkness rather than live in the light. Cut those words on my barrow-stone. They are as close to truth as any.

But we would make Britain weep with us. Our magic would draw Artos to me.

So we rode. We left a trail of death through the land of the Parisii and Brigantes through the winter, and in the spring our magic hit its mark. Artos and Gwenhwyfar had warred against each other. Artos came north to meet with his queen and make peace. I sharpened my knife, rubbed fresh mutton grease into my bow and chose among my best arrows.

Agrivaine and his men lie dead on the moor, the last bait for Artos. My folk have broken from cover, dashing away to the north. A good trick most times, but a fatal mistake today. Over open ground they cannot hope to out-run combrogi horses. If I live through this day, I will go to Wolf fhain, to Eddaina and our children. If not, if we have said farewell until we meet in Tir-Nan-Og, then so have Artos and pale Gwenhwyfar.

The combrogi follow my riders. Only Artos and two others remain. Now the three of them descend from the hilltop toward the field of the dead that the ravens have already found.

One of the dead is your scout, Artos. The man you believe to be him is a changeling in your man's ring-mail and helmet—waiting, his back to you, arrow nocked to the bowstring, until you are too close to miss.

How bright and hot it is as I wait; as you near the killing
mark, Artos. There is a hard light over both worlds now,
that which I can touch and that within me. Morgana could
see tomorrow in it, but I only night falling and falling
forever.

Artos finds Agrivaine's body. Moments now. A few
more breaths.

How to tell you, Father? That night in Camelot I could
have yearned for you and loved you beyond all else with a
folly to match my mother's. Even now, as my changeling
draws his bow and I sight myself on your broad back, I
keen for the three of us, Mother and you and me. For what
might have been. What could never be.

Sweating in the heat of Lugh-Sun. A fly buzzes past my
ear, hurrying to the carrion feast below.

I could not believe in her dream, though for one moment in Camelot I reached for it and tried. Barred even
from that.

Kill him! Now!

Hit.

Artos staggers back with the arrow in his belly. Mine
will be next. I draw it as Morgana strung and drew my
whole life taut to her purpose, aimed at your heart.

Love makes and take life.

Holding and—loose!

So *I* touch you, Artos-father. Murderer. Liar. Did leave
her. Did leave me.

Uallannach.

I met SUSAN SHWARTZ *at Lunacon '85, where we proceeded to dominate a late party doing all the parts in Hamlet. An editor, scholar, critic, and novelist, Susan is also charming and quicksilver dinner company, and a short phone call to clean up a point usually turns into an hour's congenial rap, interrupted frequently by her cat, Merlin.*

A Ph.D. from Harvard, Ms. Shwartz taught medieval literature there and did her doctoral dissertation on the prophecies of Merlin. She has edited two fantasy anthologies, Hecate's Cauldron *and* Moonsinger's Friends, *and one of science fiction,* Habitats. *At this writing she has just completed the first draft of a fantasy novel of the ninth-century Silk Roads for Tor Books.*

Her main sources for the present story were the Book of Taliesin *and* The Mabinogion—*older sources which, as she wrote: "freed me to emphasize what I have long thought to be one of the main aspects of Arthurian legend . . . the bond between Arthur and his warriors."*

"Seven from Caer Sidi" has the atmosphere of the older unglossed legends.

Seven from Caer Sidi

by Susan Shwartz

After Arthur the King and his men crushed the Saxons at Badon Hill, they sat feasting in Camelodunum and they were all a little mad. Arthur, more sensitive to his men's moods than to his wife's, ached at the sight of so many empty seats in the hall, so many wounded who would never bear arms again, or see from both eyes, or cut their meat without assistance. Too much laughter rang too loudly in the hall, as the men caroused the way people who have been exposed to plague drink and play in a frenzy, eager to pile up pleasures before they too are struck down.

Arthur remembered a night years ago when Caball, his hound, lay sick, how he had watched with him, comforting the beast with hands and voice. If he still missed the dog, how much longer would he grieve for the loss of his warriors? The men in the hall watched him, eager for anything he might say or do, in just the same way, confident that he could help them. He rose from his chair. The men fell as silent as they had been boisterous before. In the torchlight, their eyes gleamed too brightly from wine and grief and victory.

"Let us have no precedence here," he announced, step-

ping from the high seat to sit by Gwalchmei, his sister's
son, "for we are all brothers." Shouts of *Ave, Imperator!*
and *Artus bach!* roared out. Arthur acknowledged them
with relief, clasped Gwalchmei's shoulder, and sat to toss
down a few with the people he valued above all else.

A robed figure, slender and female, appeared at the
door. How she had slipped by Cei's guards, they both
would want to know. Cei rose to intercept her, but she
brushed past him to the center of the hall, lowering her
gray hood to reveal a pale face and hair like wheat. She
seized up the nearest goblet and raised it to Arthur.

"Hlaford cyning," she said in a husky voice that made
every man's blood run hot and cold at once. *"Waes hael."*

"Ronnwen! By all the gods!" shouted Gwalchmei. He
slammed his cup down and the wine spurted red. "Vortigern's damned slut! You dare come here—"

When the wine was in, Gwalchmei's wits were usually
out, Arthur thought, as he vaulted over the table. He had a
reputation for strength and speed, both deserved, and for a
moody, vicious temper, inherited from generations of Orkney
men, not to mention Arthur's own sister. He could turn
murderous in the blinking of an eye.

"Not here, nephew!" There was no way in hell that
Ronnwen, the Saxon sorceress who'd blinded the old High
King to his former vows, could be here; she'd burnt years
ago, before Gwalchmei had been born. He grabbed for
Gwalchmei's arm, but too late. With one hand he grasped
"Ronnwen's" long gold braids. With the other, still clenched
on the knife he'd used at table, he slit her throat.

Arthur thought he had become used to the sight of blood
at Badon. He had that thought after every battle, and there
had been a lot of battles to think it after. But this blood,
staining the tables and fine clothes of his hall, steaming in
puddles on the floor, shocked him and his men to horrified
silence.

It wasn't that Gwalchmei had slain a woman. He'd done
that once before, and performed embarrassing penances
thereafter. The horror lay, rather, in the supposed identity
of the woman he had slain, and in the fact that the body

shrouded in its spattered cloak refused to lie still. People died when their throats were slashed, but this "corpse" shuddered as if parts of it were reassembling in a new form.

"Make it stop," came an almost-whimper from one man in the shadows who had had too much of wine, blood, and sorcery. Another rushed forward with an axe.

Arthur held out one hand. "Summon Myrddin," he said.

"Too late for your wizard, little king!" What rose from the floor was no woman. Arthur would have staked his sword on its being not human, but still another of the manifestations from the Other World who came to challenge him at every feast.

"And you, Orkney's son, would you be a woman-slayer?" it taunted. "How can you slay what has lain in the Cauldron of Tyrnoc?"

A robed shadow brushed Arthur's elbow: Myrddin, less frightful than other magicians because more familiar, and his loyalty known. The king glanced at the man who was prophet, advisor, and friend.

"Three virtues has the cauldron," Myrddin intoned. "It will not seethe a coward's food; it grants visions of what lies hereafter to any who dares glance into it; and, should a man lie in it, he will never die."

Never to die? By heaven, if Arthur had had that cauldron, there might be no empty seats in the hall today, and the sense he had had all evening, of grief festering into a mad wildness, would be swept away as sulfur banishes the smells of pain and death from a sickroom.

"Ahhh," purred the figure. "So you want my cauldron, do you, king?" A glint of crown shone above its head: no circlet, but a shadow-crown that looked bronze and branchy. "Come and take it. Come to Caer Sidi! And bring the woman-slayer with you, or, by the Hollow Hills, he shall not survive the satires my bards will make of him."

Came a sound like a sigh, and the figure was gone, leaving behind a crumpled, stained gray cloak that only Myrddin would take charge of. He muttered over it, and exchanged somber looks with the chief bard, Taliesin.

The mood had to be lightened, Arthur thought. He poured wine into the nearest cup and raised it overhead. "Not by that thing's command but by my will, my lads. I go to Caer Sidi to win us immortality. Who sails with Arthur!"

"I do!" "I!" Already men were shouting their names, banging on the table, cheering. Gradually the shouts melded. "Hail Arthur!" Even those cheers sounded frantic tonight, but it was a madness Arthur found familiar and comforting.

We must still be mad, Arthur thought as his ship *Prydwenn* pitched beneath him on unfamiliar waters. Sea and sky reflected on another like two halves of a giant shell, shutting down upon them. Clouds and waves were troubled. A mist was rising to meet the sun—and conceal whatever rocks might jut from the sea. Not even Taliesin, poet and navigator, could predict when they might see land.

The bards sang of eight fortresses in the Other World. So far they had visited seven—and the gaps in *Prydwenn*'s crew (more gaps than crew, to speak truthfully) showed that the visits had not been pleasant. Now they sailed on the last and greatest of those fortresses, Caer Sidi. If he had had the cauldron on his voyage, those men might not be dead . . . but that dream had started them on this wild journey.

The seas that warded the isles of the Blessed were treacherous. It might be that before sunset they would all lie in the great cauldron of the Ocean, cheated of their dream of immortality.

Gwalchmei, relieved from his turn at the oars, came over to Arthur. "My curst temper," he said. It distressed Arthur to hear him so abject.

"No," said the King. "If it hadn't been your temper, they would have used something else to test our mettle. And now we will show them how keen that mettle is." Fine words, but he could see that they did not convince the man beside him.

"Land!" Taliesin cried, relief in his fine-trained voice.

The youngest and keenest eyed of Arthur's men, Gwair and Amren, strained their eyes to see it. The mists parted, and then they all could see. The island rising from the sea looked like Orkney—a high talon of reddish stone standing beside cliffs of that same stone, flattening at the top and covered by vivid green. Overlooking the channel between the rock fang and the island itself stood a broch, one of the round stone towers built ages ago, some said, by the people of the Hollow Hills.

Was that Caer Sidi? Arthur ordered the men to steer toward the channel between island and rocky spur. Between cliff and fang might lie protected water: it would be well to anchor before dusk. The fang's shadow fell across them, and smaller shadows besides. "Ravens," Arthur heard young Amren mutter, and saw him make the sign against evil. A rock fell from the cliff below the broch. The sound of its fall, clattering down the rocks, splashing into the sea, echoed and made the men shiver with more than the wind that rose as the sun set.

It was treacherous, steering between spire and island, since the channel was marked by a line of sharp rocks. Beyond them lay a boiling cauldron of a tidal pool.

"Who comes here?" The voice boomed out over the hiss and bubble of the pool and the tidal rush beyond it.

"What land is this?" shouted Arthur. He was High King, and he did not approach Caer Sidi like a thief sneaking by night into a lord's treasury.

"What man asks it?"

"I am Arthur!" His name rang against the rocks, and echoes took it up as if legions shouted it. But they sounded faintly jeering.

"Who comes with Arthur?"

"The best men in the world!" This time his name *was* shouted. Ah, that won a cheer from them. In the waning light their faces were flushed with excitement the way they'd been after Badon. Their bodies were a little too taut. They needed the relief of battle or some other successful end to this venture.

Torches glimmered to light on the broch and beside it, opening a path of reddish fire.

"Drop anchor," Arthur ordered, and glanced aside for one moment.

Taliesin's gasp whirled Arthur around again. Descending from the broch's headland came a bridge—and such a bridge! It looked like the blade of some immensely long sword. As it slid from the gateway, it twanged with a sweeter, more deadly note than any longsword or *spatha* Arthur had ever tried.

Clearly, here was the first challenge. Did Arthur and his men dare to cross such a treacherous bridge? One misstep would hurl a man into the boiling cauldron below. Several of his men—Pryderi, Manawydan, the Irishman, Gwair, and Amren surged forward, but Arthur held up his hand and looked to Taliesin.

"We might wait for dawn," suggested the bard, wise with many songs.

"And have them draw that blade back and laugh in our teeth?" asked Gwalchmei, who was already under one threat of death by satire. "I say we climb now!"

Arthur listened to the men wrangling, relishing their deep-throated argument as something known, and therefore welcome in this strange realm. He studied the swordbridge, then reached for his spear. He would use it to balance himself as he ascended.

"Before the sun sets, my lords, let's feast in Caer Sidi," he cried. "Pray God they have wine enough. I have a noble thirst." Gwair cheered and pushed forward, but Arthur swung the bole of his spear gently, tapping him on the center of his chest, restraining him.

"One moment," he said. "I lead."

There was sunlight enough for Arthur to see the youth, little more than a lad yet, blush. "I thought to carry a torch and blaze the Imperator's way for him," he stammered.

"Torches have been provided us," replied Arthur. "If we hurry, we shall not need more light. But I go first. It is my duty to lead you—and my proudest right."

Gwair grinned at him. His blue eyes flared and made him resemble something out of the Hollow Hills himself and not the lordling from around Sinadon whom Cei had ushered into the hall shortly after the vow to take the Cauldron had been sworn.

He was lithe, with a promise of strength when he reached full growth, and he asked only to serve the king, a favor Arthur was glad to bestow: he needed young men like this one.

"But what else will you have of me?" Arthur had asked, jovial with relief at having that spectre out of his hall. The Roman in him urged caution, but wine and the exuberant courtesy of his land ruled his tongue. "You shall have any favor your head and your tongue shall name, as far as wind wets, as far as sun runs, as far as earth extends, save only my ship and my mantle, my shield, sword, my dagger, and my wife."

The Roman in him had been right, of course. Young Gwair had knelt. "By the names of your best men, I beg to accompany you—and them—on the quest for the Cauldron of Tyrnoc," he had said. Arthur had already chosen the men to go with him. They were veterans. But Gwair had begged permission to come along, and asked it in their names. The Celt in him could do nothing else; the Roman ground his teeth in silent rage every time he remembered.

He held his spear out before him like the crosspiece of a hilt and started up the swordbridge. It whined and sank beneath his weight. But years in the saddle had made his balance true, and he climbed swiftly. From time to time he could feel the blade quiver and twang, and knew that yet another of his men had stepped upon it. The metal was well-tempered; he decided it would bend rather than break.

Finally he reached the safety of the cliffs and dared look down. He was appalled at how near the water the blade curved. All the men but Gwair and Amren had made the climb. Gwair swarmed up the treacherous blade with the ease of one who had climbed good British cliffs almost as early as he had walked, but Amren stepped heavily and faltered. His friends shouted encouragement at him, and he recovered heart. Then ravens swirled above him, and he looked up, overbalanced, and fell into the spume and sharp rocks below without even time for a scream.

Another good man lost. Now we are eight, thought Arthur. Tears stung his eyes. Beside him Bedwyr made the sign of the cross. Taliesin raised harp and voice, singing a stave that no one but he could understand. "It is always thus," he told Arthur. "One enters the Other World only at the price of a death."

That reminded Arthur. Hexameters clanged in his memory, clashing with his grief at Amren's loss. *Facilis descensus Avernus* . . . He couldn't remember the rest. His tutors had despaired, but he'd always been more intent on Caesar's wars than his Virgil. It was easy to descend into Hell, but . . . that was right . . . to return to the light of day, ah, there the task, there the trouble lay. Only after Palinurus, Aeneas' steersman, had drowned, could he enter the underworld. They were far-off kin, Arthur remembered, and took heart from it. Kinsman, aid us now, he thought.

To encourage his men, he controlled his shudder and his suspicious glance roundabout, or his tendency to search for a golden bough to jut from these rocks where no trees grew, nor ever had.

Rocks tumbled down before them, a rough stair. More torches revealed the broch's doorway and their path within. Naturally it lay downward. He seized the nearest torch and entered Caer Sidi.

They had marched for hours along a path that spiraled down and farther down until by now, Arthur thought, they must have passed the base of the cliffs. Perhaps Caer Sidi extended beneath the sea. His back tensed as if he bore not just armor but the weight of rock and water above him. The walls of the passage quivered with the eternal surge of the sea, and water trickled by their feet: salt, undrinkable.

Taliesin drew his harp from its hide case, muttered once about the dampness ruining its strings, and began the songs with which a bard accompanied troops into battle. His voice echoed in against the spears and shards of rock they passed.

Gwair and Gwalchmei, whose ears were keenest, tensed.

Arthur signed to Taliesin to cease his music, heartening as it had been.

"What do you hear?" he asked.

"Don't you hear it?" asked his sister's son. "Hounds."

Their belling was faint, almost a vibration in the rock more than sound itself. Perhaps a rear guard, with drawn blades, Arthur thought, might protect them all against whatever monstrous hounds coursed on their tracks. But surely their greatest danger lay ahead, and they had no protection from that. The belling of great hounds came again, more strongly now.

"Shall we quicken step?" asked Manawydan.

"No help," replied Gwair. "If the hounds here are like Irish wolfhounds, they can pull down horses."

"We do not hurry," Arthur said. "And we do not draw swords. Whoever rules here may be watching to see what we do. I fear him as little as I fear his hounds." He signaled to Taliesin, and the song of victory, of courage, and good cheer rang through the passageway.

"Our torches are going out," Pryderi interrupted after a time. "And we have no spares."

"Then our host will provide light for us," said Arthur. "We have all made night marches without torches. We go on."

The torches burned down into reddish light that made the rock spears dripping from the ceiling or stabbing from the floors look like weapons in flight. Then they went out altogether, leaving only a reek of smoke. Taliesin's fingers idled on his harp, and they heard the hounds again.

"They're closer," whispered Gwair. Arthur would have wagered his life that in the darkness Gwair's fingers shaped the sign against ill-luck—if his life had not already been in pawn to this adventure. The hounds' voices died. He heard his men's harsh breathing, as well as his own.

"Slowly, my lads," he said in the hoarse voice he usually had before a battle. "Feel your way."

Using his spear to tap out a path, he edged forward, always downward. The footsteps behind him were slow, uncertain. After a time, it seemed that the darkness became easier to bear.

Taliesin's hand dropped down on Arthur's shoulder. "Up ahead," breathed the bard.

Up ahead Arthur could see light. Was this some trick, either of the lord of Caer Sidi or of his own, light-starved eyes and mind? He walked forward, even more cautiously. Ten yards farther and he was certain that the light was real, welling from a species of golden moss growing from the rock itself in streaks, pooling on the rocky floor, glinting off—

"By all the gods," breathed Gwalchmei. "Veins of gold in the rock. Gems. This entire land is a treasure-house."

Arthur raised his spear, ordering an advance. No one stooped to scoop up a gem or nugget, and for that he was proud. Their angle of descent did not seem as steep now, and the path was smoothing out. After a long time, it softened. Now they were walking not on stone but on sand, and the light grew in intensity. It was strongest in front of them. Up ahead loomed an arch, with brightness beyond, and the sounds of harps and pipes.

"Play!" he ordered Taliesin, "and you others, sing. Put your hearts into it!"

Like a triumphal procession, Arthur and his seven surviving men entered the secret hall of Caer Sidi. It was a vast underground cave, lit by torches set in sconces of glittering rock. Sand was raked into orderly patterns underfoot; ahead of them stretched a huge table hewn from stone, a dais, and a high seat, a chessboard on a table beside it.

A cloaked figure sat enthroned, toying with the glittering chess pieces. But as they entered in parade, he rose. At first Arthur could not see his face clearly, but then some mist seemed to melt from his eyes, and he saw the features of a man in his prime, strongly marked and proud. Above the deepset eyes and high, polished forehead gleamed a crown of bronze and gold branches. Arawn Penn Annwfn. Deathlord—but not demon.

"My lord of Britain," said the master of Caer Sidi. "It's been very long since I had guests. I bid you welcome." He raised his hand.

From behind his seat paced nine cloaked figures. Only their lightness of step and the way their dark cloaks swung about their heels suggested that they were young women. Each bore a cup. One handed hers to the dark lord; the others came to Arthur and his men. There being nothing else to do, they took the cups and raised them as did the man on the dais.

"Come feast with me," said Penn Annwfn. "Or, as I once said to you in your own hall, *'Waes hael!'* "

Gwalchmei reddened, but drank with the rest of them.

"Ah, king's son of Orkney, this time you do not strike me down?"

Gwalchmei stood silent.

"And you, Arthur of Britain, you have come for the Cauldron of Tyrnoc, have you not? Well, I promised that you might have it."

"I regret I brought no gifts of equal worth for you," Arthur replied.

"Did you not? Your presence in my hall is gift enough. And perhaps, afterward, you will join me in a game of chess. For now, though . . . you have had a long journey: sit, wash and eat."

As the men sat, stone bowls of apples and flagons of dark ale appeared on the vast table. The maidens reappeared. Eight circled with linen and warm water, smelling of brine and of sweet oil. The ninth drew a curtain woven of glinting threads behind the high seat. There stood the cauldron they had come for, bubbling gently, though no fire burned beneath it. Except for the pearls that glistened on its dark rim, and the way it drew the eyes, it could have been any goodwife's cooking-pot. The women gave the cauldron a slight push, and it moved forward.

"Doubtless, your bard has told you that the cauldron will not seethe the meat of a coward, will reveal the future to whatever man dares gaze into it, and will bestow immortality on anyone who lies within it. After we dine, you may see its gifts demonstrated. Or you may prefer to play at chess. It has been weary ages since I have had a game. But first, food . . . assuming that the cauldron will cook your meat."

Behind them Arthur heard barking and a scrabble of long claws on stone. The hounds of Caer Sidi erupted into the hall, sand spraying underfoot as they ran toward the table and the men who sat there. They were huge, easily the size of Irish wolfhounds. Their fur was cream-colored, except for ruddy patches at their ears and masks around their flame-green eyes. One barked joyously and hurled himself toward Arthur, resting massive paw and heavy head upon his thigh.

"Feed your hounds first, my lord," Arthur said, "so we may dine in peace."

The maidens drew collops of meat from the cauldron, laid them on stone platters, then set them before their guests, together with sharp flint knives of workmanship so fine that Arthur had difficulty believing that they were not metal, the work of a cunning smith. Forcing his attention from the cauldron to the food, he tossed a chunk of meat to the great hound beside him, who hunkered down to eat.

The deathlord laughed, and Arthur laughed with him. After a long moment, so did his men. A pleasant harp music sprang up, and the nine women sang. Their voices were very sweet, and so was the wine.

There was nothing wrong with the food, nor with the drink that accompanied it. Arthur was proud that his men neither drank to excess nor offered any attention beyond courteous thanks to the women who served them. Not even Gwair the youngest, and especially not the sorely chastened Gwalchmei. Arthur reached for an apple, and wondered what the price of this hospitality might be. If the truth be told, he feared the master's hounds—especially the one who lolled at his feet, lambent eyes never leaving him—far less than that chessboard. Games had been played before with kingdoms as the stakes.

The maids circled with warm water and towels once again. The Lord of Caer Sidi leaned back in his chair and sighed with contentment. "I had forgotten how good it was to dine in company. And now, perhaps, lord Gwalchmei, a game of chess?"

Arawn should not have kept hounds, Arthur thought, but cats. There was something feline in the way he toyed with the small band.

"You honor my nephew," Arthur cut in smoothly, "but we should like to sail on the dawn tides. You do permit that we take the cauldron?"

"Certainly, certainly." Penn Annwfn was all charm, all suavity, and Arthur was suspicious. It had been easy to descend into Caer Sidi; it didn't make sense that its master would feed them, give them the gift they came for, and then send them merrily on their way. But overt suspicion would antagonize the man. Perhaps that was the test. The semblance of trust must be Arthur's best defense now, for himself and the men who sat, poised and watchful.

He rose, half bowed to his host, and walked toward the dais, his boots scuffing in the sand. The hound rose and tried to follow him, but a snap of his fingers made it sit back down on massive haunches. One step, and he had mounted the platform, reached the cauldron, was reaching for it. He had his hands locked on the gem-studded rim. Ah, he thought, this felt right! He realized he had been longing to lay hands on the cauldron from the moment he had seen it. It was his now, and with it, the promised gift of immortality to take back to Camelodunum. But first, he would stare within. Then the water in its depths rippled, and he knew himself bespelled past his power to look away. The trick had not been the chessboard but the very prize Arthur had come to seek.

On a bloody plain, Arthur kept struggling though his men lay dead, and his spirit died within him. He faced one last enemy, fought, and finally thrust his sword through the breast of a man whose face was a blurred and younger version of his own. The man was dying, gouts of blood spurting from his mouth, but his sword had been raised to hack, and it struck with the hate of a dying man . . . Arthur reeled as if the blow had sheared through his helm and pierced his brain pan.

Again the water rippled. *Ranks and ranks of men marched across a field made hideous by a harvest of arrows, by ranks of shouting men wearing steel. The leader fell from his horse, an arrow jutting from his eye.* Arthur stifled a gasp of mortal anguish.

The water shifted again. *Flames whistled from the sky above a wondrously transformed Londinium like the red dragon and the white of which Myrddin had prophesied, and the city's spires quivered, then spurted fire. Beneath them burning figures ran this way and that, or lay crumpled beneath rubble. Destruction howled down from the night sky.* Arthur tried to cover his ears, but found he could not move his hands from the cauldron's rim.

"No," whispered the King. Arawn of Caer Sidi leaned forward, his pose as gracious, if indolent, host forgotten.

The water rippled, and this time . . . "My God, the burning, burning, burning . . ." His eyes were melting, swift fire pierced his very marrow. An instant more, and he would be but fire and white-hot air himself, then darkness thereafter, for him and all the world. Still he could not avoid the sight the cauldron showed him, of a flame like a mushroom, hotter than any Greek fire alchemist could devise, sucking up first a city, then an entire world to feed itself.

His head sank, and he felt his knees sagging. Behind him he could hear murmurs. His men were afraid. For him! That was not right. He owed them better than that. Though the struggle bathed him in sweat and left him gasping, he pried a hand free of the cauldron's rim, and gestured his men back, unwilling to let them share the cauldron's deadly visions.

He could not free the other hand, could not turn from the cauldron and walk back to his men. Now he could hear fear in his men's voices, and pain: not for anything they might suffer, but for him.

He was hurting his men! The very thought stung him back to awareness, and he set his will to fight. Not for himself but for his men, and for Britain, the world ravaged in the cauldron . . . he must get free. If his will were strong enough, perhaps the cauldron might bring him comfort visions, might release him . . . *I cannot believe that*

*only burning and death lie ahead. Show me the other face
of it,* he commanded silently. *Damn you, show me!*

Ripples came and went. Slowly, new visions formed: a
man with a hillman's face and a cleric's garb, telling
taller, blonder conquerors, "His name shall be meat and
drink to tale-tellers," and knowing that the man meant
him. Other tellers of tales clamored up from the visions:
harpers in court; dark-robed, ascetics crawling in secret;
and, in a prison, a man who looked as if he once had
borne arms and now bore imprisonment with patience, and
grace enough to tell Arthur's stories; a thin, nervous man
who laid aside his pen and his fears to fight for all mankind in the name of a once and future king.

Last of all came their hearers, men and women in
strange garb, speaking stranger tongues, in which he could
hear his name and know himself remembered. These were
the folk who lived through the battles Arthur had but
foreseen, who listened, looked at one another, and seemed
to ask, "Will Arthur never return?"

The burden was even greater than he had dreamed. Such
a temptation to shrug it off, to sit here, in this pleasant
cavern, and play chess through eternity with Caer Sidi's
chief, rather than shoulder what no man should have to
bear. The weight was unthinkable—but it was equally
unthinkable that he back away from it.

"I'm coming!" His great, inward scream blotted out the
treacherous visions. High King. Their king. And no cauldron's slave.

Arthur flexed the hand still grasping the cauldron's rim.
He could not release it yet. For the sake of the men in the
hall as well as those countless others he had foreseen, he
must free himself. "In their names," he gasped silently.

"Unwilling to leave?" purred the lord. "Stay then. I
grow lonely. Stay and bear me company."

"No!" Gwair's cry and Arthur's shattered the silence of
the hall as Gwair flung himself across his king, and made
the cauldron rock upon its base. Water splashed from it
and drenched them both.

Arthur's hand came free, and he clutched Gwair, dragging him away from the cauldron. Gwair was only a boy; he could not bear the visions that had almost shattered his king's will.

"Young idiot!" he cried to the youth. Arawn Deathlord rose from his chair and walked over to them.

"You do realize that once that cauldron has—I suppose we should not call it 'baptized' you—you are changed?" he asked.

It had been immortality Arthur had sought. He realized with a grisly humor that now that he was on the verge of receiving it, he'd have done anything to avoid it, if it meant staying here.

"Still, since you have eased my loneliness, I will not insist that both of you remain. One will suffice. You choose which one."

"But you will release all the others?" Arthur asked cautiously. This might be the last bargain he would ever make. "And the cauldron too?"

"All that I promised, and a fair wind to sail home with," promised the lord.

"Then," said the King, "I am well content to remain, knowing I have brought my people such a gift. Tell Cador my heir for me . . ."

All order, all discipline was forgotten as Arthur's men surged around him, protesting, lamenting. Even the hounds bayed until the hall echoed.

"*I* shoved the cauldron, *I* should remain," Gwair protested.

Arthur grasped him by the shoulders. "You're young, boy, young, and with all of life to look forward to. I've had a full life. Let me stay."

"He ordered you to bring me here," Gwalchmei cut in. "I should be the one to stay!"

Gwalchmei's temper was just an excuse, Arthur started to say: a way to lure them in. But then Taliesin's voice rose, and Taliesin's hands struck the strings of his harp, overpowering the other voices. "By your leave, King," he spoke when all were silenced, "that is not the nature of the royal sacrifice."

"Bard, I've spent my life for Britain and my men," Arthur snapped. "Don't presume to tell me what my duty is."

"You've used your life for Britain and for your men . . . for *all* of them, and for as long as you live. If you were a simple warrior, you might sacrifice your life in a final charge or hopeless stand, or trade it, as Gwair offered. But you are the king. Your sacrifice may not be just to give your life—though the time may come when that, too, is required—but to lead, to keep going on when dying would be easier. To offer your life, never knowing when the gift will be accepted." The beautiful voice modulated and turned rich with compassion. "As Gwair's gift must be. Arthur, my friend, my king, Gwair knows what he did. And accepted the price."

Arthur turned to his youngest man. Now he could never attend his wedding, or see his masters-at-arms train his sons. Gwair would never ride alongside him to battle, or sit near him afterward, thankful to be alive, grieving for the loss of their comrade. *But no one else need die*, a voice whispered within his head. *Not while Arthur ruled the cauldron.*

"I would have saved you too," he told Gwair in a broken voice. He would have wept, but kings do not weep when there are people to see it and despair. "I would have made you, and all the others, immortal."

The young man drew closer. "I don't think it is death that Arawn has in mind. He's lonely, he said. I think I may be more a hostage than a victim."

And if Gwair were a hostage, there was always the chance that some battle or stratagem might free him. "That's right!" he whispered, and returned Arthur's bear hug with the fervor of a child. "And even if it weren't, you and my brothers-in-arms go free. That makes it all worthwhile."

Gwair walked over to Arawn Penn Annwfn and bowed. "I shall stay here. May my king and the others leave?"

The master of Caer Sidi gestured at the cauldron, which floated from the dais toward the door. "You have been fine guests," he said. "I regret that you will not stay longer. Believe me, you are always welcome to return."

As one man, Arthur and his remaining men saluted Gwair, who watched them a little desperately, then marched toward the passage and the long, spiraling climb back toward light and water. Behind them came a disconsolate howl.

"King Arthur!" Arawn's voice rose slightly. "You had better take Luath with you. He seems to long for the outside world." The dog bolted toward Arthur and whined at his heels as they started the climb. The cauldron floated alongside the king, the gems on its rim lighting the way.

The first turn of the path put the hall's light behind them. Arthur heard the deathlord's voice one last time. "Now then, friend Gwair, do you play chess?"

Arthur sat hunched on the *Prydwenn*'s deck. He had not moved since they had emerged from Caer Sidi at dawn, crossed the swordbridge to the ship, and weighed anchor. The deathlord had been true to his word; the weather was fair, and the winds blew them swiftly back toward waters that Taliesin knew. The dawn stars were fading, but they were stars Arthur could recognize, and the sky wore crimsons and golds instead of the strange gray that had wreathed Caer Sidi.

"My lord?" Gwalchmei approached him with a cup.

"Get away from me!" Arthur cried. He had let none of the six other survivors come near him since they set sail. Gwalchmei, Arthur thought, with his courage and his uncertain temper: if he gazed into the cauldron, it would surely destroy him. No, Gwalchmei must not be permitted to look within . . . not he, nor any of the others, not even Taliesin.

He laid one hand possessively on its rim, and with the other stroked the hound that accompanied him from Penn Annwfn's hall. The hound's body was firm, warm, the only reassuring thing in his world since he had seen that cauldron and gazed into its appalling depths. How would he bestow the immortality it promised upon his men? What would that do? He would have to speak to Myrddin . . . no, Mryddin might be seduced by all that power . . . he could trust no one but himself. Luath the hound whined, and Arthur petted him.

The men weighed oars, trusting only to sails now. Several crouched across from where he sat, staring at him. They seemed far away, removed from him more than by the mere width of the ship. But beside him was the gift he wished to make them—*the gift Gwair had died for,* he thought, though the hurt seemed even more distant from him than his men. Immortality lay in the cauldron's depths, covered against the sea spray by a thick ox hide. But Arthur knew what lay beneath, if only a man's will were strong enough to force the cauldron to do it.

Desire to test himself once more, to see those generations upon generations of people who knew his name, perhaps to see their cities, their triumphs, grew hot within him, though the wind blew cold. All he had to do was remove the cover. Taliesin rose, one hand going out, but he moved so slowly, as if he moved through mire rather than clear air. If he were a warrior, Arthur might have slain him thrice in the time it took him to raise his hand . . . but now none of his men would ever die again, thanks to the cauldron.

Beside him, Luath whined. Unlike Caball, *this* hound would never sicken and die: he would be an immortal companion for an immortal king, a man greater than the master of Caer Sidi himself.

Luath growled. In the instant Arthur moved to jerk away the leather that covered the cauldron, the hound sprang. The jaws that might have severed his hand at the wrist closed on his wrist and merely gashed the skin.

The unexpected pain made Arthur drop the cover. He stared at the hound, which forced its body between the king and the cauldron just as Gwair had.

As Gwair had . . . Gwair had chosen captivity in Caer Sidi to protect Arthur. But he was king, he needed protection from no man, and never had.

But protection from a cauldron that promised him surcease from the pain he hated most? Taliesin was still moving. His mouth was open, but Arthur could hear noth-

ing. He could only see the despair in the chief bard's eyes
as he realized that no power of his could aid his king.

The cauldron and its master had lured him from the
start. *Promise him immortality*, Arthur thought. *Not for
himself, but for his men, and watch him grasp at it the way
a hound snatches at a tidbit.* And once he had grasped
immortality, Annwfn would own him, bought by that promise, by the dreams within the cauldron: no better than Caer
Sidi's slave as long as the cauldron lay within his reach.

Already it had put a gulf between him and the companions who had dared the fortresses of the Other World with
him. Endless years of this would make that gulf irrepara-
ble. And they would go down the centuries, as isolated in
the world of men who lived and died as the deathlord was
in his island fortress, as isolated from mortals as though a
bridge of swords divided them, one from the other.

*At least Arawn would have Gwair to play chess with
down the ages*, Arthur thought in sudden wrath. If he
succumbed, he would be alone.

The hound pressed against his leg. Its body was warm
and solid the way Gwair's had been when he hurled himself between the cauldron and the king.

Immortality, the cauldron had promised. But there were
many forms of immortality. One was the death-in-life that
had reduced Arawn to an elegant spectre, setting traps for
men who still lived and struggled in the upper air. Out of
love and loyalty, Gwair had entered just such a trap. But
his sacrifice was not the only form of immortality.

The cauldron had shown him a man in a black robe . . .
what was it he had said? "His name shall be meat and
drink to tale-tellers everywhere."

Wasn't that another form of immortality? To fight, perhaps to die in battle, but ultimately to die having fought
one's whole life to make that life into something worthwhile and, at the last, to leave it to the people who would
follow him. That was why Arthur had fought at Badon.
That was why Arthur's men had died at Badon, to preserve
their friends, their land, and their king—who would never
forget them.

Immortality? By all the gods, what did Arthur need the cauldron for when they already had it in their hands? He had snatched at a promise like a hound when even Luath knew better, an immortal hound who chose to leave the spiral paths of Caer Sidi for the light and sounds of the world where hounds grew old and sick, but died, mourned by their masters, as Arthur mourned Caball.

For once the Roman and the Celt in him agreed. *Dulce et decorum est pro patria mori,* the line of Virgil's he had found easiest to learn. It was sweet and proper to die for one's country—and those who did were never forgotten.

Arthur plucked away the cover from the cauldron and gazed within. No visions but his own reflection stirred within its depths. Odd: he had thought that during the "night" they spent in Caer Sidi, years might have passed. But his hair and beard were no longer, no more stippled with gray than they had been the night before. Only his eyes had changed. Though they were tired, red-rimmed the way they got after a battle, still they seemed serene, able to accept what he had seen, as he was able to live with it. With that acceptance came joy. He laughed, and saw joy blaze up out of those mirrored eyes. As he laughed, his hands closed upon the pearl-studded rim. The gems, that had been so splendid underground, seemed dulled and cheap in comparison with the morning sunlight on the clouds, on the back of a gull that soared above the ship, or the tears in his men's eyes.

He had been the one to uncover the head of Bran the Blessed where it had been buried by the shore, because he preferred to defend Britain by his strength alone. If he'd rejected the help of a creature that some people called a god, what did he need an old cauldron for?

He lifted the cauldron and hurled it overboard. It filled and sank within a cauldron infinitely greater than itself, and Luath barked at the splash that it made.

The sounds released the spell that divided Arthur from his men and they surged forward, laughing, clasping arms or shoulders to reassure themselves that he, and they, still existed and were together—as they always would be.

After the tumult died, and the men returned to their oars, Taliesin came and sat with Arthur and his hound. His fingers moved upon his harp, slowly, in a reverie of songcrafting.

> I am of fair fame.
> My song was heard in the four-cornered four-sided city;
> My first saying it is from the cauldron that it was spoken;

The deathlord had promised Arthur immortality. Now Taliesin made his songs. In them, and the thousands that would follow, lay the only immortality Arthur and his men ever wanted, the only immortality Gwair would ever have. And it was enough.

> Well-furnished was the prison of Gwair in Caer Sidi.
> And in the presence of the Spoils of Annwfn dolefully he sang;
> And our bardic prayer shall last till Doomsday.
> Three shiploads of *Prydwenn* we went thither;
> Except seven, none returned from Caer Sidi.

Arthur turned his eyes south, eager to return to his kingdom.

At this writing (January, '86), GREGORY FROST has recently seen his second novel, Tain, *published by Ace Books. His first,* Lyrec, *was also from Ace, and there are appearance credits in* F&SF, Asimov's, *and* Twilight Zone, *as well as theme anthologies like* Liavek *and* Magic In Ithkar.

Tain is based on the Irish Cycle *Tain Bo Cuailnge and—as Damon Runyon would say—a story goes with it.*

Ace sent me the manuscript of Tain. *I didn't have time to read it all but couldn't resist the first hundred pages, delighted by the clear writing and the unaccustomed sound of intelligence. I grabbed the phone and invited Greg Frost to Camelot. "The Vow that Binds" is the happy result.*

Greg has an educated taste in single malt scotches and does excellent impressions of British actors. Two good reasons to get together ASAP.

The Vow that Binds

by Gregory Frost

In Cornwall there is a tale that still gets told around fires some cold nights, of a handmaiden from Castle Dore and a strange man who spoke to animals. The events of the tale occurred when Mark was king, but many years prior to the trouble that arose between him and Sir Tristram. The maiden's name was Eirian, and the forest dweller who spoke to animals was called Lant.

Those who had encountered Lant described him as dark and tall, and they furthermore claimed that his eyes changed color with the leaves through the seasons, from winter gray to summer green. No one knows where he came from or how he arrived in the woods: these elements of the tale did not survive, if they were ever known at all. The rustics roundabout called him Lord of the Forest, although such a title implied an awareness of prominence, and he seemed to have none. He wore leathers, and dark cambric shirts, in winter adding heavy furs. Only rarely did anyone chance upon him, and stories wove up like ivy around these encounters, of his turning from man into beast or bird. There were plenty of simple fools more than willing to believe such maggots. The certainty of the matter was that he had a phenomenal gift, seemingly no longer available, which allowed him to commune with the animals that dwelled in that forest. Their multifarious squawks and howls became words and phrases in his mind, and his words in reply were understood by the creatures he spoke to, more as if he could share his thoughts with them than as if he made their sounds. Of all the animals in Cornwall, there was only one that Lant did not speak with. This was the Raven. He knew its words—that wasn't the reason. When the Raven spoke, it had one purpose in mind: to cheat, to deceive, to do harm. It could foretell events but always altered what it saw in order to cause calamity. With such a fiend, Lant refused to converse, and by his example the other animals in that wood denied the Raven their company as well. The ostracized bird grew bitter, and it plotted hard to seek revenge upon the Lord of the Forest.

The forest itself spread out for miles and miles—to the sea in one direction and to bracken and, finally, moors in another—and the castle dwellers frequently entered its quiet confines, sometimes for a stroll after a meal, and sometimes to hunt. Trails of every sort crisscrossed through its depths.

One autumn afternoon, the maiden, Eirian, went walking in the forest and, despite great care to stay on known paths, found herself in a part of the forest she did not know. Eventually, she might have made her way out again, except that she became the prey of a boar, which had picked up her scent. The hairy monster charged after her through the brush; its angry grunts warned her of its pursuit. She grabbed her skirts and ran for all she was worth. She leapt tree roots, rocks, and logs that lay in her path. She cut through patches of brush like a sprinting deer, shredding her cloak, finally abandoning it as she raced down one hill and into a stream. The rumbling boar gained steadily.

On the other side of the stream, she must ascend again, this time through an extrusion of rocks. Eirian climbed and clawed her way. She imagined the heat of the boar's breath, the stab of its tusks. At the top she leaned against an immense outcropping of rock and, glancing back, found the boar scrabbling scant feet below her on the winding path. Panic-stricken, she turned to flee, when a figure dropped from the rock onto the trail between her and the boar. She could see only his back, and that was clothed in dark leathers.

He fell to one knee, lowering his head. His hands he put to the sides of his head, splaying his fingers like antlers. The boar lumbered up and skittered to a stop in front of him. It tried to turn away but seemed snared by the lure of the man's magic. The boar's wild eyes rolled in its head. It backed up a few steps and began to swing its ugly tusked snout from side to side. Then, abruptly, its legs buckled and it crashed down in a heap. After a few moments the man rose up, still precautiously attentive to the boar, then faced her. The irises of his eyes were the orange of the autumn leaves. Eirian had heard many stories about these woods, and she knew who he must be. She wanted to thank him, but the shock from her near-impalement overtook her; she had to lean against the rock as on weak legs, she let herself down beside the path.

Lant moved beside her. "You're safe," he said. "He'll sleep for hours."

"I owe you my life."

"Maybe. But you were a fast runner. I think you might have eluded him."

A rabbit appeared across the path. It sat up and stared at the man. *Terror visited the hill just now,* it spoke to him. All Eirian saw was the man's head tilt to one side, the way people sometimes do when they listen to a distant sound. He made a sudden clicking sound against his teeth, then shook his head. *The terror passed safely,* he was explaining. The rabbit turned away abruptly and bounded out of sight.

"You really do talk with them, it's not just a story," Eirian said in amazement.

"There are stories about me? I suppose I shouldn't wonder. I speak with them, though, that's true enough. They have much to teach anyone who'll listen."

"You mean anyone who *can* listen. You don't appreciate your uniqueness. The rest of us don't have such abilities as yours. There's no one in Castle Dore who can speak with animals—not even the Man of Knowledge, who's easily many heads above me."

"You've very sure of your capabilities, or is it your incapabilities?" he suggested. "I think all of you could do as I do—if it were important enough to you."

How impertinent of him, she thought. "Then, I suppose it isn't." Bracing herself against the rock, she stood, and found her legs to have regained their strength. "Now I should get back. If you'd show me the way . . ."

"Gladly," he replied, and gestured her past him on the path.

Eirian followed the path back the way she had come. As she neared the boar, she skidded on a loose stone. Inadvertently, she kicked the sleeping beast and it squealed and swung up its head. One tusk slashed across her leg. Eirian fell back in pain. Lant danced around her in a dizzying spin that scared the boar from charging. It skittered back, slid, and tumbled down the hill and into the stream, where it gathered itself up and ran off into the underbrush.

Eirian leaned against one of the boulders beside the path. She held both hands over the wound, but blood spilled from between her fingers. Her tight face had lost its color. Drawing nearer, Lant winced as he shared her pain. "That's a bad gash he's given you. I think you won't be walking the distance home today. I have a dwelling near here—we'll go there for tonight, so that you can heal." He sounded regretful, and Eirian thought that it must be regret over her encroachment upon his world. The supposition angered her, but she could only nod her consent to all he proposed; she was afraid, if she opened her mouth to speak, that she would be ill.

Supported against him, she hobbled carefully along the path that snaked across the ridge. The forest sounds rang in her ears as if through a tunnel, echoing. She thought the sun was burning through the top of her head, and at some point she lost consciousness.

High above, silent and nearly motionless on a tree branch, the Raven watched his enemy take the woman in his arms and carry her deeper into the woods.

Eirian awoke on a straw pallet, in the dimness of a hut, or so she thought at first. When she looked more closely, she saw that the dark walls were of rough stone. A small fire in a brazier somehow filled the subterranean chamber with warmth. Within a few moments of her awakening, she saw Lant emerge from the shadows. He carried two mugs, one of which he handed her as he sat beside her. She smelled the steam rising from it—smelled apple and honey.

"I cleaned your wound and dressed it," he said as she drank the mulled cider.

"Will it be all right?"

"Oh, assuredly. It's a bad scrape but not too deep." There seemed to be something more he wished to say, which he held back. Eirian hardly noticed. She was seeing him as if for the first time, as though the man who had annoyed her earlier had been someone else altogether, someone irrelevant. Here beside her was a man as beautiful as the forest itself.

"Bad," she echoed dreamily, "but it wouldn't, for instance, keep me from kissing you?" Lant did not know what to answer and finally shook his head. She leaned forward and kissed him gently on the cheek. When she drew back she found him staring at her with almost painful intensity. "What is it?" she asked.

"It's—it's my fault, what happened to you. The boar should not have awakened, and wouldn't have if I had been paying attention to what I was doing. My mind—" He could not go on without telling her about the strange feeling that had come over him on the trail, that was right now burning in his chest. He had met women from the castle before, some must have been as lovely as Eirian. No, he thought, none lovelier, none that even came close.

"What was it you were going to say?"

He lingered upon her gaze and became bold. "Just that, you might kiss me again if you think it will help the pain." It was his own pain that he spoke of so obliquely, and he hoped to be transported past the point where pain had any meaning. He watched her eyelids flutter as she leaned towards him. Just before her lips brushed his, he let his own eyes close. As with the moments when he spoke to the denizens of the forest, his mind fell back and the sensations of another swelled within him. He did not hear her thoughts, but the moist pressure of her kiss became everything he knew. Her lips parted slightly and the tip of her tongue teased him; he thought he could hear the sound of her laughter distantly in his mind like bright sunlight bursting across the land. He thought: *I will learn to listen to her unspoken words, too,* and he knew she was the one for him. No other woman would ever be so much of him. This is the way of first loves, that they ascend higher than any that come after, because the wings are new.

Lant and Eirian spent the next few days in complete bliss, almost oblivious of time passing. Their love rose and fell like a range of mountains, each peak higher than the one preceding it. They might have continued in that manner to seek uncharted heights if a search party from Castle Dore, seeking news of Eirian, had not come upon Lant. He told them that he knew where she was and described what had befallen her, how he had looked after her, tended her wound. Their appearance in the forest and their questions so flustered him, it was not until after he had spoken that he realized the full meaning of their presence here. Eirian's leg had healed; nothing now prevented her from returning to the castle, and these knights expected her to do so in their company.

The searchers waited while he returned to his cavern.

"Did you find the strawberries?" Eirian called to him.

"Yes," he said distractedly. "And more besides. They've come looking for you—your friends from the castle. They're worried about you." She turned and looked at him, a face full of conflicts that he could not read. "They want you to come back now that you're . . . all right." He had finished reporting now, and all that remained was to ask the one question he least wanted to ask. "Do you want to go back with them?"

"I don't know. I guess I have to—I have duties, Lant, people who depend on me, and—"

"How can they depend upon you more than I do?"

She went to him, took his hands in hers. "Or I you. You could come back with me," she suggested, but knew better. The forest lived within him. Listening to his tales of wry adventures with foxes, of his runs with deer and encounters with all other forms of life in the forest, she had come to know that he would waste away if removed inside castle walls. The animals would never dare to come there. The deer would be slain on sight, and the jumbled voices and emotions of a bustling castle would confuse and dismay the rest who spoke to Lant. He would be a snare, a deadly lure to most of them. But Eirian remained uncertain whether or not she could live without the people she had grown up around, without friends. "Could I learn to speak with your animals? Could you teach me?"

He smiled sadly. "I said before, you have only to listen. This is nothing I know to teach. I never learned it because it was always there."

From outside, people impatiently called her name. She looked at him, then at the pathway leading up to daylight. Ultimately, the pressure of the choice became too much for her and she fled past him. He hung his head and did not try to follow. She had decided, and he accepted woefully that she had decided against him. He sat down and placed on the cavern floor the small basket of ripe strawberries he had gathered for her, forgotten till now. He imagined Eirian eating them, imagined their juice on her lips and a light of joy in her eyes. Soon he was recalling the scent of her hair, the wetness of her skin against his at the apex of their passion. The cavern still thrived with her presence, and he could not abide where her ghost remained. He ran up the path to daylight, kicking over the basket of berries. Outside, he sought a glimpse of her as the castle party departed. He raced through the woods back to the height where the boar had attacked her, but the group from the castle had chosen some other way to return, and Lant saw no one. Maybe, he thought, she would come back.

In a tree overhead, the Raven squawked down at him, and he looked up coldly, distrustfully. The bird cawed, "Eirian, Eirian. You will be her destiny." Then it fluttered and swooped out into the sky, gone from sight.

Eirian had believed that, once reunited with her people, she might find consolation—if not cheer, then at least absorption in the routine of a day-to-day life that was second nature to her. Lant, she thought, was just a brief hour's walk away, in no way lost or given up. She tried in vain to allocate places for him in her heart and mind where he might be mastered; but he leaked from these at any moment, like water out of a fractured vessel, pouring disruptively into view. His image began to plague her: she saw his ghost in shadows on the castle's narrow landings, in the steam of boiling meats in the cramped kitchen. The earthy smell from the stable next to her quarters brought a reminiscence of the musky odor that surrounded him in his cave. Eirian began to think that he was trying to contact her, that his magic allowed him to appear in this way to her that he might plague her. If such trickery were real, she should be angry with him; but the thought of him actually appearing in her confined little room, in her bed, made her heart race. She could not find anger in herself. If the visions were from him, then he loved her enough to make the effort; if they were from within herself, then she must love him more than she knew. The meaning, in either case, left her in no doubt of what she needed to do. A castle so grand as Dore could always acquire more servants. Where, though, was she ever going to find another Lant?

Having reached this decision, she tried to tell her friends, but they disregarded her or told her she was under a spell and should go see the Man of Knowledge. They did not remotely understand what she felt; they only made fun of her, resurrecting the numerous tales told about the Lord of the Forest, but now with a mocking tone. Not one among them comprehended the depth of her love. She would not miss these people. She would not even do them the courtesy of saying good-bye when she left.

* * *

Lant found the forest to be deathly silent, more quiet than he had ever heard. Over the past week he had gone out less and less; each time he had emerged from the cave, Eirian's absence from the landscape made it seem dark and cold. Worse than that, he had found the voices of his friends hushed, as if the animals were keeping their thoughts from him or moving slowly, steadily away to some other part of the woods. He returned to the place where he had left the search party the day they had come to fetch his lover. To his horror he discovered that someone had killed an animal there. Probably a deer: he found a wide red smear on the rocks, and an arrow beside it. He picked the arrow up. A shred of bloody tissue still hung on the tip, a piece of some creature's heart. It was cold to the touch, the victim long dead. Why had no one come to tell him? He raised his head, listened for the animals. *Rabbit!* he called. *Fawn! Goshawk! I've always come to your calls of grief, where are you all for mine?* No reply answered him from any direction. The forest might have been dead and decaying. *Why won't any of you speak to me?*

"I'll speak to you," came a reply from right behind him. Lant swung around in desperation. The Raven stood on the dead branch of a fir tree at the level of his head. Its black eyes gleamed.

"Where are—"

"The others? They won't come to you now. They're afraid of you because you've surrendered to a human. You've given her everything and left nothing for any of us. They can sense it, even at a distance. I alone come to your pitiful call because it's all the same to me—you've never had anything for me."

"I could never trust your deceit."

"Deceit? How can I be deceitful when I've had no dealings with you at all?" asked the Raven.

Lant wondered if he could have misjudged the bird. It was true—his mistrust had been founded entirely on what the other animals had told him, not on fact. And in the past week not one of the others had come to see him in the grotto. "Will they return to me?"

"After so many years of rejection, you'd ask me to give you your future? My, I really don't know what to say."

Lant stepped forward. "You started to—the day she left me. You said I was her destiny."

"Did I?" The Raven cocked his head. "I might have done. When you can look into the future so easily, you are sometimes taken by the visions, whisked away as on a sudden gust of wind. What I said then was nothing but a glimpse, a flash of insight. That's all."

"Say that you'll look into my future and see if she is in it. Tell me that she is."

"I can only tell you what is, not what you want, no matter how badly you want it. There are a thousand ways two futures can mingle. Are you sure you want this knowledge?"

"Of course I want it. I can't go on living without knowing."

The bird raised its head imperiously. "All right," it said. "I'll look for you. For you and the woman . . ."

"Eirian."

"Eirian," echoed the Raven, abstractedly. "She is in your future, yes. More than that, she is the turning point for you. Oh, I see it clearly. Eirian—you will *kill* her. You will take her life with your own hand."

"What lies are you feeding me?"

"Not what you wanted to hear, was it?" replied the bird. "You will kill her because I want you to, just as I brought you together with her to rob you of your gifts. I made her lose her way. I set the boar upon her path. I even turned your magic so that the hairy thing would awaken at her passing. Now I speak with your friends, with all of them, and you will speak with no one. It was nothing to make them understand how you had given up your heart to a castle dweller, simple to turn them from you. And now for me you must kill the very thing you've come to love beyond everything else." The Raven flapped his wings restlessly.

"You conniving, feathered monster—you've hated me as everyone warned."

"I do," said the bird, and it seemed to grow larger as it flapped its wings again. Lant drew back, but the bird continued to expand. It meant to devour him, and its raucous shriek pierced his soul. Blackness consumed his view of the tree on which the bird had perched. Huge wings enshrouded him like a pall. Through the screech of the Raven's voice, he heard the forest voices, all crying out at once. Stung, betrayed, he thought they sided with the monster that tried to smother him. The cold, oily feathers pushed against his face. He choked for breath. The arrow—he still had the hunter's arrow clutched in his fist. Now, while he had some power left, he raised the arrow and stabbed into the Raven's breast, felt the tip go deeply into the bird's flesh. A sharp wail shot through the roaring squall. The blackness became smoke, thinning, dissipating. Still he held the arrow lodged in flesh. The smoke blew apart . . . as on a sudden gust of wind. Eirian stood before him, though only because he held her up by the shaft of the arrow. Her head hung to one side.

Beyond comprehension, he could only state the obvious. "You came back," he said.

"Of course she came back," the Raven answered hideously from the tree overhead. "She couldn't live without you. She couldn't live without the Lord of the Forest. *Lord of the Forest!*" Lant looked up at him with eyes that opened on a shattered soul. The bird said, "So, and I told you your true fate, now fulfilled. Remember that you demanded it. Remember that this is what you sought." Then the Raven swept up off the branch and through the autumn trees, leaving behind two bodies—one drained of life and the other of its reason to live.

The maiden was not seen again in Castle Dore. They thought at first she might have some lover in the settlement close by; but when she failed to appear after a full week had passed, a party went seeking her again. They called to Lant but he did not appear. An arrow shaft and a smear of blood lay ominously on the stones where he had met some of them before.

No one saw the maiden or the man throughout the winter, and the hunting was the poorest in memory, as if the animals had for some reason deserted that part of the forest. It was not until late the next summer, when the girls from Castle Dore went into the woods to pick strawberries, that they came upon the strange sight of a creature gray as ash kneeling as if in prayer over a ripe patch of berries. At their approach he fled into the brush. The strawberries where he had been were the largest the girls had ever seen, red and splendid, glistening; but no one wanted to pick any, and they returned to the castle emptyhanded. When asked why, they explained in subdued tones that the berry patch itself had been surrounded by a dozen tall stakes, and on every one of these the body of a raven had been impaled.

The forest has been pared down over the years and Castle Dore reduced to a ruin; but on sultry late summer days when the berries are sweetest, one can often find the ravens devouring them frenziedly in a desperate attempt to eat them all before the ghostly Lord of the Forest returns to his lover's grave.

MADELEINE E. ROBINS *is perhaps not as well known now as she's going to be. Suffice to say that, in 1981, Algis Budrys named her one of the 10 most promising new genre writers. She has published five historical romances, including Regencies, stories in* Asimov's *and* Fantasy & Science Fiction. *Still quite young, Ms. Robins is "a New Yorker by birth, training and inclination" and has been, in the last ten years, "a nanny, costumer, secretary, actor, slush-reader, teacher, and repaired hurt books."*

Whatever she's been, Madeleine E. Robins is a writer of subtlety and power. "Nimuë's Tale" contains a truth deep and central to the Celtic imagination—if love creates sunlight in the heart, it cannot escape making shadows as well.

Nimuë's Tale

by Madeleine E. Robins

One who plays with time barely notices its passing. The green of the forest trembled on the verge of autumn when Malla's husband Oulen told me there were strangers in the village.

I knew. Why else did my heart beat with such heavy strokes, my hands tremble as I put my work aside? By the time I had taken off my apron, unpinned the sleeves of my tunic to hang properly from my elbows and smoothed my hair from my forehead, and had instructed Landra to have wine and honey ready to refresh the visitors, they were in my courtyard.

Pelles looked well, but older; brash enthusiasm given way to a sterner carriage. His attention was all for his companion; he had dismounted and was at her side before I stepped from my door. She smiled at him, then turned and let her eyes meet mine, as if it had been moments, an hour, a day since she sent me forth from the Lake House.

"Nimuë, how brown you've become," the Lady said.

All my learning deserted me.

I was a girl trembling in a cave:

One last time the old man's hands stole up to tweak my breast (and him watching slyly, thinking I would not notice it). Once more, apology in his wet-mouthed smile (as if a smile could atone for the twelvemonth of listening to his ancient rambling boasts while I tried to remember to simper up at him). One more time I leaned away from the old enchanter's narrow shadow, all the while trying to make myself lean toward him, seeking to intoxicate him with my scent and nearness. I was a very bad seductress.

I did not mean to destroy him.

He had backed me toward a wall to explain some trifling relic: one more of his interminable lessons. As he talked I watched from the corner of my eye: his hand moved stealthily up to toy with the fiery plait of hair that lay across my breast. The thousandth gesture, the sum of a thousand gestures. It made my stomach turn. With no idea what I was doing, no more hope than to get away from him, I reached into myself, and out, pulled down and away and I knew not how, stretching and pulling, venting my rage and disgust: that he should want me. That he should dare want anything young and fresh and beautiful.

The glittering cave began to tremble. Pyrite-streaked stone crashed down around us and I pulled away from him and ran with all my strength through the chambers, up the rough-hewn stone steps, tracing the branching path back to sunlight and clean spring air.

For long minutes I stood in the adit and waited until my pulse slowed and the world lost its film of red panic. The rumble and crash of stone had ceased and there was silence behind me in the cave. When I could think enough to realize that I must do something, there was only one thing to do, as natural as breathing. Our horses were tethered to a gnarled apple tree near the cave mouth. In a trembling dream I loosed Merlin's old mare and set her running. Then I mounted my own and turned her toward home: not Camelot, whence the enchanter and I had ridden out that morning. I turned east, toward the House of the Lake and my lady.

In that same dreaming way I rode through a green and

blossoming countryside I did not see. When I was not minding the road (or seeking it anew; I was often lost), I tried to imagine a homecoming to the Lake House after a year. How Sister Eilon would look when she found me standing at the oaken gate; the smell of beeswax, incense, and clean rushes in the Chapter hall; the murmur of women's voices in the workroom. All the things I had longed for in the year of bright noise and bustle in Camelot.

I thought of the Lady. I told myself she would understand my flight, what I had done—what *had* I done?—to the wizard. After all, she herself had told me of men, had shared dismissive laughter after each of her dealings with them. She *would* understand, I told myself with one breath; with the next, I remembered that I had failed her, and I trembled.

And when I had lulled those fears from my heart and rode on, half asleep, I would have a vision of old Merlin under half the sparkling mountain, struggling for the last stale taste of air, trapped in the cold darkness and cursing me.

It was a blessing to find myself lost again, and in finding the route clear, forget my fears for another few miles.

I arrived at the House near dark of the second day, hungry and dirty and fearful and so grateful to be home that I nearly wept. Sister Eilon made one startled exclamation at the sight of me, then opened the gate, saw that my horse was taken to the stable by one of her helpers, and brought me herself to a room where I could bathe, eat, and sleep.

The Lady saw me in the library after Terce the next morning. She was more beautiful than I remembered, tall and cool in the green morning light. She smiled and my heart rejoiced and I knew everything would be well. I schooled myself not to show my joy too openly, to stand with my eyes downcast, waiting for her embrace. It came, a brief touch of her cheek to mine that turned my heart to water. Then she took my chin in the palm of her hand and tilted my face up to read what was written there.

"What happened, Nimuë?" Her voice was poised at the edge of concern, sweet and low.

I made myself brave and told her: "My lady, I think the enchanter is dead."

I could not read what she felt at the news: something like a smile was quickly gone and replaced with a frown and a tiny nervous tic in her brow. "Merlin dead? *How*?" Then, "You *think* he is dead? And why have I not had some word of this from Camelot?"

I began to explain—I told her of the stone quaking around us, and how I had run and heard the walls crashing down behind me, sealing the old man in. "Lord Merlin often disappeared for days to the cave, even the King himself knew better than to seek for him. I don't know how long it will be before they miss us in Camelot."

She nodded without hearing. "But are you sure he is dead? How? Who could have done such a thing?"

I swallowed and looked at the floor. "My lady, I think—I'm afraid—I did."

"You?" She looked startled; her hand dropped from my chin. "Did you learn so much in Camelot?" Her eyes were avid. I ached to please her, to be able to tell her yes.

"No, Lady. I don't know what I did, I don't know how I did it. I just . . . did."

She stood away from me, walked the length of her chamber until she was hidden in a spill of morning light from the window. Her shadow trembled. "You just *did* what?"

The words outran my tongue as I tried to make her understand. "I could not bear it any longer, he kept touching me, grabbing at me." I waited for the nod of understanding which surely must come. I filled the silence with more words, waiting for her to stop me. "I don't know what I did, my lady, but he reached for me again and I could not stand it, I *could not*. It was something inside me that came out and . . . and brought the cave down, like a flood. I was so angry, him with his boasts and his lies! He told me he'd never seen an aura of power like mine, he swore he'd teach me everything, but it was like sifting barley to find a dram of wisdom in his brags. I could have waited forever for his true secrets!''

She stood like a statue in the light; I could not see her face. ''You destroyed him.'' Her voice was wondering. ''Because he touched you.''

I nodded.

''He *touched* you?'' She stepped from the masking light and her face was tight and there was fear or rage in her eye. ''You fool, he must have touched you a thousand times in the twelvemonth. That was your purpose, to smile and fawn and listen and be *touched*. To suffer whatever the old man would do to you to gain his secrets.''

A great trembling took me; I grew small under her anger. Somewhere inside, a tiny rebellious voice insisted that it was all very well to talk of failure, but *she* had not been pinched and patted by those palsied hands, not suffered whispers in *her* ear. But when I looked up at the fine planes of the Lady's face, burning cold with rage, I forgot anger and was miserable.

''What did you do?'' she hissed. ''Why didn't he break free? How could *you* destroy him?''

Again I tried to tell her of the fear and disgust that had broken in me, of the reaching and twisting and tearing, of murmuring words I did not know and could not remember. Nothing I said softened her expression. She listened with her arms crossed before her, hands tucked into the wide dark sleeves of her robe.

''I don't know,'' I finished. ''It was as if something burst inside of me. It did the damage, *it* sealed old Merlin in the cave. Not *me,* my lady. Please . . .''

I thought my confusion moved her at last. She came toward me and reached a hand to me; I was to be forgiven. She took my chin between strong fingers—no softness now—and looked long and hard into my eyes. I made myself stand without shrinking, trembling with pleasure at her silken touch. When I looked into her dark eyes I prayed for her to understand, forgive. To love me again.

''You will go,'' she said at length.

I started to make reverence. "Yes, my lady." She stopped me with her hand on my shoulder.

"Do you understand? You will leave the Lake House. Today. And you will never return unless I bid it."

The light in the room receded, darkness surrounded the burning whiteness of the Lady's face, her fierce eyes watching me. When I tried to shake my head, the weight of the gesture carried me to the floor; I fainted, still unbelieving.

I woke in the company of one of the lay sisters, a thin, pinched-looking girl with worried eyes and an impossible number of freckles. She said her name was Malla; her accent was heavily Breton. As my eyes adjusted to the dimness, I realized we were not in my cell; this was a small damp room with the smell of rotting silage. A room over the stables, kept to accommodate the groomsmen of visitors. "Madam Abbess said you was to rest here until you was fit to travel." The girl drew away from me as she said it, as if she feared a blow. "I'm to take you out of Britain. There's your horse, and a donkey for me below. And she give me this for you." She held a purse out to me. I opened it wide enough to see a sparkle of gold, then drew the string tight again. "Madam said it's your dowry, mistress. Soon's you feel up to travel—"

"No, I have to talk to her." I pushed myself upright and fought my dizziness.

The girl shook her head. "Can't, mistress. You'll not be given entrance. They give us some food, if you're hungry." She nodded at a saddlebag filled to bursting and left sitting by the door. "Are you hungry, mistress?" she asked hopefully.

"No."

"Then I s'pose we'd ought to start away," she said sadly. I let her raise me to my feet and dress me like a child. She tucked a cloak around my shoulders and pinned it with a silver brooch old Merlin had given me. While I sat unseeing, Malla dragged the heavy saddlebag downstairs and slung it onto her donkey; my horse already bore

a chest with my few possessions in it. Then she returned
for me, saw me mounted, and clambered onto her donkey's back. She took the rein of my horse and led me from
the House yard, past Sister Eilon at the gate, into unprom-
ising dusk.

The girl kept up a stream of comfortable chatter as we
rode. I heard none of it until she asked if I was a good sea
traveler.

"Sea travel? What are you talking about?"

"My home, mistress. Brittany, where my folk are. And
kinder folk than you find in your Britain." She made a
scornful sound of it: Bree-t'n. "My old aunt Landra'd take
us in. But be a good sea traveler?"

I was not. The voyage from the seaport of Clausentium
to the Breton coast was one long grey misery. I listened to
Malla rejoice at being so nearly home: I could not share
her joy. My home was behind me, across the sea, a place
wrapped about a person; that any other place could become
my home I doubted.

Malla's aunt lived in Rugonde, a village of a dozen
cottages, close set in the Breton forest. The forest, called
Broceliande, had a presence of its own; at night in Landra's
tiny cottage the deep green fastness seemed to embrace the
village; I remembered that Merlin often spoke of Brittany
as a place of strong magics. Old Landra, fat and tooth-shy,
took us in without question, and I was let to sit in the sun
or by the fire, healing my hurt. By and by the ache in me
gentled to a thin grey longing, a pale film that stretched
across my thoughts until I no longer noticed it.

Still, it took a fever that swept Rugonde and would have
killed a dozen or more, to pull me from my fog. Watching
folk sicken around me, *willow bark and strawberry leaf*, I
thought. *Don't they know?* It seemed they did not, and I
spent hours in forest and field searching for flowers, leaves
and bark, and more hours decocting a tisane to take the
fever away. When the sickness had gone, I had found my
occupation making tinctures and cerates, dispensing medicines and learning to read sickness in the eyes of folk who
came to me.

I had cause to bless Merlin's lessons. So many of them had seemed trivial, a mixture of nonsense—cats slaughtered to cure warts, salt cast over the shoulder to avert ill luck—and cookbook magic. Now I recalled his healing spells and recipes, and cures learned in the stillroom from my Lady. I had believed myself an indifferent student, trying no harder in my studies than would please her. Now I had reason to remember and to learn anew.

So I earned my keep: when I cured the baron's son of the lung-flux I was granted a small draughty stone villa in payment, and brought Landra from her mud-and-wattle cottage to cook and see to me. I delivered babies, closed the eyes of those I could not save, learned the franker speech of country folk, forgot in some measure my convent-bred niceness. Malla was betrothed, then wed to Rugonde's miller; a year later I was both midwife and godmother to her girl child.

I could have forgotten—almost—that there was another world outside the green shadows of Broceliande, but from time to time strangers rode through the town. I cared less for their tidings than for the pleasure of hearing different tongues: Latin or British. Often I invited these strangers to my hall to dine and tell me their gossip, and I smiled and poured more wine when they toasted me, the gracious lady of Rugonde.

One traveler, Pelles, was of Arthur's court and returning from a mission to Rome. Having sped across the continent on the King's business he undertook now a more leisurely return for his own pleasure. I thought him very young, fair and open and just a little brash, but he was three years my senior and a veteran—to hear him talk—of several hair-raising campaigns in Arthur's service.

I liked him. The first night that he dined with me I laughed often. The second night I barely noted what I ate, so deep were we in talking. By the third night I looked for his coming and would have been disappointed to take my meat with only Landra for company. Pelles reminded me that I had been accounted pretty; listening to his tales, the nonsense he could spout with gorgeous ease, I remembered Camelot.

"I was there," I told him. "In Camelot. It seems a long time ago."

"No, surely I'd remember a woman so beautiful and so charming—"

"Truly, among so many?" I teased. "I was there for a year. *You* must have been off on one of your quests."

He gave me a look full of heart and laughter. I remembered seeing men and women carrying on such dalliance in Camelot; I had scorned it there and never realized its airy pleasure.

Three more evenings he dined with me. We laughed and exchanged stories, he urged me more than once to come to Camelot with him. "Astound them, let them remember how fair you are, how talented, how gracious." He waved his arms in exaggerated circles and grinned. On the storming night when he made his farewell I was sorry to see him go. We screamed our good-byes over the thunder and watched as lightning shadows made a giant of the stone lintel over the courtyard gate.

"Visit again and bring me stories of your heroism," I yelled.

He took my hand and pressed it against his heart. "Come back with me," he yelled back. "Come back . . ." He hesitated. "With me."

After a moment I pulled my hand away. It was cold outside his grasp. "My place is here. They need me." *I can never return.* "Go safely!"

Rain plastered his fair hair to his skull and water ran off the corner of his smile. He stayed a moment longer, told me to go in before I was as wet as he. So I turned back to my fire. I was pouring more wine when I heard it happen: thunder, the scream of the horse, the grate of stone.

I ran for the courtyard and saw him: his horse had shied in the lightning and brought the wall down; Pelles was pinned beneath the lintel stone.

Through a haze of panic and anger I reached into the heart of the stone lintel, pulled up and twisted away, only half knowing what I did. As I ran stumbling across the rain-slick yard, the lintel rose, obedient to my command, up and off Pelles's body. He was free before Landra and I reached him.

Pelles made a slow convalescence. He charmed old Landra, who scolded and fussed and was entirely under his thumb in a day; with me he was more respectful—a little. I spent some part of the day and each evening with him, dicing or reading, talking. I did my work, gathered and dried herbs, pressed out oils, mixed liniments and powders, prescribed for the sick and hurt who came to me. But I had found a new study, as intoxicating as love or honey wine; Merlin would have recognized it.

I thought often of Merlin, knowing I had missed the heart of his teachings. What I had scorned as an old man's prosing were his greatest secrets, tricks he had learned over his many years to discipline and develop the great natural ability that was his. What I had dismissed as flattery I realized now was truth; the old man had recognized a power in me that even my Lady had not seen.

I struggled to learn the limits of my powers (and it was a struggle, all experiment and failure, no demure learning from scrolls or parchments), spent hours in the woods straining to do simple things without the fuel of panic, doing them easily once I achieved the proper degree of nonchalance. On the day I learned that knack I went from shifting pebbles to moving rocks, made the trees dance to my will, drew the clouds together in one great frowning congregation. While rain poured down on me I stood on the hilltop and laughed like a zany, filled with triumph.

Sometimes the learning hurt: I discovered inadvertently that the touch of the Lady's hand which I had prized as a sign of especial tenderness was, as well, a way of compelling truth or loyalty. The shadow memory of her hand cradling my chin still made me flush with longing, despite the distance of time and years. Even the power in me seemed powerless to stop that pain.

Learning so preoccupied me that when Pelles told me it was time that he returned to Camelot I was surprised (that

the time had passed so quickly) and saddened (that he
would go) and worrying over a beldame's recipe for
dream-reading.

"Will you miss me?" he asked, playing with my fingers
like a Christian telling rosary beads.

"Rugonde will be very quiet without you," I admitted.
*Storax, benjamin, labdanum and oil of lavender and . . .
what else?* "You'll be happy to be back in the city, I
suppose."

"Nimuë?"

*Camphire and damaske, with civet. All together, as a
kind of incense.* "Yes?" I pulled my attention back to
him. He looked well now, only a scar on his brow as token
of his fall; his fair hair almost covered it.

"Will you *think* of coming to Camelot? You'd be welcome, more than welcome. I promise it." He was very
earnest; it made my heart sink.

"I cannot. I'm sorry, Pelles." What there was for me in
Britain I could not approach; what he wanted I did not
know how to give. "Come visit me again," I offered,
knowing it was a cool comfort.

He refused to be comforted. "I'll leave in the morning." He said it as if he expected the words to hurt, and
curiously, they did. He rose and left the room, very straight-
backed with his anger, gone before I could say again "I'm
sorry." He never heard the words.

In the morning he kissed Landra's fat cheek and swore
undying love to her; he and I said a quiet farewell. Anger
had passed through us both. Landra and I stood in my
small courtyard and watched as Pelles rode away. Then
Landra gave a prodigious sigh and went in to her spinning.

Broceliande's shadows closed behind Pelles, sealing
Rugonde safely away from the world. I was busy with my
work in the infirmary, with household chores in which I
was Landra's fumble-fingered student. And my studies.
There was no goal to the learning, magic such as mine was
rarely called for in the Brittany forest, but I studied: the
shifting of rocks and trees, the management of clouds or
human moods; I searched for words that would unlock the

past and let me read what had happened in Merlin's cave
that day. Curiously, I never thought to read the future.

"Nimuë?"

The Lady waited for my reply. Dizzily, I tried to think
of something to say. Three years since Pelles rode from
my courtyard; seven since I set out from the Lake House.
Why now, why come now, after all these years? I was a
woman grown and still I could only stand staring at the
Lady, wanting to touch her hand, listen to her voice, be
her beloved. Finally I managed: "My lady, will you take
some wine?"

"Thank you, I will." She ignored her groom and allowed Pelles to lift her down from her horse. His hand
lingered at her waist and I was taken with a jealousy so
sharp and fierce I almost cried out. She held his eyes with
hers for a long moment, then drew one finger casually
along his jaw. Words came to my lips that would have torn
Pelles from her side—torn him to pieces—but the habit of
discipline was strong; some part of me still thought of him
as friend. I turned on my heel to lead them to the hall.

"Pelles told me such things of you, I had to see myself." She sat in a chair of carved wood just beyond the
window; rosy afternoon light touched the embroidered hem
of her robe. She no longer dressed as soberly as she had at
the Lake House: the privilege of Camelot draped about her
shoulders in embroidered linen and fine wool. "Sit down,
dear girl. Tell me what became of you after you left us."

After you left us. She made it sound as if the exile had
been my own choice. Pelles paced the length of the wall,
his eyes always on her. "There is little to tell, Lady: I
came here; I've been the healer since Malla and I arrived;
you'll remember Malla, Lady: the girl you sent with me."

She nodded vaguely. "You're too modest, Nimuë. A
country healer does not have a villa like this, or a reputation such as yours. In the villages all up the coast you're
mentioned with considerable respect. You're hardly a village herb-grannie." I watched her lips form the words but

barely heard, marveling at the soft rose of her mouth, wanting to trace its shape with my fingers, my own lips.

Pelles laughed behind me, a forced sound that begged for notice. "I told you, Lady Viviene, her powers—"

"You did, sir." She cut him off. Despite myself I felt a gleam of vindictive pleasure: *see there, she does not love you*. "Nimuë, I am tired after our journey. Is there a chamber . . ."

At once I was on my feet, calling for Landra, who had gone off to clear my own room for the Lady and to ready two smaller rooms for Pelles and myself. "I'll take you there at once. Will you sup later with me? Us?" I added, feeling Pelles's hot look on my shoulder blades.

"Of course. Pelles, see that my groom and horse are taken care of." She did not wait to see him nod; she was gone.

I paused for a second before I followed her. "Pelles . . ."

He looked at me. For the first time since their arrival he and I really saw each other, looked square and openly at each other. There was no softness in him for me now. "Yes, lady?"

"You're welcome back." It was all I could say. My heart urged warfare, promising a battle for the Lady's least word. Common sense and the hard-won discipline of my studies reminded me again that he was, or had been, my friend. When he nodded grimly I understood that his heart and mind were no less divided than mine. "At supper, then."

The torches were lit when the three of us met in the hall. Lady Viviene wore a tunic of garnet red wool, finely embroidered; it made her cool black-and-white beauty the more stirring for the reflection of rose in her cheeks. I ached to touch her, but knew better than to show my feelings too plainly. Pelles obviously did not know her as well: he followed her movement through the room, besotted.

It was a strange meal. The Lady spoke, and Pelles and I at either hand restrained ourselves from quibbling too obviously for her attention. She asked me what I had done

before coming to Rugonde, what great folk I had met in
Brittany. I was embarrassed to admit how little I knew
outside of Broceliande and how little I remembered of my
first months in Brittany; she took my protestations with a
sort of smiling disbelief. "Keep your council if you will,
child." She and Pelles spoke of Camelot while I picked at
my food and watched the radiant flesh of her throat rise
and fall with her breath.

"A toast." The Lady poured honeyed wine into my
cup; her eyes met mine. "And Pelles?" She poured for
him, then herself. "To old friends re-met."

We drank. The wine was too sweet for my taste, cloying;
I was used to taking it nearly unsweetened. Still, I met her
eyes over the brim of my cup and smiled; she returned the
smile and drank to me.

Then she rose, shimmering in the firelight, bade us both
goodnight, and was gone. We sat dumbfounded for a
moment, then Pelles smiled; not the beaming of an infatu-
ate boy but a rueful man's smile. "So are we dismissed,"
he said.

"It would seem so. More wine?"

He refused the wine, but sat awhile longer. It was
companionable, that sitting, shared bemusement between
us.

"Pelles, what brought you here?" I asked at length.

"It is just as she said. When I returned to Camelot I
spoke of you—often. They called it boasting, Pelles' quest-
tale. But Lady Viviene heard and believed me when I told
her how you had saved my life. I did not know until she
made up her mind to visit Brittany that she had known you
as a child."

I thought of our last parting. "Yes. Years ago." *And
now she is here.* I still could not compass it. In a wondering mood I bade him good night at last and retired to the
room Landra had made ready for me.

In the night I woke from a nightmare, fought my way
back to waking to find I had not dreamt all of it: there was
a fire in my throat and belly, a tearing that every breath
made worse. My heart beat too fast, my vision was blurred.

It was very hard to do what I knew I must: compose my mind to read my body and seek out the sickness. That isolated, I reached, muttering the incantations between gritted teeth, into myself, soothing the burning tissues, finding the toxins and changing them into a syrup as harmless as water, to flow through blood and flesh without damage.

When I could stand I dressed myself and went to her room.

It seemed she was waiting for me; she was still dressed in her dinner finery, sipping wine by the fire. "Come in, dear child," Viviene said. "You look pale. Some wine?"

"To try the same trick again, my lady?"

She did not seem dismayed. "That was a most potent poison; your masters would be proud of you," Her smile invited me closer. I found, to my horror, that I wanted her still; had she reached for me I would have gone to her embrace, not trustingly, but helpless to resist.

"Why?" I asked, distantly pleased that my voice had not broken.

"What else could I do? I sent you away once, I could not banish you from banishment. And sooner or later you would tire of this retreat. . . ." She waved a hand dismissively, as if to make my home, the village, all of Brittany small and insignificant. "You would come and challenge me. I could not risk that. While my reports said that you were ignorant of your power I could let be, but when that boy told me what you had done here in the wilderness, I knew it was past time. Whoever your masters are, soon or late they would demand you leave—"

"I have no master!" I cried. "Not since you sent me away from the Lake House. I've taught myself what I needed for the love of it, using what I had learned from you and from Lord Merlin."

"An old fool who knew better than to be killed by a stupid girl with a spark of ability?" Her mouth curled. "He deserved his death."

I looked at her and saw what I had never understood: "You feared him. He was stronger than you and you were afraid of him. You wanted his power."

She looked at me as if I were telling a children's tale. "Of course I did. Just as you would come to want mine if I let you." Her voice was all reason. "So I cannot let you."

She raised one slender hand to gesture. I reached, and grasped her hand to stop her, the first time I had ever touched her without permission. It brought us face to face; her dark eyes glittered down at me from her greater height, her mouth was pressed tight. For all her slenderness Viviene was strong, her will steely. I kept my grasp on her wrist and tried to break her cool stare with my own gaze.

And she was still so beautiful. *How can I know this evil and still want her? How can I know what I know and love her?* Gradually her resistance died; our hands dropped and we faced each other.

"Oh, Nimuë . . ." A very small voice, tired and sad. She was panting slightly. So was I; my hand trembled at the release of tension. When she raised her hand to cup my chin, I leaned into the palm, the gesture as natural as breathing. With that gesture and for the first time in seven years, I was *home*. Pleasure made my bones as soft as honey; there was a honey taste in my mouth. If she had asked me for my life in that moment I would have given it to her.

I raised my eyes to her face, inches above mine, near enough to kiss. Her mouth was curved in the tenderest smile; her wide brow creased just slightly as she read my face. Her dark eyes, fathomless, dancing with the firelight, were filled with love. And pleasure. And triumph, an ugly reckoning triumph which counted every minor capitulation and treasured it.

I pulled away from Viviene's hand. "I know the trick of touch, Lady. I'm proof against it."

She smiled wolfishly, the tenderness gone. "You never have been."

I felt tears start with anger. "I have *always* been. I loved you, that was what that touch was to me. Not power, love. You could have kept me, here or at the Lake House years ago, docile and biddable as you wished. I'd never have risen against you."

"It must have come to war soon or late. Look, child . . ." I looked into the fire as she bade me, and in the flames saw old Merlin in his cave. He stood, bowed and feeble, beneath the rain of stone that I had loosed, paralyzed with grief and unable to save himself. Watching the image licked by flame, I knew that he had died rather than strike me down. He had loved me.

Hot grief seized me, fed upon itself. I stood weeping, staring into the fire, blinded by my vision and hating the stupid callow girl who had killed that old man. And then I remembered why the child had been there, who had sent her. I pulled my gaze from the fire and shook my head, forcing a smile.

"You use the wrong argument, Viviene," I told her. I looked at the flask and cup from which she had been drinking, planted a thought in her. "You are too used to folk who cannot fight back." She followed my glance and her white skin paled, glowing with her sudden terror in the firelight. She raised a hand to her throat.

"What have you done?" she whispered. I imagined what she would feel; the tightness, the burning, the confusion. "You've not been near my cup," she protested. "And I'm proof against poison. Do you think I'd not protect myself against any potion I'd use myself?" She rang out triumphant again.

"It's not *your* potion, Viviene." I let my mind reach hers, let her feel the slow constriction, touched her heart and set it racing. The fire in her belly, the sickly-sweet taste of honeyed wine in her mouth, and fear rich and hot in her blood. I poisoned her with rage. "It's mine."

She staggered back with her hand at her mouth. "Nimuë . . ."

"Do you like the war of your own making?" One final twist, one last cold clutch and I drew back from her. Released, she shuddered and fell backward, knocking over a small table. While she caught her breath and tried to right a spinning world, I made myself wait, letting the enormous hurt run out of me. "I don't want to hurt you," I said at last.

She stood against the wall, one hand at her side, the garnet-colored tunic hanging askew. Her dark hair unraveled from its plait and her face was tense and narrow. *"I'll destroy you.* You cannot stand against me."

Certainty blossomed in me when I looked into her eyes: she was right. I looked at my hands and saw the bones of a child. I was frail, the very draughts of the chamber buffeted me. I was not a woman safe in the serenity of her life and her power but a girl, pretty and callow and unlearned, as naive as an infant, afraid of the world of men. I was breathless with terror, knowing that all that kept that girl—me—safe was the Lady's protection. Without that I was helpless; fighting her would be madness.

Dimly, I watched Pelles enter the room and go to her side, his face all concern, come to a wordless summoning. She smiled a false smile of near-concealed suffering, her fingers caressed his cheek affectionately. I wanted to tear his heart out and I could not move.

"N-nn-no!" I stuttered. Pelles turned and saw me: a madwoman gasping and weeping. Viviene whispered something to Pelles, who held her protectively, slightly behind him. My eyes met his—dim and sleepy, bespelled by Viviene's light caressing touch—and I was distracted from her spell, returned to myself. I stood still for a moment and let strength course through me.

Pelles spoke: "Nimuë—lady, think what you do."

I answered him from a cool dim place of power. "I know what I do; Pelles, she thrust this upon me. I never wanted to hurt her. I loved her."

"Would you destroy her because she cannot return your love?" *Was that the lie she had told?* "Think who she is, what she is; Nimuë, what's love to the ones that are the stuff of legends?"

I thought again of Merlin. "No more than food or drink or air to breathe," I told him. "To those that *are* the stuff of legends. Did she tell you she was such a one?"

He looked at me and shook his head dizzily. "Nimuë—"

"Kill her," the Lady growled. "She'll destroy me—kill her, Pelles." Her hand went again to his throat, but the caress was desperate this time, her fingers poised like talons.

"Will you kill me, Pelles? It's what she brought you to do," I said levelly. The truth was twisted in her face. "Kill me . . . and she will kill you, soon or late. Am I wrong, Lady?"

Her hand worked at his cheek, feverish. "What does it matter? You, him, that slobbering old mage—I have a right to destroy what is a danger to me. Or what I have no need for. Now, Pelles. Kill her for me." Behind the dimness in his eyes there was a hopeless spark of rage, and I knew I must help him.

I froze him where he was and watched Viviene as she realized she stroked stone, not flesh. Pelles gazed unblinkingly at me, standing like a warrior facing death.

She screeched something, wrenched the dagger from Pelles's sash, and flew at me, her face furious as a hawk's. If I stopped her now she would try again and again, knowing no other way. She raised the dagger above her head to strike me.

I reached for her, grasped her heart with my mind and twisted, crushing, feeling the flesh tear. There was no pleasure in it. It took only a moment; there was hardly time for her look of surprise before the Lady dropped the dagger. Her eyes filled with blackness and she fell to the floor.

Afterward I sat and wept for a long time. Pelles, freed from her spell and from mine, held me, and he wept too.

In the morning Landra wrapped the Lady's body in a white damask and saw that a carter was found to take the body from my house to the seaside, the first leg of its return to the Lake House. We stood in the courtyard, watching as the wagon pulled away and rolled haltingly over the rutted path, until it was swallowed by the dappled shadows of the road. Grief stuck in my throat; I had wept all my tears before dawn, for all of us.

"Let them bury her," Pelles said coldly. Freed of the Lady's spell he was angry, ashamed of his infatuation.

Two survivors still raw, sharing. "You'll go back to Camelot?"

He nodded. "You'll stay here?"

"I don't know." My exile was over. "This place tastes of ashes."

"Come to Camelot," Pelles urged again, a ghost of another urging. "With me."

I was afraid to promise too much; the leaves were tending to golds and russets, and soon it would be no weather for traveling. "Perhaps I will," I said. "Not now, but soon."

I have returned to Britain. It looks much the same as I remember, but the open spring countryside seems strange after Broceliande's green confines. The blossoming orchard before Merlin's hill turns its face up to the sun. I came here to study the old man's grave, the rock-filled adit hidden now by young trees and gorse, but there are no secrets revealed in the stone I broke; like one waking from a dream I shrug myself free of the past and mount my horse. Then, hopeful, I turn her west, toward Camelot.

CHELSEA QUINN YARBRO *has a marvelous authority with a line; when Quinn says it, it stays said. Her works stay in the mind for years. I can still remember many details from her SF novel,* False Dawn, *and the more recent* A Mortal Glamour *is one of the most inexorably horrific books I've ever chilled through, because the real horror of it is history and humanity.*

The first volume of Yarbro I ever opened was her 1978 collection, Cautionary Tales, *which contained a story, "Un Bel Di," that I can't reread even now without pain and pity. The same collection included "The Fellini Beggar," inspired by Quinn's fascination with Puccini. The first chance I get, I hope to sit down with her and argue that troublesome last scene in* Turandot.

Her present story, "Night Mare," takes Breton legend as its source, a very ancient one not often tapped by genre writers. Trust Quinn to come up with something new; after all, look what she did for vampires with Count St. Germaine. . . .

Night Mare

by Chelsea Quinn Yarbro

For as long as he could remember, he had hated horses; those enormous heads that prodded at you, those huge nostrils that blew out, those great shambling feet, those bugle voices, all of it revolted him.

His hatred set him apart as much as his doubtful paternity, and his older—half?—brothers laughed at him as much for his cowardice as for his illegitimacy. It was not surprising that he was a sullen child, nursing his wounded pride with dreams of vindication and glory.

Fergus, the oldest house-*gille*, often looked after the boy, feeling sorry for him. "You don't want to let them bother you," he said so many times that the words became meaningless and were only a gesture of comfort.

"They don't," was the answer he always gave while rage and shame went at him with twin claws. His sharp face would set, his dark brows drawn together and his eyes thunderous.

"You ought to have a word with your mother," Fergus suggested when the boy was approaching his ninth birthday. "You don't speak to her."

"Why should I?" he challenged, scowling. "She is a

dishonest woman. What could she tell me? It would be lies." He folded his arms and looked out over the wide stone battlements toward the flat grey shimmer of the ocean. "I have nothing to say to her and she has nothing to say to me."

Between the bailey-and-keep and the shore there was a cluster of tall stones arranged in an elipse with two avenues of smaller stones leading away in opposite directions. The stones were very old, and the largest in the elipse was sometimes called the Mother Stone by the crofters who farmed the area, though none of them would plant crops near the stones. Fergus looked at those stones as he spoke. "She is your mother, and she knows better than any what is yours."

Wind sliced off the ocean, taking the boy's breath away and making his eyes sting. "She wouldn't tell me," he insisted at his most sullen.

"You must try, boy. She can be the best friend you have." He put his massive hand to his beard. "Your brothers won't be any help to you, and the gods are not favoring King Uriens since he started to listen to the priests of the White Christ. Your mother must be your defense now."

"She's never helped me before," he said, trying hard not to pout. He was too angry for pouting. "Last spring I went to talk to her and she refused to give me any time. She sent me away as if I were less than a tirewoman, and said nothing more than my sleeve was torn. So I will kiss her hand at supper and I will present her midwinter gifts, and that's the end of it. She will have none of me; I will have none of her."

Fergus, who had fathered nine children and had seen six of them live, patted the boy's arm. "Give her a chance. Her life hasn't been easy for her, either. You say that you cannot speak to her, but that is not always possible for her, since she is watched so much. She and the King have become estranged, and there is little for her to rely upon. You are the one who can champion her, if you want to wear her glove."

"Why should I?" the boy asked, turning away from Fergus. "I am more an outcast than ever she was."

"Then what will you do?" asked Fergus reasonably. He did not repeat his question when the boy fell silent.

"Something will happen," he vowed, his expression fixed angrily on the stones. "Perhaps not at once, but it will happen."

"And your mother?" Fergus said, feeling the boy slip away from him.

"Let her be left to her own devices, as she has left me." He turned on his heel and stared away, only to pause and turn back. "I think she wants none of me. Why do you think otherwise?"

"Because now you are all she has," Fergus told him, shrugging to show his neutrality.

"Then she has nothing," the boy said with a trace of satisfaction as he left the housecarl to stare out over the stones to the sea.

The priest who served as advisor to the King lectured him from time to time, and as the year faded into winter, the priest sought the boy out, offering to pray for him and find a place for him in one of the monastic communities being established in various outlying points of the area designated a kingdom.

"What can you hope for, boy, but the mercy of Christ?" He gave a hard stare that swept over the room as if he feared the presence of spies or devils. "You have no claim, your mother is disgraced by you, and you cannot expect any provision from her for your living, for the King will not tolerate it."

"I will manage," the Queen's bastard answered stiffly, wishing he were with Fergus rather than this prating fool.

"Our management is found in acquiescence in God's will," the priest informed him with an expression that bordered on smugness. "You are houseless and landless and nameless; where can you turn but to God?"

"Perhaps I will turn to my father," the boy responded boldly, hating himself for not striking the man in the face. "I might persuade him to take me in."

"Vain hope," warned the priest. "How many others like you have pinned their aspirations on their absent fathers and ended up living in sties with the pigs? If your father has not sought you out by now, what convinces you that he will want you should you approach him? Why should he acknowledge you? How many other bastards has he turned away already?" The priest gloated at him, his eyes the color of stream water after rain. "You are not going to be able to reach him, this father of yours. Why not seek for him where you are always welcome—Our Father in Heaven? Why not embrace Him rather than seek the favor of an earthly lord?"

"My father will take me, he will legitimize me, and I will inherit all he has!" the boy declared as he flung himself out of the room and into the courtyard. He had to get out of the castle, if only for an hour. The most direct way lay through the stables and across the grazing field, but that meant horses, and he would not go near them.

There was another gate, hidden in a fold of the enormous walls, heavy and stiff with rust. It led to an ancient path that went to the standing stones and beyond into the woods. None of the servants would walk it after sundown. The boy laughed angrily as he closed the gate and strode away.

It was late autumn now and the air was full of the promise of storms. Wind bludgeoned the cliffs and flogged the trees into bowing submission; it drummed on the tall, silent stones. The boy ran, only the sound of the wind in his ears, away from the shore, toward the copse that lay hidden in the define. His dark hair was tangled as it whipped across his face, and in his rage, he longed for nettles instead. His contempt for the world was enormous.

Once in the shadow of the wood, it was chilly, and the ground held no warmth under the oaks and the beeches. The boy folded his arms tightly over his thin chest and ground his teeth together to keep them from chattering. He was glad now that he had a destination in mind.

The woodcutters had huts deep in the copse, hidden in brambles from beasts and men. They boy had learned the

ways years before, when he had fled the taunts of his half
brothers, preferring to be left in the woods than to listen to
more insults. Now the woodcutters knew him, and in their
strange way had sympathy for him.

"It's the lordling, then," said the toothless old man
who sat in the doorway on every day that it did not rain.
He had lost a hand years before and his one remaining was
gnarled and tight as the roots of the trees he had felled. His
beard reached halfway down his chest and was matted so
that it, too, looked like weathered lumber. A wide-bladed
hatchet was tucked in his belt.

"They want to make a monk of me," the boy said
without any greeting. "They want to be rid of me, to shut
me within walls so that they can forget about me. They
want me to disappear."

"It's the White Christ again, isn't it?" the old man
lisped; only four tilting teeth remained in his head.

"You know the King," the boy said, feeling suddenly
very tired. He dropped down at the other end of the short
log that served as a bench.

"We hear," was the oblique answer. "There are always
rumors. Men say that the King has forgotten the old ways
and prays to the White Christ instead of the other gods."

"The King falls on his face before a book and repeats
the prayers his priest has taught him. He banished his
bailiff for sacrificing a white bull, saying that it was not
permitted any more. Most of the soldiers were disgusted,
for they claim that their god is the same as the White
Christ. They say that the two are brothers." He grabbed
his elbows more tightly. "The King is a fool; I'm glad
he's not my father."

"Father doesn't matter. Who knows what man plants
the seed? It's the mother owns the children," the woodcutter declared. His tongue made sucking sounds as he spoke.

"My mother does not want to own me," the boy protested. "She won't talk to me. She hates the sight of me.
Everyone says that I shame her."

"Still, you're hers." The old man got slowly to his feet,
his knees sounding like harness leather. "The others will
be back soon. You can eat with us if you like. It's rabbit."

"I might," said the boy, "if the others don't mind having a bastard at the table."

"Another bastard, you mean." The old man grinned. "It's always good to have the Queen's son with us. Who knows when she might show us favor on your behalf? That's the old way, and old ways are best."

"Not she," said her son. "She wants to be rid of me as much as the King does. When she thinks it's safe to send me away, she will. There are lords and ladies who want pages and men-at-arms who need squires, and she will give me to one of them before too many more years have gone by."

"Then she'll offer you first to your father," said the old woodcutter. "That's the way it's done."

"If she does it that way, I'll be grateful, but she won't, not she." He put one hand up to his dark, unruly hair. "She will be rid of me, and then they will not whisper about her, and she will rejoice. She will tell me that she has found a place for me, and I will be gone, and that will satisfy her." He hated the tears that stung his eyes.

"Your father will do you honor," the old woodcutter decided. "I've told you before, any man would take a son like you."

"Because my limbs are straight and my eyes are good and my wits aren't addled?" the boy challenged. "Fine legacy for one night of rutting."

The old man shook with soundless laughter. "Wait until you've done your share of rutting, lad, before you condemn those who do. Only the priests of the White Christ would have us believe that there are joys beyond the flesh that are better than a stout branch in an open door."

The boy looked quizzically at him. "A stout branch in an open door?" he echoed.

"You'll learn soon enough," the woodcutter promised him. "You're young still, but youth flies faster than hares from foxes. In a year or two you'll feel the sap rising, and then you'll think differently than you do now."

"Oh, that," said the boy with disgust. "They couple in the fields during harvest, if that's what you mean. They grunt and it's silly."

"That's your innocence speaking," said the old man smacking his gums for emphasis. "Later on you'll understand."

"I wish everyone would stop telling me that," the boy complained. "Later on I'll understand what caused the King to turn from my mother to the White Christ, and I'll know why my mother took a lover and disgraced herself and me, and I'll know what she has told my father of me, if anything. I'll know what makes the birds fly south in the winter as well." He kicked at the loamy earth. "It's all useless."

"Not useless," said the old woodcutter, and motioned to the boy. "You'll see." He indicated the way back to the castle. "You'll be returning tonight?"

"I don't know yet; does it matter?" His smile was more bitter than any the old man had seen on the face of a child.

"It matters, whether or not you believe it." He cleared his throat and spat. "Your mother would know if you were not there. She's like that, being Queen."

"Mother to all the people, the way it was long ago? Not likely, not her." He got up and abruptly began to pace. "I want to run away. I want to go out on my own. I want to find my father and ask him to take me into his service as his son."

"Then do so," said the woodcutter. "Find out who the man was and where he is now. Your mother cannot deny you that."

"She has so far," the boy declared. "She has said that she will not add to disgrace by admitting the name. The priests have said that she must reveal the name if she wishes to be forgiven her shame. She will not tell them, to spite the King."

"Everyone says that it was a goodly man who fathered you, and who wanted your mother for his." The old man reached out and patted the boy's head. "Take care, lad. You'll find your place in the world yet. Leave a gift at the Mother Stone when you go home, and it will show you the way."

"The Mother Stone," jeered the boy.

"Don't mock her; she was here long before the White Christ came and she will endure long after the castle has crumbled to the sands. The Mother Stone is part of the earth and she endures."

"Mother threatened to make me a stable boy," her son muttered. "Because I hate horses. She wanted to punish me."

"Or she might have wanted you to end your fear. Horses are the right of the great ones. She wanted to give you honor."

The boy laughed harshly, turning at a sound in the wood.

"My sons are returning," said the old man with great satisfaction. "We'll have food soon."

"Rabbit?" asked the boy.

"Rabbit. No one minds if we kill rabbit. Sometimes"—he winked broadly—"our rabbits have antlers, but you won't tell the gamekeepers, will you?"

"Not I," the boy promised, and turned to greet the other woodcutters coming back through the trees.

The meal was plain—rabbit stew with turnips and onions all washed down with thick ale. The woodcutters said little to each other, and their women tended to the cooking and serving. They paid little attention to the Queen's bastard.

"You'll find your way safe enough?" the old woodcutter asked the boy as they stood in the gathering dusk. "There's always a place for you to sleep by the fire, if you want it."

The boy set his jaw. "I'll find my way. I know the path."

The old woodcutter shrugged. "Here, then. Leave this by the Mother Stone and you'll have nothing to fear." He pressed a handful of grain into his hand.

"That's foolish," said the boy.

"Then why not do it? It would please me, and you've eaten my bread." The old woodcutter patted his beard. "Leave it at the foot of the Mother Stone and watch for her sign."

The boy sighed. "All right," he agreed, and closed his fingers around the offering.

"Come back again when you like. You're welcome here at any time." He raised his one good hand in farewell and then went back into the hut, taking care to spit before crossing the threshold.

The boy watched him with a mixture of disgust and envy. He resented the comfort he found in this place as much as he resented the desire to be here. With an impatient gesture he turned away from the hut and set his feet upon the path back to the castle.

While it was true enough that he knew the way and had walked it many times, in the last light everything seemed strange. There were limbs of trees where he did not expect them, and roots snagged his steps. There were sounds in the woods as well, sounds he did not hear during the day, and they brought back all the tales he had heard of restless ghosts and ravening beasts. He tried to walk faster and stumbled, almost dropping the grain that he held.

"This is stupid," he whispered to himself, and tried to let go of the grain, but could not persuade himself that it would be safe to do so. Cursing his own gullibility, he kept grimly on, trying not to hear noises that alarmed him.

Finally he saw the break in the trees ahead, and with more relief than he could ever admit, he stumbled toward it, gasping as if he had been in danger of drowning. He wanted to run to the castle and pry open the old gate, but the grain in his hand pressed on him, and reluctantly he turned his steps toward the avenue of stones.

The moon, nearing full, glistened in the sky, fuzzy with the promise of mists to come. There was no other light to guide the boy and he tried to keep his pace slow as he went down the pathway between the stones.

The Mother Stone stood a little apart from the rest, dominating the elipse. In the dim light it seemed much larger than it did during the day. The boy stopped a short distance from it, filled with scorn at his own fear. With a nervous laugh he stepped closer to the Mother Stone, holding out the handful of grain. "Here," he said, feeling

foolish. "This is for you." He opened his fingers and let
the grain fall to the ground.

An owl floated over him, hooting softly.

"What . . .?" The boy turned, lost his footing and fell,
his head striking the Mother Stone a glancing, dizzying
blow. He cried out, then his vision wavered and his eyes
closed.

When he came to himself, not very much later, he felt a
tickle of long, stiff hair on his cheek, and when he moved,
a sudden burst of warm air and a low whuffle greeted him.
He looked up, then recoiled in disgust at what he saw.

At the foot of the Mother Stone a pale-coated mare
stood, her large, tranquil eyes directed at the boy. She was
more delicate than many of the horses the King kept, and
not quite as tall. Her ears, pricked forward, were small and
well-shaped, and her mane and tail looked as if they had
been combed only a moment ago. She carried her neck in
a good arch, and when she moved, it was in a slow
prance.

"Get away!" ordered the boy, striking out at the soft
muzzle with his arm. "Get out of here."

The mare cocked her head and stared at him.

"Go on! Go away!" He backed up, trying to get to his
feet while he moved away, and to his dismay ran into one
of the other stones. He used this to help him rise; all the
while he watched the mare.

Delicately the mare approached him, making a low
rumble in her throat. Her coat shone where the muted light
struck it.

"Go *away!*" the boy ordered in a quavering voice.

The mare continued to advance, coming slowly nearer.

The Queen's bastard stood it as long as he could, then
he bolted and ran for the protection of the wall of the
castle. He paused only once, panting heavily, and glanced
back. He saw the mare standing within the stone elipse,
watching him.

For the next several days the boy remained within the
castle walls, keeping moodily to himself. He refused to
explain himself and when his brothers teased him, he

became more sullen than ever and retreated to the small, dark chamber that served as the muniment room for the castle.

Fergus found him there one cold afternoon when it was coming on to rain. "You're holding aloof, aren't you, boy?"

"I suppose," he answered vaguely. He was frowning over one of the sketches that had been made of the castle when it had first been built, more than four generations ago.

"Looking for something?" Fergus was determined to bring the boy out of himself.

"I don't know. Perhaps." He drew his finger along the line of the avenue of stones. "Where did these used to lead, do you know?"

"Well, one goes into the woods and the other follows the cliffs out along the spit of land to the four tall rocks. They say that the men who built that place used to live in the woods and kept their boats at the other end of the stones. I don't know if it's true or not." He waited, looking at the boy. "Does it matter?"

"Where did they keep their horses?" the boy asked.

Under other circumstances Fergus might have given a light answer such as "In pastures," but he knew the boy was troubled and so he said, "I don't know that they had horses. They probably kept them near their houses if they did."

"In the woods," the boy added.

"If that is where they lived. I don't know for sure. Some of the crofters around think that the stones were raised by the old gods and that they still dwell there." He folded his arms. "Are you coming out of there sometime?"

"Not yet," said the boy defiantly. "I have to find out some more things." He had rolled up the old parchment and taken another from its pigeonhole.

"What things? I might be able to help you." Fergus was a patient man, but the boy could test him more sorely than anyone he had ever met.

"If you know where the old horses were kept, then you

could help me." He was going over the older parchment.
"Was there a castle here before this one was built? Was
there a fort or something like that?"

"There probably was," Fergus said carefully. "The
King says that it was his family who built the castle where
nothing had been before, but who's to say." He paused,
hoping that the boy might tell him something more.

"They told me once that the old Romans had a camp
here. Did they?" He had not bothered to look up from the
parchment he held opened on his knee.

"It's said that the old Romans had camps on every hill
in Britain," Fergus said with a trace a laughter.

"They kept horses, didn't they? The Romans, I mean?"
He scowled as he tried to make out something on the
parchment before him. "The ink fades so on these old
plans."

"The Romans kept horses and regiments and all the rest
of it, if the legends are even partly true. They went all
over the world and they showed the way to the apostles of
the White Christ, even though they killed the Christians,
or so the priest says."

The boy looked up. "Did the Romans raise the stones?"

"I don't think so. They made great buildings, but according to the stories, the stones were raised long before
the Romans came and long before anyone else was here. It
may be that the crofters are right and the old gods put them
up." Fergus reached for the guttering oil lamp that stood
at the boy's elbow. "Come away. You'll wreck your
eyes."

"And then only the priests will want me," the boy
remarked as he rolled the parchment and returned it to its
proper place. "Where is the King's clerk who looks after
these parchments?"

"With the King and his priest, listening to the teachings
of the White Christ," said Fergus.

"What does the White Christ say about horses?" the
boy asked as he followed Fergus toward the main hall.

"I don't know that the White Christ has anything to say
about horses. The priest says that the White Christ rode on

donkeys when he didn't walk.'' Fergus motioned to the boy to walk beside him.

The boy was silent, glowering down at the rough stones underfoot.

''Are you still worried about horses?'' Fergus sighed inwardly, knowing that a squire without an understanding of horses was all but useless to men-at-arms, and few nobles wanted pages who could not or would not ride.

''I don't like them,'' he said.

''You can learn to. Many horses don't like men, but they learn. You can learn as well.'' He patted the boy on his scrawny shoulder. ''Your father is probably a great horseman.''

''My mother would say that,'' he muttered.

Fergus searched for a defense of the Queen, but nothing occurred to him that he had not said before. ''What's all your talk about horses? Since you don't like them . . .''

After a few more steps, the boy said, ''Who has a pale dun mare, do you know? One with a white mane and tail.''

''Pale dun?'' repeated Fergus. ''Old Mirnith has a dun, but the mane and tail are dark. I don't think I've ever seen a dun mare with a white mane and tail. Why?''

''No reason. Have any of the King's guests had such a horse, do you remember?'' They were near the main hall, and so the boy stopped and waited for Fergus to answer him.

''I don't recall a horse like that. One of the Silure chiefs rode a light chestnut with a flaxen mane and tail, but that was a stallion and was no better behaved than the man who owned him.''

''I know about that one. It's a mare I'm trying to—'' He broke off and turned sharply on his heel, walking away from Fergus toward the dining hall.

Fergus watched him go with growing concern; the boy was more isolated than ever and there were many who resented it. Fergus hoped to find a way to persuade the boy to change his actions before he put himself beyond a servant's help.

Fergus' concern was not shared by the boy's stepbrothers. The second oldest was also the most mischievous, and he often took advantage of his position within the family to plague the sullen child. Not long before the Midwinter Feast, Agren found his half brother outside castle walls. With a whoop of delight, he set his big chestnut horse in a canter, aimed right at the younger boy.

"Agren!" he shouted as he started to run, loathing the sound of hooves at his back. "Stop it!"

"Mordred is a bastard, Mordred is a bastard," Agren chanted as he thumped his mount with his heels.

"Stop!" The boy was almost at the bank of the stream, and he had seen ice on the slow-moving water earlier that morning. He did not want to slide into it.

Agren laughed merrily and pulled in his panting horse so that he came up on his hind legs, his front feet passing less than a handsbreadth from the boy's head. "Frightened, little brother?" he asked innocently.

"You shouldn't have done that," the boy muttered.

"Why? You think the big mean horsey will hurt you? He only hurts the ones I tell him to, and I held him back, didn't I?" Agren was clearly amused by what he saw. "Another few steps and you'd have been in the creek."

The boy did not let himself say any of the cutting rejoinders he wanted to; Agren would go to their mother, and then there would be trouble.

"Gawaen is going to leave soon," Agren said when his half brother remained silent for a short while. "Did you know that?"

"Where is he going?" the boy asked.

"Mother has arranged for him to go to the chief at Camelot, with the men-at-arms. He'll be trained to be one of them. Don't you wish that could happen to you, Mordred?" He pulled his horse back a few steps, his cherubic face coloring with the effort.

"That's Artus," said the boy with envy.

"Mother knows him, and she made a special request. I've asked her to do the same for me in a year or so. I'll be twelve then, and that's old enough to go for training." He was boasting now, and it was evident that he relished his half brother's shame.

"She'll do it for me, too," the boy declared, more with defiance than conviction.

"For you?" Agren burst out, crowing with laughter. "*You*? her bastard? You'll be lucky if they find you a tradesman to take you as an apprentice! You, a man-at-arms?"

"Well, I will be," the boy insisted.

"For Artus, of course." Agren chuckled. "Artus wants bastards in his army."

"He'll take me, Agren." His cheeks were hot and his words were loud enough to startle Agren's horse.

"Why should he?" Agren asked, still amused.

"I'm his son," said Mordred.

Agren screeched, so overcome with mirth that he had to hold on to the chestnut's tangled mane. "Your father! Naturally!"

"He is! And he'll take me. And he'll make me his heir. You'll see. *He will!*"

Agren shook his head. "You i-i-idiot!" he stammered, to keep from laughing again. "Artus your father! Make you his heir!"

"He will," said Mordred fiercely. "He will."

The chestnut whinnied with distress and shook his head.

"Get that beast out of here!" Mordred ordered his half brother.

"You're scared of him," Agren teased. "You think he's going to hurt you. Artus wouldn't like that."

As much as he wanted to believe what he had said, Mordred was resentful of the derision Agren showed. "That's just a horse," he scoffed deliberately. "Anyone can master them—they're stupid animals."

"A man-at-arms needs a horse," Agren shouted, his mirth extinguished. "And you're afraid of horses. Fine son you are for Artus!" With that he dragged the chestnut's head around and set it cantering back toward the castle.

Mordred stood on the edge of the brook and stared after

his half brother. "I will go to Artus," he vowed. "I will be his heir." On impulse he turned away from the castle and went toward the woods. Since his encounter with the light-dun mare, he had not ventured beyond the edge of the wood, still too unnerved by his experience to risk having it a second time. If there were horses in the woods like the pale mare . . .

He found the old woodcutter stripping the branches from a felled beach tree. The old man used a rough bow saw for his work, grunting as he tugged at it with his one arthritic hand. He was grateful for the opportunity to stop his labor. "It's a cold time, boy," he said as he put the saw down and dropped onto a fallen log.

"The Midwinter Feast comes soon," said the boy. "And then the storms."

The old woodcutter made a gesture of acceptance. "All things come in time," he said philosophically. "While the storms blow themselves about, we'll stay indoors and sharpen our axes and hatchets and make new handles for the ones that need it. We'll be ready for the spring, and we'll do well."

"Is it hard, cutting wood?" He watched the old man carefully.

"It takes a strong back and good sense, like many another sort of work, but it isn't hard the way going out in ships is, or riding to war, or building in stone. Those are tasks that bring a man down. The gods don't forgive errors in cutting stone or on the sea."

"I . . . just wondered." The boy sat down, putting his arms around his raised knees. "What lives in the woods?"

The old man laughed. "What doesn't live in the woods, except fishes? All the creatures of the world live in the woods."

"What are they?" the boy persisted.

"The lords of the air and the lords of the earth are here," he said with great contentment.

"But what *are* they?" he prompted.

"Hart and hind, and all the families of foxes and wolves. Some bear, but not as many as there used to be. Badgers

and ferrets and stoats. What are you looking for, boy?''
This last, shrewd guess was leveled at Mordred with a
keen look.

"Cattle? Horses?" Mordred asked.

"Some of each, from time to time. Foals run away from
their dams and end up out here. No one can catch them,
and if they don't die, they have herds to run with. Why are
you asking me about this? What happened to you?" He
shook his finger at the boy. "You saw something, didn't
you?"

"I hit my head," Mordred said.

"Where? When?" The old man leaned forward, interest
animating the seams and fissures of his features so that his
face looked like a grainy extension of his mass of beard.

"When I left the grain you gave me," he admitted. "It
was dark and I dropped the grain. I stumbled and hit my
head, and I thought I saw something, that's all."

"What did you think you saw?" demanded the old man.
"What was it?"

Mordred looked away. "It was dark. I thought I saw a
mare."

"Ah!" cried the old man. "And what then?"

"Nothing. I ran away. I probably didn't really see her,
in any case. I probably just had a dream because I hit my
head in the moonlight."

"What about the mare?" the old man asked. "The mare
is for the Mother Stone."

"There wasn't a mare, I just dreamed it," said Mordred.

"There was a mare. She's one of the Wish Horses, you
young smirchpate!" The woodcutter got to his feet and
paced the length of the felled beach. "You actually saw
her. What was she like?"

"Pale, probably dun with white mane and tail," said
Mordred more reluctantly than ever.

"It was her!" The old woodcutter spoke in awe. "I've
heard about the mare, but no one has seen her, not for
generations. Some even said that the Wish Horses left
when the priests of the White Christ came. But you saw
the mare."

"I might have," Mordred conceded. "I told you, I hit my head. It might have been nothing."

"A pale mare with white mane and tail under the moon at the Mother Stone?" The old man crowed with pleasure.

"But where does she live? In the woods?" Mordred allowed himself to be interested, at least until he had a few more answers.

"She lives in the Mother Stone, of course," the old woodcutter said as if he were teaching a simpleton. "They all live in the stones, the Wish Horses. They *are* the stones."

Mordred laughed uncertainly. "Tales."

"There's truth in many a tale, boy, and well you know it. So you've seen the mare. Well, what did she give you, since you gave her grain." He rubbed his hand against his leg, making it serve for another hand.

"She gave me a fright, and that was about all," said Mordred, his jaw set.

"Didn't you ask her for anything?" the woodcutter inquired.

"What . . . why should I ask an animal for anything?" He brushed the dark hair from his eyes.

"But she always gives favor for favor. If you go to her, she'll give you what you ask for. She'll grant you your wishes. That's why they used to make sacrifices to the Mother Stone, so that the mare would grant them favors."

"Oh, come!" said Mordred in disbelief. "A mare cannot give favors. Horses aren't smart enough. There's nothing they can give."

"Don't spurn her," warned the old woodcutter. "You'd be worse than a fool if you do."

"Then I may be worse than a fool," he suggested laconically. He was starting to think that the old woodcutter had lost his wits and that the tales were more to entertain children than to remember the gods of the past.

"Hush!" the old woodcutter commanded him, bringing his hand up. "Never say that. Do not say such things."

"But . . ." Mordred began, letting the words stop.

"If you speak against her, she will take back as much as

she might give and more. You take the things she will give you. You take another measure of grain, and you go to her and you tell her that it was because you hit your head that you did not ask anything of her before, but now you want her gifts.''

"And then what?" Mordred asked, becoming more interested—there were so many things he wanted.

"She will give you what you ask for. She will grant you your wishes.'' The old woodcutter sighed. "When I was a lad, not much older than you, I went out to the stones and I left a dead pigeon for her, but that was wrong; horses don't eat pigeons. So the father of the King gave permission to the crofters to clear two more fields and I lost some of the timber that by rights should have been mine. It was years later that I realized my mistake.'' He shook his head. "The old priests offered lives and blood, but that's why the White Christ has come—horses don't like lives and blood, either.''

"You gave me grain," said the Queen's bastard as he watched the old man with narrowed eyes. "Why?"

"Well, there's favor should have been yours that you've been denied. I thought it was time that you had the chance you ought to have. If your mother was blind to her obligation, then I thought that perhaps the Wish Horses might give some notice to you.''

"You don't really believe that, do you?" scoffed Mordred.

"I believe it as much as the priest thinks that the White Christ was lifted into the sky by a dove,'' answered the old man seriously. "The King has faith enough to make it bad for those of us who do not want to bow down before the White Christ.'' He waited while the boy thought over his words, then he went on. "You can choose to be what you wish to be. If the Mother Stone receives your offering, you can have what you want to have.''

"What I want is a proper father, one who will recognize me and make me his heir," said Mordred, deep in thought.

"Ask it, and leave grain for the Mother Stone. The Wish Horses will come to you, and it will be yours,'' promised the old man.

"Perhaps," said Mordred with a distant look in his dark eyes. "Why not? Where's the harm? I don't have to touch the horse, do I?"

"No one ever has," said the old man. "The mare is the best of them. If you see her, you know you will get your wish."

"All right," he said, shrugging to show he thought it was a game but he would go along with it for the sake of the old woodcutter.

"If you mock her, she will know it," the old man warned, reading Mordred's expression accurately.

"I won't mock her," he sighed. "I'll try to be respectful, all right?"

"Don't try, do it," said the old man, and looked away into the woods. "She will give her gifts generously to those who please her, and she will give dangerously to those who do not. Don't challenge her—she's like all mares, and she will not take bad handling without getting even."

Mordred winced, thinking of the hooves that struck like maces. "If you insist."

"It's not I who insist, it's her. Keep that in your head when you go to the stones tonight."

"Must it be night?" asked Mordred after a pause.

"That is when she is there. Leave grain in the day and the birds will eat it." The old man made a whistling sound around his few teeth. "You're taking a chance, boy. But there's no one else to gamble on you, is there?"

With a sour smile, Mordred said, "No."

So, late that afternoon Mordred walked to the stone elipse and sat down, a measure of grain in the leather wallet tied to his belt. He crossed his legs and leaned against one of the smaller stones, turned so that he could face the Mother Stone. The setting sun made the shadows very long and stark, and he watched these with fascination and dread. "I'm being an idiot," he said to the air, then added, in a more subdued voice, "It's not because of the stones. I'm missing my supper." He thought he was being more foolish than ever, but he could not help but cling to the chance that there might be some benefit in leaving the grain, and in his soul he knew he was desperate.

A flock of seabirds flew overhead, their cries coming down to him weakly, making him feel more alone than ever. Tonight they would be drinking mead at the castle to celebrate Gawaen's natal day. One of the women would be sent to his bed tonight, and tomorrow everyone in the castle would want to know how many loaves he put in the oven. Mordred sneered at the thought and vowed that he would never give anyone the opportunity to treat him that way. No woman would laugh at him, and no man.

He wished he could doze, so that the time would pass more quickly, but his mind was too alert for that. As the first trailing wraiths of mist crept in from the ocean, he watched them, and told himself the chill he felt was from them and not from fear. When at last it was dark, he got stiffly to his feet and walked up to the Mother Stone, untying the cords that held the wallet to his belt.

"You grant wishes, they tell me," he said, squinting up at the stone; it glistened white as the thickening fog. "I have a wish that I want granted. I come to you for it." He opened the wallet and poured its contents on the ground in front of the Mother Stone. "I've been told you like grain because horses like grain. In exchange for this I want—" He stopped abruptly as he heard the soft clop of unshod hooves.

When he spoke again, it was less certainly and with many pauses as he peered into the darkness around the stones, trying to find the horse he knew was out there. "What I want . . . is a father. I want Artus to be my father. I want him to acknowledge me and make me his heir, so that I will rule after him. If I am a bastard, I want to be his bastard, and I want everyone to know it."

The sound of the hooves was nearer, and Mordred looked around fearfully, afraid that somehow the animal would sneak up behind him and snort or paw the earth or do some other horrid thing.

"The grain is for you, so you'll give me my wish." He took two careful steps backward, and it was then that he saw the mare again.

She was inside the stones, not far away, her neck arched and her nostrils flared. She came forward, whickering as she caught the scent of the grain.

"It's yours," Mordred said, his voice cracking for the first time. "Go ahead, eat it. I brought it for you, you stinking horse."

The mare minced nearer, neck stretching out and down as she came to the Mother Stone.

Mordred stared at her as he backed up another half-dozen steps. He watched her upper lip wiggle over the grain; he covered his own mouth in distaste. He listened to the grinding of the mare's teeth, and it made him want to yell at her. Only the warning from the old woodcutter kept him silent while his mind jeered relentlessly.

"No one knows who I am," Mordred said very softly. "I want them all to know, and to remember me forever. I want to be as famous as Artus."

The mare raised her head and turned to look at him. She stood very still.

"Well, that's what I want: to be Artus' son, to be his heir and to be remembered as long as he is remembered." He whispered but there was deep-burning defiance in his voice and his dark eyes were smoldering.

The mare bent her head to the grain once more and continued to eat, taking care to get all the grain that had been spilled.

Mordred waited, expecting something to happen. After a time the mare raised her head as if listening, her ears pricked forward. She gave a loud whinny that made Mordred jump, and then wheeled away, vanishing into the gathering mists. Mordred made fists of his hands and then trudged back to the side door in the wall of the castle, wishing he had the chance to fight someone.

There was noise and jollity in the main hall where Gawaen was being feted. Even the King, for once, had graced the occasion with his presence. He did not sit near his wife, preferring to have his priest at his side instead of his Queen. If anyone thought that this was improper, no one said so. Mordred stood near the entrance to the hall, bitterly aware that he had not been missed. His clothing was damp, there were circles under his eyes, but not one of the revelers saw. Mordred listened to the carousing and singing for a short while, then made his way to the small chamber in the keep that he shared with two clerks and a scribe. He lay on his bed, his face turned toward the wall, and cursed himself and everything he had done that night.

Three days later there was another celebration, but this one was not as happy, since it marked Gawaen's departure for the company of men-at-arms who were gathering around Artus. Most of the household gathered to see the young man off. The King made a speech and the priest blessed him. Gawaen was presented with two horses and a mule and the oldest son of the chief archer to be his squire.

"Bring us honor," the King admonished his oldest son. "We have great hopes of you."

"I will do all in my power, Father; you have my vow." Gawaen looked like a grown man in his bright new scale armor. The sword that hung from his belt had been forged in the summer and was the best to be had.

"And may God the Father and His Son the White Christ and the Spirit of Christ go with you and keep you." The King glanced at his priest as he said this. "We will remember you nightly in our prayers." He stepped back so that his wife could speak to her firstborn son.

"Your two older sisters were married away from me, and that was bitter enough, my son," she said in her deep, sensual voice. "Now you leave me, and soon Agren will go, as well. Then I will be so bereft that I will live wholly without comfort."

Mordred, hearing this, wanted to shout, to remind her that he would not leave her, that he was with her, and that he was better than any of them.

"I will think of you always, Mother," said Gawaen, sounding embarrassed by this outpouring.

"You're a good and dutiful son, and I ask you to recall what you have learned here from me as well as from your father." She spoke so clearly that there had to be a private, a secret message in her words. "I trust that you will not fail me."

"Never, Mother," said Gawaen. "I keep to the old ways as much as the new."

"Then go, and take my love with you; loss of you, my son, is a canker in my side from this hour until my death." With that she walked away from Gawaen and the King, returning to the keep-and-bailey with only two of her women accompanying her.

Mordred followed her with his eyes, hating the sight of her and furious with her for ignoring him now, and always. He folded his arms and watched his half brother turn his horse, ponying the second behind him, his squire bringing up the rear on the mule. All the crofters and artisans from the village were gathered to see Gawaen off, and Mordred felt disgust and envy roil within him as the King's subjects cheered.

"They'll do more than cheer me," he muttered. "One day they will bow to me."

Later that day, when everyone had returned to his labors, Mordred went down to the elipse of stones and examined them. He found a dead cock at the foot of the Mother Stone along with a cup of wine. He smiled nastily— horses didn't like meat. He would ask the old woodman later if they liked wine.

The night of the Midwinter Feast was cold and sleety; all the King's subjects who had gathered for the celebration came wrapped and bundled in all the layers of clothes they possessed.

"There's another big storm coming, mark my words," said Fergus to several of the villagers, and they nodded in agreement. The room was filled with people and noise, with the smell of them and the smell of food so thick on the air that it was hard to breathe it.

"The priest is going to give prayers to the White Christ before the meat is cut," one of the house-*gilles* said, clearly disapproving of this. "That's the way they do it—prayers first, food second."

The miller shook his head and clucked his tongue. "It's bad enough that he cut off the Queen's boy, but this is going too far," he said to Fergus. "The King has lost his senses."

"It's that priest, taking over with his new ways and that White Christ who never touched women and was killed for it." The complainer was one of two clerks employed to keep the household in order. He stared at the miller. "How was the harvest for your crofters this year?"

"Not bad, considering. With the new land cleared for growing, we have more to harvest, but the early rains ruined some of it—the grain took rot and contagion and could not be used." He folded his arms. "Next year ought to be better, if we take precautions."

"Be careful how you do it," the clerk warned. "The King doesn't want any more offerings left. It offends the priest."

"Then we'll leave it at night," said the miller pragmatically. "It's better that way, in any case. I won't watch crops be ruined so that the priest can smile."

Fergus nodded in agreement. "Talk to the Queen. She might be willing to help you. It's better coming from the Queen in any case. The Mother Stone is the mare. The rest are her colts."

All the men laughed, then separated to join the other revelers. From his concealed niche Mordred watched them and scowled. He had to get out of the castle again, never mind the weather. He went to one of the house-*gilles* and said that he was dizzy with wine, and in case anyone asked for him, he would be walking in the courtyard.

Leaving the castle, he detoured through the kitchen, taking three of the honied buns that were set in heaps on trays. A few would never be missed; scullions took them all the time. He tucked them under his tunic, glad that they were still warm, and drew his old woollen mantle around his shoulders before stepping out into the howling night.

He slipped twice going down the path from the hidden door, and by the time he reached the stone elipse, he was sodden and shivering. He stumbled to the Mother Stone and held out the three cakes defiantly. "This is the last time!" he shouted at the massive front. "If this doesn't do any good, then I'll know it's all a lie." He flung the three buns at the Mother Stone and smiled as they struck. "I will be Artus' son, or I will be a monk, and which is up to you!" With that he turned away and trudged back to the castle, his skin growing numb with cold.

The next day his head was sore, but so were most of the heads in the castle, and no one thought anything of it. The day after he had a slight, dry cough, and it was enough to make Fergus suggest that he have the cook prepare an infusion of rosemary and honey to drink. The boy did as he was told, and went sullenly to the younger clerk for more schooling.

In the night the cough worsened, and the next day Mordred was flushed and dry with fever. One of the sewing women was sent to nurse him, and when she saw him, she was alarmed. She summoned Fergus, who called for the farrier, who tended men and beasts with equal success.

"The breath tells it all," the farrier explained. "We know there is fever, but if it is from putrid humors, the breath changes. The boy has a corruption within him and it must be purged." He then gave the sewing woman orders for tending to the boy and went off, shaking his head.

For the next four days Mordred tossed and coughed and burned, his body lost in misery. His thoughts were jumbled and he often did not know the difference between his dreams and the world. He wept with misery when he was forced to drink the various concoctions prescribed for him. Once he called Mayren, the sewing woman for his mother, and once he dreamed that there were horses everywhere as he flung his arms out in feeble defense. Since his dislike of the animals was known, this was regarded as a very bad omen.

When it was feared the boy would die, the King sent his priest to pray for him. "In His mercy, God is calling you," he said to the Queen's bastard as he stood by the bed. "The suffering on earth will bring glory in the life that is to come. You will thank God for the kindness He is bestowing in taking you from your shame to His side."

"I'm not going to die," croaked Mordred, barely loud enough to be heard.

"It is not for us to challenge the will of God," the priest said. "You have been vilified in the world, but for that you will find reward. Give thanks that you are spared the sins of those burdened with flesh."

"I'm not going to die," the boy repeated.

"If you go with God's blessing upon you, no, you will not die. That is the promise of the White Christ." He started to make a sign on the boy's forehead, but Mordred turned away and would not let the man touch him. The priest shook his head. "I've done all that I can," he said to Mayren and Fergus, who stood in the doorway.

For another day they waited, each hour expecting to find Mordred still and cold. Then, late at night, the fever that had held him in its grip for so long, broke, and the hacking coughs gave way to steadier breathing. For most of a day and a night, Mordred slept.

His eyes were sunken and his cheeks hollow when he left his bed two days later. His body, always skinny, was gaunt and he moved weakly, tiring quickly. Fergus was overjoyed and Mayren kissed him before going back to sewing. Agren told him he looked like one of the stick men he practiced his swordplay on in the courtyard. Mordred said nothing to any of them.

When another ten days had passed, he felt strong enough to go into the woods. The day was clear and chill, so he took one of the bearskin cloaks usually worn by the men-at-arms on watch at night. The heavy garment kept him warm but slowed his progress, so it took twice as long as he anticipated to reach the hut.

The old woodcutter had an arrow nocked as Mordred approached, but lowered it as he caught sight of the boy. "Take care that the wardens don't mistake you for game," he warned with a rough chuckle. "They told us you were dead."

"No," said Mordred. He noticed for the first time that the old woodman smelled of loam and sweat.

"They said the King's priest gave you up."

"That's true enough," the boy agreed. "They all wanted me dead. I disappointed them. The Queen never bothered to find out if I lived." He sat down. "The Mother Stone has done nothing."

"It takes time," the old woodcutter said philosophically. "Not everything happens at once."

"This had better, or I will let them make me a monk." He got the end of his cloak snagged on a loose branch as he tried to pull it more tightly around him. "I made three offerings."

"That's generous," the old woodcutter said. "She won't deny you if you've done that."

"Won't she? How can you be sure? The priest says that all the tales about the Mother Stone are foolish myths for little children and simpletons. He told everyone that praying to the Mother Stone and leaving offerings for it was wrong, and it offended his God." Mordred's sarcasm was strong, but there was a deep crease between his brows revealing his uncertainty.

"And you believe the priest?" asked the old woodcutter in surprise.

"Not really," Mordred hedged. "But I don't really believe about the Mother Stone, either. Nothing has happened."

"Suppose something does happen, what then?" The old woodcutter rubbed his one hand on the leg of his trewes. "What do you require to be convinced?"

"I would need my wish to be granted, I guess. Then I would know that the Mother Stone had power." He looked away. "Unless I really am Artus' son. Then it wouldn't mean anything."

The old woodcutter shrugged. "You will have to choose what you believe, boy." He stared off into the woods. "It's getting late, and you will want to be back in the castle before sunset. You've been ill and you don't want to take another fever."

Little as he wanted to admit it, Mordred was offended at this suggestion, for it called to mind the many times he had been sent away out of shame and embarrassment. He put one hand on his hip. "Then you want me gone, too."

"Until you are recovered," the old man said vaguely.

"What have I done to make you . . . dislike me?" Mordred insisted. "You're trying to make me leave, aren't you?"

"Yes," the old man said candidly. "If you have lost favor with the Mother Stone, we who live by her aid cannot afford your friendship." He hawked and spat, deliberately avoiding Mordred's eyes.

"All right," said the boy, getting to his feet and gathering the cloak around him against a chill that was not only in the air.

"I hope that the Mother Stone accepts your offering, boy, but until she does, stay away from here." The old woodcutter cleared his throat. "I like you, lad, and I feel for you. But I have to live here."

Mordred nodded once, abruptly, and walked away into the woods, keeping to the trail and whistling, just in case one of the wardens should be waiting. There was a tightness in his chest which he decided came from the aftereffects of his fever and not from grief.

For most of the early spring the skies wept. The first of the early lambs did not thrive, one of the cows strayed into a bog and drowned, and in the stables the horses were plagued with hoof problems that kept the farrier busy for the greater part of a month. Many of the fishermen did not put to sea, and those that did kept near the shore. Merchants who traveled from town to town and kingdom to kingdom came later than usual, and brought tales of unusually severe weather in the north. Often dead birds were discovered at the foot of the Mother Stone. The priest of the White Christ exhorted and threatened the people of the castle, but to no purpose, for the offerings continued.

Mordred resigned himself to studying with the clerk and tried to picture himself in a monk's habit. He watched Agren training to be a man-at-arms and it sickened him; envy burned in him as keenly as fever had.

Finally the skies cleared, and soon after there came a messenger carrying the eagle standard of Artus and bearing greetings from Gawaen. He was welcomed with more enthusiasm than pomp, and the villagers held an impromptu fair, decorating the doors of their houses with wreaths of wild roses and sweet thyme. In the castle they feasted for two days. It was assumed that when the messenger returned to Camelot, he would take Agren with him to join his brother.

Then word was sent to Mordred that the Queen wanted to see him. The boy was so startled that he forgot his resentment long enough to answer her summons promptly.

"My . . . son," said the Queen as Mordred came into her quarters where she sat with her women at the looms. Beside her the messenger from Camelot waited.

"You sent for me?" Mordred said, kissing her hand as he was required to do.

"I have to speak to you." She glanced uncomfortably at the messenger before going on. She was over thirty and her figure was shapeless from her eight pregnancies; her hair showed tracings of white and the skin under her jaw was growing loose. Ten years ago she had been a great beauty, or so everyone said.

"What is it?" asked Mordred, becoming more guarded.

"This messenger . . . brought me word from Artus . . . in Camelot. He sent a request that I must . . ," She fidgeted with the empty shuttle she held in her hands.

"What is the message?" Mordred inquired, not letting himself hope.

"You have to understand, Mordred." She sighed. "Your father . . . It was Midsummer, and there was feasting and drinking and more entertainments than you can imagine. There were many men from Camelot here, and the King received them with magnificence. He . . . the King had recently started to follow the White Christ, and he no longer came to me. I thought, that night, that with the wine and the celebrating, that he had—"

"What has this to do with the message?" he demanded, growing impatient.

The messenger spoke to the boy directly for the first time since he had arrived at the castle. "Listen to your mother, Mordred. She has much to tell you."

Annce rose, casting the shuttle aside, and began to

move restlessly and aimlessly about the room. "I was so happy that night. My lord had come back to me. The wine and the dancing had brought him. I was . . . so drunk with him and his sweet body . . . I had left birds at the Mother Stone for over a year, and finally he had come back to me." She stopped and stood very still. "All night long we lay together, and never had I been . . . "

The three women who were at the other looms had fallen silent and did not bother to pretend to work.

"In the morning, when I woke, I was alone. And when I went to the King, he denied that he had been with me. He had spent the night with his priest keeping vigil. He said such things then." Her cheeks turned scarlet with the memory.

"And he called you a whore," said Mordred flatly, "and disowned your child."

Annce nodded. "Nothing I said made any difference to him. He wanted no part of me after that. He had wanted little enough before."

Mordred stared at her, feeling only contempt for his mother and for the King. "Why do you remind me of this?"

"Because . . . because there has come word from your . . . your father." Annce looked around nervously, afraid that one of the women might laugh or that the messenger might change his mind. "That is what the message said, isn't it?"

"Yes," agreed the messenger.

"Why are you bringing word?" Mordred asked the man. "What does it matter to Artus?"

"It matters that you are his son," Annce said, and started to cry wretchedly.

"Artus?" Mordred repeated as if he had never heard the name before. "My father?" It was the thing he had wished for, the thing he had wanted above all others, and it made almost no sense to him.

"He has learned from your half brother that King Uriens has not taken you as his own, which is his right. Because of that, your father wishes to exercise his rights in this circumstance, and legitimize you.'' The messenger held out the small baton with the eagle standard. "He sends this to you as his pledge."

Mordred shook his head, dazed. "This is mine?"

"Take it," Annce whimpered. "There is nothing that anyone else can give you. Take it.'' Her weeping had reddened her eyes and the tip of her nose was pink.

"Take it," the messenger said. "I am Caius, and Artus is my stepbrother. He knows what it is to be without heritage. He will not offer false coin to you, boy.''

As Mordred's hand closed around the baton, he had to control his trembling. It had happened. At last it had happened. He looked up at the messenger who was called Caius. "I will come."

"Artus has a wife; she is young and she has no children yet,'' Caius went on. "There is no claim before yours.''

"No claim before mine," Mordred repeated with grim satisfaction.

"Go to him, Mordred," said his mother. "If you stay here, there is nothing I can give you. The King will force me to send you away, so that I won't remember so much. Every time I look at you, I remember." She had stopped her tears, but her voice was unsteady and hollow, as if she had suddenly grown very old.

Mordred did not look around; he said to Caius, "Tell me when I am to be ready."

"I leave morning after next. A horse will be ready for you." Caius smiled at Mordred. "Artus will be pleased."

"A horse," Mordred said with distaste. It was expected, but he still hated the idea. "Very well." A horse was a small price to pay for legitimacy.

"Take what you need for the journey. Your father will see to your needs after we reach Camelot.'' Caius looked at Annce. "I will let you be alone.'' With that he left the chamber, and at once the three women fell to work with such purpose that at another time Mordred would have laughed.

Annce stood very still, facing her son with an expression he did not understand. "Tell your father," she said after a time, "that I will never forget him."

"If you wish," Mordred told her. He doubted he would say anything to Artus about his mother unless he asked.

The silence between them lengthened. At last Queen Annce made a gesture of dismissal and looked back toward her women. "We have more weaving to do today," she said vaguely.

Mordred, his hand holding the baton, saluted his mother and left her alone. He walked through the halls, aware of the looks that were directed toward him. Word had already traveled through the castle, and suddenly he was no long invisible, but someone to reckon with. He swung his arms as he walked so that everyone could see the baton.

That night Mordred sat at the high table next to the messenger Caius. He looked down on the others and gloried in the feeling it gave him. He turned his head so that he could see Agren at the other end of the table, and was pleased to note that his stepbrother was pouting—he had not yet been invited to Camelot. When Fergus gestured to him with his wine cup, Mordred ignored him.

It was nearer dawn than sunset when the revels ended and Mordred made his way toward his chamber. Most of the company were already asleep, but a few had remained in the great hall, listening to Caius describing the exploits of the men-at-arms gathered around Artus. Mordred had hungered to hear more, but Caius's voice had grown hoarse and his eyes bleary; Agren insisted that they all retire, and as the son of the King, his word was law.

On impulse, Mordred decided to walk down to the stone elipse. He thought that perhaps the pale dun mare would be grazing and he could satisfy himself at last that she was real.

The elipse was empty. The ground within the elipse was marked by many unshod hooves, but of horses there was no sign.

"Just as well," muttered the boy as he stood facing the Mother Stone.

The wind, fresh off the ocean, was damp and smelled of salt more than grass. The moon, like a broken silver coin, hung in the western sky, making a single bright streak on the dark waters.

Mordred paced back and forth, his senses sharp. "Well?" he asked a bit later. "Well? Was it you? Is that why I'm being taken to Camelot? Is Artus really my father? Or is this your doing?" There was no answer. "How am I going to know? If you don't tell me, how am I going to know? He might not want me at all; you made him do this, and I'm no more to him than a crofter's get."

There was a high, distant sound, possibly a gull drifting over the land, perhaps a whinny from very far away.

Mordred held up the baton with the eagle crest. "Is this really mine? Is it? Or is it all a lie?"

Silence answered him and remained with him until he went back to the castle to prepare to leave for Artus and Camelot.

SHARAN NEWMAN *makes the most delectable peach pre-serves I've ever tasted.*

She is better known at large for her trilogy: Guinevere, The Chessboard Queen, *and* Guinevere Evermore. *Ms. Newman has a style as delicate as it is difficult to de-scribe, like her preserves.*

"The Palace By Moonlight," intended to fit directly into the trilogy canon, has a lovely light/bittersweet touch that will reward more than one reading. It makes its strongest emotional points with the sparest use of language, and sometimes with none at all.

The Palace by Moonlight

by Sharan Newman

Miniffer coughed noisily, scratched his nose, coughed again, took a long gulp of milky-white ale and cursed the universe. He started with the splintery bench he was sitting on and worked outward to include the whole of creation. It took most of the night, but it was satisfying work and he had nothing better to do. As his imprecations grew in range, his voice grew in volume until he attracted the notice of the bleary few in the dilapidated inn who still remained awake.

"Stuff it, Miniffer," Old Tamas said genially. "We all know what you think of life. You've bellowed your damnations so often they ha'n't no more power than a whore's blush."

"Too true," one-eared Urbgan sighed. "It's not like anyone here disagrees. Things ha' gone mightily hard since Arthur's time. So give us a night's rest. We got our own swearing to do."

Various grunts and belches indicated that the majority agreed, and so Miniffer reluctantly desisted, still muttering into his glass about the degeneration of government, society, and life in general in the thirty years since Arthur had left the earth. It had gotten so that a well-trained bard, capable of reciting the genealogies of all the great houses of Dumnonia and Powys, not to mention Cornwall; of chanting the most stirring sagas of military splendor; of giving the slyest turns to the old favorites of love and betrayal . . . a man like that, Miniffer grieved, was reduced to sleeping under the table in a disgusting inn which hadn't had a cleaning since Vortigern the traitor had married his Saxon bitch and started all the troubles a hundred years ago.

Even while descending into his nightly stupor, Miniffer couldn't stop himself from thinking like a showman.

The next morning he was awakened, as usual, by the tavern dogs licking the grease from his face and hands. This was accompanied by a sharp kick in his midsection. The innkeeper, while not a tidy man, had grown tired of having a sodden poet cluttering up his establishment.

"Out, you!" He emphasized his suggestion with another kick. "We know all your stories. We're sick of hearing how great it was in Arthur's day. Arthur! Wha' do you know of Arthur? You wasn't even born when he died."

Miniffer roused himself, carrying his head with him gently.

"Arthur isn't dead!" he insisted. "He's just gone away awhile. He'll be back; you'll see. Leading all his knights, charging down through this valley . . . in all their shining, wondrous, holy splendor. And he'll—"

"*Will* you leave it for once, Miniffer," the innkeeper sighed. "Those days is dead, like all them knights and whatall. And I never heard they was so great, anyways. My own grandmother used to tell how one of those knights came riding by one day and had his way with her without not so much as taking off his boots. Don't sound so holy wondrous to me."

Miniffer started to make a comment on the probable veracity and virtue of said grandmother, but reflected in time how close his host's foot still was.

Sitting in the glaring sunshine by the side of the road an

hour later, Miniffer wished he had spoken. The innkeeper's words were being echoed far too much lately. It wasn't right, after all King Arthur had done, for him to be forgotten so soon. Or remembered like that! As if a knight would ever rape someone's grandmother! It was all due to the lack of respect for learning these days. They weren't turning out proper bards anymore. Not like in the old times.

Miniffer forced down the bile in his throat, then, upon consideration, let it do as it wished. After some unpleasantness, he felt better. Well enough, in fact, to lift his head from the ditch in time to see the messenger ride by and to be spattered with dust raised by the racing horse.

There, Miniffer thought, as he pulled himself indignantly back onto the road. That's what we've come to! No thought at all for a poor bard who might have been blinded by the flying pebbles. He shook his fist at the retreating rider.

"Here, you!" he shouted. "You could have killed me, charging by like that! Why don't you watch the road, you big—"

Miniffer stopped in horror as he saw the rider pull his horse up and turn around, coming back to confront the quaking poet.

"Sweet Saint Catherine," Miniffer moaned. "I don't need this. I thought he was too far away to hear."

There was nowhere to run, so Miniffer sat down in the dusty road and awaited his doom. Soon he felt the hot breath of the horse on his neck and heard the clink as the rider dismounted. A hand dropped heavily upon his shoulder, raising him to his feet with no intention on his part. A large, ruddy, exceedingly young face confronted his.

"Have I hurt you?" the rider asked worriedly. He looked at Miniffer carefully, as if trying to decide how much of the damage he could reasonably be blamed for. "I am sorry! I didn't see you there, with your head in the ditch. I expect I thought you were just a log or something. I'm Brien, king's rider from Dumnonia. Are you all right?"

He peered more closely, coughed, and pushed Miniffer to arm's length.

"Whew! You smell like you've spent the last month in an ale keg! Oh, sorry! I didn't mean to offend."

Miniffer, mindful of the weight on his shoulder, smiled wanly. "No offense taken, sir. Actually, I think it was closer to two months. One loses count of the days in such Stygian dark."

Brien let go of him so quickly that he collapsed into the dust. With more apologies, he picked the bard up again, brushing off the top layer or so of detritus with his hands.

"Sorry!" he said again. "I didn't expect you to talk elegant like that. You sound like old Durriken at the court, you know. Look, let me give you a spare tunic of mine. It'll be a bit big but—"

"It will cover the holes in my trews," Miniffer finished. "Thank you, but I'm not a beggar. I earn my way. Now, if you'd care to hear a saga of Arthur or a tale of Gawain while you eat your midday meal, I might be persuaded to accept it as remuneration."

"'Remun . . .'?" The youth's face clouded, then cleared, "Oh, you mean payment! All right, tell me about King Math, who could only live if his feet were kept between the legs of the maiden, Goewin, unless, of course, he was fighting, and the time Gawain and Gwydion raped Goewin and Math changed them into a stag and a hind so that they coupled and produced Hyddwn, the fawn, who, when baptized, turned into a human boy and then—"

"Hold, lad!" Miniffer covered his ears in genuine horror. "Is this what my art has come to? That's nothing but a lewd tale, fit only for the kitchens and stables."

"It's very popular at King Constans' court," Brien muttered.

"No doubt it is," Miniffer sniffed. "But in Arthur's time such things were kept in their place. At the king's court only tales of valor and honor were allowed. That is why all who served him, even to the lowliest potboy, lived pure and holy lives."

Brien decided that good manners had gone far enough, especially to a smelly, ragged, cast-off human being such as this.

"I don't believe a word of it," he stated firmly. "My own grandfather was a soldier for Arthur and would have been a knight, if he hadn't lost his arm in a battle with the Saxons. He could have told you a thing or two about Camelot and the court. I think you're addled. Here! Take the tunic. You can pay me when you've learned some real stories."

With that, Brien roughly thrust the tunic over Miniffer's head and shoulders and, mounting this horse, galloped off.

"Insolent, ignorant, bastard!" Miniffer yelled at the top of his lungs when he had freed himself from the tunic. But by then Brien was a good mile down the road. Miniffer sighed and started wearily in the opposite direction. His heart ached even more than his head.

Sick of the world and heedless of danger, Miniffer turned into the great forest, tracing his way along leaf-deep paths, eating what came by and falling often in the busy spring rivulets. The water tasted dreadful, of bark and moss, and he thought tenderly of the innkeeper's new ale, but with a wistful yearning of the sort he felt for vanished Camelot.

One day he came to a quiet glade, high in the hills. Bees murmured hypnotically, and the grass was soft and embroidered with wild flowers. Miniffer stopped and looked around. Gently he set his harp on a cluster of daisies. Then he lay down. It was almost too much effort to close his eyes.

I believe I will die here, he thought softly. He felt his body begin to merge with the earth and was content. No point in living in such a cruel, ugly world where glory had been murdered and honor was a jest. One tear slid across his temple and through his hair. He composed himself for the end.

"Hello? Hello! Wake up, man! Are you all right?"

Miniffer was annoyed. That was no way to welcome a poet to the afterlife. He opened his eyes.

Looking down on him was a sun-beaten face with eyes burnt almost to gold. They lit like candles when they saw Miniffer was alive and the man grinned in delight as he put an arm about him and lifted the poet shakily to his feet.

,"A good thing I came out to check Timon's bees or I might not have found you," the man continued. "I haven't seen any travelers about here for years. Can you walk a bit? My home isn't far."

Too befuddled to think, Miniffer let this strange being half carry him to a stone hut set among the trees. A stream ran by, making a curious music that confused him still further. His host brought him inside and laid him gently on a cot covered with soft lambs' wool. Miniffer wriggled down into it and gazed in wonder at the man who had succored him.

"Excuse me," the poet stammered. "But have I died yet?"

The great laugh that greeted his question reassured him somewhat, and the reaction of his stomach to the smell of fresh bread convinced him. His host ripped a hole in one loaf and ladled a scoop of vegetable stew into it. He gave this to Miniffer with a wooden spoon.

"I see I found you none too soon." He laughed again. "I was going to apologize for the lack of meat, but you seem not to miss it. Now, while you're restoring your body, I'll introduce myself. My name is Domin. I came to live up here about ten years ago, when I came back from searching for the Grail. Timon the Roman lived up here then, all alone after his sister died and I decided to stay. Lucky for you that I did, eh? Oh, wait, here, let me help you!"

Domin rose in alarm as Miniffer choked on his bread.

"N-no. I'm all right." Miniffer coughed. He swallowed "It's just . . . did you say the Grail?"

"Yes," Domin answered. "I went with my father, at least Mother said he was my father, and we agreed to believe it. Anyway, we went north into the land of the Picts."

His voice became more remote. "We saw things I still cannot explain, strange monsters and fire that danced in the sky. The Picts caught us and enslaved us for a time, until Father earned our freedom by saving their queen from a bear. We stayed too long, and when I came back, everything was changed and poor Mother had died. We never saw the Grail. Galahad found it, they say. I think the Round Table tried to tell us he would. We just didn't understand.''

Miniffer's breath came quickly. His stew dripped unnoticed into his lap. He tried to speak, but he kept squeaking.

"You *knew* Sir Galahad?" he managed to force out.

Domin was puzzled.

"Of course. We played together. Is that strange? He was the best snowball fighter at Caerleon, but I always had to give him a leg up climbing trees. He was a fine boy. Never reminded us that he was Lancelot's son and the queen's favorite. Lord, was he good at wangling extra rations from the cooks!''

Domin laughed again. Miniffer stared. Sir Galahad, the finder of the Grail, the boy knight, holiest of all, wangling drumsticks? This couldn't be! Who was this man? How dare he! And yet . . .

"Did you really live at Camelot?"

Domin smiled at him. "You're very young. I see that now. Not much over twenty, are you? Yes, I was born at Camelot, and I would wish nothing greater for anyone. My mother was lady's maid and friend to the queen. I was sent off to my grandfather's farm until I was seven. But that year Galahad came to be fostered by Guinevere and they sent for me, to be his friend. God's eyes! That was a time to be a boy!''

Miniffer forgot that he was hungry, forgot his longing for ale, forgot that he had ever wished to die. He leaned forward, his mouth opened as if to catch the memories on his tongue.

"Tell me all about it," he begged.

Domin smiled sadly. "I was still a boy when I left. By the time I came back, it was all over. Gawain and Gareth and Mordred were dead. Arthur was gone. The plague had gotten most everyone else. Queen Guinevere still lives, I think, and Lancelot. Gaheris is in Iberia, a bishop they say. The last time I saw Camelot, the walls were overgrown with vines, and peasants in the fields told of ghosts

on the ramparts. It was too long ago. I don't remember
what you want to know.''

But Miniffer wouldn't be cheated.

"Gawain. Do you remember Gawain? Was he as strong
as they say? Did he really slay the Green Knight?''

Domin was silent awhile. "Gawain," he breathed. "He
was . . . like a god. He strode though life in an aura of
gold. It would scorch your eyes to stare at him in the noon
sun. And he could laugh! All the jokes they played on him
and he still laughed. Even fate played with him. Poor
Gawain! The Green Knight was a joke too. I remember it,
though I couldn't have been more than eight. That great,
ugly head rolled across the floor and jeered at us all, then
calmly hopped back on its body. I was so frightened that I
wet myself. And Gawain knew he had to hunt the Knight
out and bare his neck for the axe. He took advantage of it
too. He bedded half the women at Camelot that year, since
it was to be 'the last time.' ''

"But that's not the way I heard it!" Miniffer wailed.
"They say he spent the year on a quest.''

Domin reached up to a shelf and took down a flask.
Miniffer brightened as he saw the honey-dark mead pour
into the cups. Domin handed him one.

"I warned you. Truth is never like the tales. I know.
I've heard a hundred versions of how Modred betrayed and
battled Arthur. There were a thousand heroes there that
day. I don't know how Modred could have dared attack,
since every man I've talked with swears he fought for the
king. You'd think the traitor would be afraid to challenge
Arthur without an army.''

Miniffer sipped his mead and comfort slid through his
body. It gave him the courage to ask the question he feared
most.

"What of Arthur?" he asked. "No one saw him die,
they say. The tale speaks of a huge ship with a wild and
fierce crew that sailed down the river, swooping him up
and carrying him off to help in the wars against the false
emperor in the east.''

Domin nodded. "I have heard that. It may be true.

There are so few still alive. It was a long time ago. Each person has his own story, his own belief. For all I know, each of them is true. I've given up wondering. All that matters to me is that the bees stay in my meadow and my hearth glows bright this winter. The rest is only dreaming.''

He yawned and smiled at Miniffer, who couldn't grasp it. Domin was an ordinary man, aging, his hair getting thin. He was dressed like a peasant, in gray woolen tunic and trews. How could he have been part of Arthur's world? And yet, the glow on his face when he spoke of Gawain . . . It was something to mull over.

Miniffer stayed on, unwilling to lose the nearness to lost wonder. He worked for a while in Domin's gardens. He helped cart mulch for last autumn's leaves and raked it into the turnip beds. He pulled weeds and went into the woods to hunt for berries. His fingers, which had been cramped by holding a harp or a cup, slowly straightened. His chest expanded from breathing deeply in exertion. He was beginning to look like a man again. And all the time he wondered about Arthur.

One day he and Domin followed a narrow path to a glade thick with berries. Miniffer sat on the lush grass, reaching into the thorns as carefully as possible to pluck the largest fruit. Absently he looked down and yelped with pain as his arm was jabbed and scratched.

"Domin! Look at this!" he cried.

"Oh, now. You've hurt yourself," Domin tutted in sympathy. "Do you want to go back home and wash it?"

"No, no, it's nothing!" Miniffer pointed to the earth under the bushes. "I mean the flowers. What are they?"

Domin frowned. "I don't know, exactly. I never saw them anyplace but here. Timon called them 'Guinevere's Roses' and had a tale about how she grew them with the old magic. But it may not be true."

"And yet they still bloom." Miniffer gazed at the strange, warm blossom.

"Yes," Domin agreed. "Each year, they still bloom."

He put down his basket and studied the poet's face a long while.

"I think, Miniffer," he said. "That it's time you were on your way."

Domin sent him back to the world better garbed than when he had left it. His harp had been oiled and restrung. Brien's second-best tunic patched and washed, and a new cloak made for him of the thickest, softest wool. As winter was coming in, Miniffer was grateful for the warmth. But Domin had given him something more, a purpose. Like the knights after the Grail, Miniffer sought the unattainable. And he sought it with the pure flame of absolute belief.

He would find the truth about King Arthur, Merlin, the knights, the ladies, all those days of glory, and he would compose a tale of them that would ring in the souls of all who heard it.

The first snow of the year was falling when Miniffer knocked at the door of the shepherd's hut. He heard the grumbling as the bolt was drawn. An old woman peered at him through a crack.

"What be ye wantin'?" she croaked.

"Directions and a bed for the night, good woman," Miniffer answered.

The door opened a bit more as the woman leaned out for a better look.

"Can ye pay?"

"I can chop wood for your fire and give you a song."

"Well enough. Shake off yer boots and come in."

The hut was crammed with humanity, most of it young, and Miniffer was grateful that they would let him have a bed. There didn't seem to be places enough for those already there.

"My son's wives, and their bairn." The woman nodded at the crowd. "The men all be bringin' down the sheep, but they'll be back before morning so ye can forget any ideas of dallyin'."

Miniffer doubted he could have found floor space to dally. He took off his cloak and moved into the seat they cleared for him. They gave him a bowl of barley soup and he gave them his songs. By the time he was done, the children were all asleep in little clumps on the floor, using each other's bodies for blanket and pillow.

"That were nice chantin', lad," the old woman said. "Good enough for court, I'll be bound, even the one up the hill."

The fingers of all the young women moved simultaneously to ward off evil. Their mother-in-law gave them a scornful glance.

"But ma'am, there's wicked things up there. Old, dark, magic. You know it!" one protested.

"There's no evil up at Camelot!" the old woman snapped, and Miniffer's eyes lit with excitement. "Any ghosts there be gentle, sad ones, only wantin' to go back to the good days."

"And what of Merlin, the wizard?" another whispered. "They say he brought the big table through the Old Ones' world and that they struck him down for it and trapped him. There's lights up there, sometimes, bright flashes. It's Master Merlin, atryin' to break free."

"In the daytime? Use your wits, child. What sorta dark magic works in the sunlight?" The woman picked up her spindle, reminding the others that they had let their hands lay idle all evening.

Miniffer leaned forward, "Is it close, Camelot? Have you been there?"

The gnarled fingers deftly held the thread taut as the spindle dropped.

"Aye," she said casually. "Often, in the old days, until King Constantine moved the court to Dumnonia."

Miniffer was shaking with impatience. "What was it like? Did you see the Knights, the king?"

"Aye . . ." A long pause. "It were beautiful then, great white towers and bright flags in the wind. They'd come ridin' by, all shinin' with silver and gold, and laughin'. The ladies were so beautiful and clean! Sometimes they'd stop at the well and they'd smile at me. Once the queen saw me gawkin' at her hair and she laughed and tossed me her scarf."

She stopped as the others stared at her in disbelief. "Ye didn't know that, did ye, girls? Well, I have it still. Here."

Pushing aside several of the children, she knelt before a rough wooden chest.

Inside were extra lengths of wool. She reached far down to the bottom, rummaged a bit and come up with a leather pouch. Holding it reverently, she returned to her seat and undid the thongs.

The firelight caught the shimmer of it, blue and silver, of a thread so fine it might have been spun on the wind. Miniffer's gasp was echoed by the others.

The old woman stroked it gently. "I wore it at me pledging with Tammas. It goes to me eldest granddaughter at hers, and I'll hear no complaint from ye others. Ye may each touch it once, though. And remember, Arthur's Guinevere wore it!"

Miniffer let his fingers brush the delicate cloth. Then he pulled back. Was this all the closer he could come to it, memories and relics? There must be more. He stood up.

"Thank you for the food and company." He bowed to the granny. "I must be going now. If you could point the way for me to Camelot . . ."

They all gasped at his request, and some moved away from him with a shudder. The old woman grabbed his arm at the door.

"Are ye daft, lad! It's the middle of the night! Ye'll not be able to see a thing and likely enough, break yer own neck trippin' over the fallen beams and stones."

"You said it yourself," Miniffer answered. "Magic won't show itself by daylight. If I'm to find it, it must be now."

She shook her head in disgust. "Find yer death, lad, that's all. But if ye last till cockcrow, come back. Tell me what ye saw and I might tell ye somethin' more. Not all from Camelot are dead, ye know."

She gave him a sly smile that he found distasteful. He answered sharply.

"I'm well aware of that. I've talked to one much closer to the court than you. Domin is his name."

She raised her eyebrows. "Sir Bedevere's son? I'd heard he'd come home. Well then, ye'll not care to know where Sir Lancelot is."

"Lancelot?" Miniffer squeaked unprofessionally. "You know where he is? Tell me!"

"First ye must stay the night up yonder." She cackled. "Then ye must ask me nicely. Now come along. I'll point the way."

Miniffer drew his cloak tightly around his shoulders as he climbed the hill. The snow had ended and the sharp autumn wind had blown away the clouds, revealing a moon full and at its zenith. For this he was thankful. The old earthworks were overgrown and blocked in places and, without the brilliant light, he might have fallen just as the old woman had predicted. Sometimes, when he stopped to catch his breath, he thought he heard voices on the wind; laughter, singing, shouts, someone calling.

"I'm coming!" he called back. "Please wait for me!"

Miniffer snapped his mouth shut over the words. Had he really said that? By all the saints, he must be going mad! His heart pounded and his knees wobbled. He thought about going back, but pride and longing made him move on. At last he came out of the maze and stood before the gate of Camelot.

Once it had been white, but time had beaten it to gray and left it open at a crooked angle, stuck in mud and debris. A lone post was all that remained of the guard tower. Through the gap Miniffer saw a weed-grown court-yard. The buildings were in ruins. A balcony hung from a window by a single slat. The roof of the chapel had caved in. The weeds rippled in strange patterns, as if still trod upon by passing feet.

Miniffer swallowed. He was frightened but could sense that the old woman had been right; the place was not evil. It was lonely and grieving. Miniffer longed to wrap his arms about something; to comfort it. He unslung his harp and stepped into Camelot.

Timidly he began to pluck the accompaniment to the

Lament for Gereint. It was the sort of tale he hoped to compose, full of gallant battles against great odds. He tried to chant the words, but they caught in his throat. His fingers froze against the strings. Across the courtyard a door was open. Through it streamed a cold brightness.

Miniffer searched himself mentally and managed, by gathering in every bit of nerve, to come up with enough courage to walk toward the doorway. Behind him whispers skitted along the lost paths.

As he came closer, he realized that the light was caused by the moon, shining through a large opening in the ceiling. Glass shards still glittered from it. The light was focused on the only thing remaining in the great room; a table, perfectly round. Miniffer knew it at once. He wondered if it were possible for a man to die of happiness. As a pilgrim to a shrine, he approached and rested his hand on the letters, still legible in untarnished gold, ARTURUS REX. Weeping in pure joy, Miniffer fell asleep on the place where his god had once stood.

The first shaft of sunlight caught on the glass above the table and reflected a bright beam right into Miniffer's face. He woke with a start, thinking that he heard someone laughing. He looked around sharply, but no one was there and the sound diminished as the sun rose higher. Hope faded; he was alone.

"There was magic here," he insisted to himself. "I can feel it. This is the very place where Merlin wove his spells, where the Knights watched before they left to find the grail. Here . . . !" He started walking around it, his fingers tracing the fading letters. "Here was Sagremore, and Gareth and Percival and Gawain and Lancelot and . . ."

The letters had been bitten away at the next place, as if someone had spit curses at it until they had cut into the wood. There had been more here than just a name, Miniffer saw, and he knew whose seat it had been: Galahad's. But who could have done this, and why? There was such a viciousness about it.

"Modred did that, with his aunt, Morgause." The voice

behind him was mild, but Miniffer shrieked as if the devil himself had howled in his ear. He turned around and saw an elderly priest watching him in amusement.

"I am sorry." He smiled. "I thought you had heard me come in. My name is Antonius."

His smile shut as he gestured at the table.

"I saw them in here night after night. They were determined to desecrate this bastion of Arthur. The things they did are not fit to tell, or to remember."

"But why Galahad?" Miniffer asked. "Why did they hate him so?"

"Oh, I don't think they hated him. No one could hate Galahad." He sighed. "I met a lot of men in my day who were named 'Saint' by their followers, but Galahad was the closest thing to a pure and stainless being that I have ever known. And that was why they needed to erase his name."

"I don't understand," Miniffer said wearily.

Antonius shrugged. "I can't explain it, really. It was a time of evil. You would have had to have known them all and lived through that dreadful summer. It's not something I would recommend."

"But Father, I *want* to know them all. If only I could have been born then!" Miniffer wailed. "Please help me. I'm a good poet. I was apprenticed seven years in the court of Powys. I'm going to make a saga that will tell Arthur's story so that it will never be forgotten. What was it like? Please!"

He looked so like a begging puppy that Father Antonius was forced to laugh.

"I came late to Camelot and missed the best years, they say. But come with me and I'll try to give you a bit of what you want. Are you hungry?"

Miniffer consulted his stomach and found that it was still too unsettled for anything new, so he shook his head.

"Thank you, Father. A woman down the road promised that if I came back this morning, she would tell me where I could find Sir Lancelot. I should go to see her first."

Father Antonius laughed again.

"That would be old Magan," he said. " I doubt she'll be expecting you now. She saw me coming up here. Now don't worry. I only came by to have a look at Camelot and say a prayer in my old chapel. I was on my way to Glastonbury. I'll take you with me, if you like. That's where Lancelot is now."

Getting to Glastonbury meant climbing another steep hill, this one treacherous with mud. Miniffer groaned every time he slipped and splashed some on his cloak.

"How can I meet him looking like this?" he complained.

The priest gave him an undecipherable glance.

"He won't mind, Miniffer," was all he said.

At the top of the tor was a small community of monks of the new Benedictine order. Some were chopping wood or carrying loads of peat, others worked to cover the gardens or boil down herbs. All were busy at something, even a poor, old blind man, who sat in the sun and laced up sacks of grain to store. Miniffer stared eagerly about for the great knight, but no one there looked as if he could have ever wielded a sword in his life. Where was Lancelot?

Father Antonius gave him a gentle tug.

"I have a message for the brother over there. Come with me a moment."

Grudgingly, Miniffer followed as they went to pay their respects to the sightless man.

"It's Antonius," the priest said gently as he knelt by the aged monk. "How are you?"

The man's fingers stopped their work and reached out for Antonius' hand.

"Is she well?" he asked, and in his voice was a longing so great that it brought tears to Miniffer's eyes.

"Very well. She sent me to see if you needed anything for the winter. I have a flask of wine from the cellar at Cameliard for you."

The old man took a deep breath and shook his head.

"All I need are the words you have brought. Thank you."

Antonius paused. "I have a man here with me who wishes to know about the early days at Camelot, of the battles and the Grail. Will you speak with him, Lancelot?"

Miniffer nearly cried aloud. This blind, broken thing the supreme knight, Lancelot? It wasn't true! It was a cruel trick. He glared furiously at the priest.

The old man's sightless eyes seemed to find him.

"Those days shouldn't be forgotten." He spoke haltingly. "Arthur was the greatest man, the best friend I ever had. He championed me when I was a pompous ass and he forgave me when I took from him the thing he loved most. But please don't ask me to live it all again. I see them all too clearly. No, Father, tell him I can't. Perhaps Guinevere will help him."

Antonius motioned Miniffer to stay silent.

"Shall I take her any message?" he asked.

For the first time Lancelot smiled. "She needs none. She knows."

When they were out of Lancelot's hearing, Miniffer turned to Father Antonius in anger.

"Why couldn't you have told me he was like that now?" His voice was that of a hurt child. "What happened to him?"

Father Antonius made him sit and gave him some bread and cheese. He gnawed his own meal for a bit before answering.

"When I first saw Sir Lancelot, he was the shining example of Arthur's men; brave, strong, devout. Yet by that time he had already gone mad once for over a year, been on innumerable quests, and been deceived into fathering Galahad. All his life he was tormented, by others and by his own mind. He wanted something . . . well, I don't pretend to understand another man's soul. But he succeeded enough in his private quest that he was allowed to see the Grail unveiled. No human eyes could bear such glory. I don't know why I brought you to him. Perhaps it was just to shock you into some sort of understanding, although I hope I'm better than that."

He took another bite of bread and continued.

"I've heard the tales about Arthur, about his knights. In all of them they are greater than true men. They slay their foes without effort. They never doubt or fear. Only treachery can undo them. But Arthur was so much more than that! He was a man who felt and hurt and . . . Oh, damn!'' He stopped in annoyance. ''Yes, I will take you to Guinevere. Perhaps she knows the words. But please don't embarrass me again!''

''I won't,'' Miniffer promised sadly. ''If she's as toothless and stooped as old Magan, I'll bow over her hand as if she were the fairest queen in Christendom.''

Antonius snorted doubtfully, but said nothing.

In the next few days Miniffer tried to get the priest to tell him more about his years with Arthur, especially the great quests and magnificent feats of courage he performed.

''They say he fought off the Saxons for three days, alone, carrying a cross on his shoulders the whole time!''

Antonius shook his head. ''That was about the time I was born, but I know the story. Only Arthur's cross was on his shield, not his shoulders. Even he couldn't swing a sword under those conditions.''

Miniffer pouted. ''You weren't there, though. He might have done it.''

''Yes,'' Antonius conceded. ''I knew Arthur. He might have done it.''

Winter had settled in hard and fast by the time they arrived at Cameliard, Guinevere's family home. It was an ancient Roman villa, the first Miniffer had ever seen that was not in ruins. Before he could meet the queen, Father Antonius made him sit for almost an hour in the calderium, until the last few months' dirt had floated away. Then he had to take a metal stick and scrape off another few years accretion. Finally he was allowed into the main room for the evening meal.

At the table, several women were seated. Miniffer tried to pick out Guinevere, but forgot his intention when he saw the face of one near the center. She was past her first youth, perhaps thirty, he thought, but there was something about her that made him think of spring. Her head was covered and the veil drawn tightly across her forehead. He felt the need to push it back and touch her hair.

"Who is she?" he whispered to Antonius. "Not even Helen could have been so lovely."

"Who else could she be?" the priest answered. "My Lady Guinevere, this is a bard of Powys who wishes to sing for you and speak with you. Miniffer?"

Miniffer took out his harp, noting with fury Antonius' amused expression. He gave them one of the old Celtic stories of the birds of Rhiannan. The women seemed pleased, but he had no idea, then or after, how he had sounded. He felt nothing but the presence of Guinevere. Looking at her, all the stories became possible again. She *must* agree to talk with him. She would know about magic, about demons and wizards and monsters slain by brave knights for her sake. With her help, he knew he could make Arthur's court live forever.

After the meal she sent for him.

"Father Antonius has told me that you wish to create an encomium for my husband." Her voice carried the Latin intonations of a former era. "I will try to help you. Tell me what you already know."

So Miniffer told her about the battles and the glorious quests; how each knight was brave and each woman virtuous. He spoke of Arthur's dream of uniting all of Britain under one law, and how he almost achieved it. His face shone as he described how the sorcerer, Merlin, had prophesied Arthur's coming and his eventual return. He sang of the Grail, and she wept. He whispered what he knew of Modred's treachery, leaving out the rumor that Guinevere had aided him. When he finished, he was as dry as a pomegranate seed sucked of its juice.

He waited, but the queen said nothing. He swallowed.

"Lady," he asked. "Is that the way it really was?"

She wiped her eyes and looked at him steadily.

"Yes," she said. "That's exactly the way it was. Let no one tell you anything else. Arthur was the greatest king ever to live; the noblest, the wisest, the kindest."

"And was there magic?"

"Yes. We breathed magic. It was in the very air of Camelot."

"And dragons . . . someone told me there were no dragons!"

Tears spilled down her face.

"They were wrong. There were always dragons and brave men to challenge them."

Miniffer grew so excited that he forgot himself and knelt beside her, grasping her hands.

"Thank you, Lady! Thank you! I promise I will make people hear the truth about Arthur." He added rashly, "I will even write it in a book and leave it where it will be found, even after I have died, so that no man may change it."

Her smile made him dizzy.

"Then I thank you," she said. "When you have finished making your tale, will you come back and tell it to me again?"

"Yes, Lady."

As he backed out of the room, her maid slid off her veil to prepare her hair for the night. His mouth opened in childlike joy. Loops and coils and curls of living gold fell to her feet. It glistened in the candlelight. She turned her head and it rose like a flock of butterflies, floating in the air.

"Oh, yes," Miniffer breathed. "It's all true."

He spent the winter working on the saga. He left the warmth of Cameliard to test the parts he had finished in the courts and inns. And when spring came again, he knew it was right. But when he came back to sing it for Guinevere, it was too late. She had died quite early one morning, they told him, with the sun full in her eyes.

"We kept a few strands of her hair," one of the women told him. "If you would like it, you may have one."

He had a small box of silver, a present from a lord he had sung for. Into this he wound the strand. He muttered thanks and left without saying good-bye.

It was some weeks before he found the monastery he had heard of, where men and women sat day after day, in heat and frost, to copy the holy books. He presented himself as a novice. When they heard that he already knew his letters and some Latin, they put him to work at once.

He was given a life of St. Illtud and materials to copy it. The new brother Miniffer chortled over his lectern. Now he had all he needed; parchment, ink, time. He would put it all down, just the way it really happened, as Guinevere had assured him: brave deeds, great devotion, dragons and wizards. Everything. He picked up his pen and began.

Quandam . . . no, was it Quandum?

Oh, well. He went on. He scratched a few lines more.

Illius . . . no, maybe illiud, or was it . . . ? And what about this . . . *draconis metus civitas delebat et*—et what? And what about the endings? And anyway, that wasn't what he wanted to say. He wanted to tell how a dragon, a dire tyrant of a dragon, an appalling apparition, had swept up from the dark caverns of the earth like a scorching, engulfing tide and paralyzed the countryside with terror until the mighty soldiers of King Arthur had . . .

Miniffer sighed and wished for his jar of ale. He threw down the pen. Latin! A sterile language, good for nothing but laws and morals, for the dusty miracles of forgotten saints. But for Arthur! How could those stiff conjugations ever express the wonder, the enchantment, the rich, shimmering, heart-breaking perfection of Camelot! No. Only one tongue was great enough for this tale; his own. It could only truly live in the musical language of Rhiannan, of Llyr, of the ancient magic woven into the very earth of Britain. Yes, in the British tongue the matter of Britain would blossom and flourish forever.

He started again. This time his pen moved surely and, as he wrote, he saw it all before him, just as he knew it had been. The Golden Age of Britain; the time of glory that was and was to be again. The time of Arthur.

※※

Axiom: if you care about your characters, the reader will.

JANE YOLEN cares and makes you care as much as any writer I can think of. If that isn't good writing, what is? The lady is as charming and warm on the page as she is in person. She can be touching or uproariously funny; these are separate accolades. It's easier to impress someone with your narrative skill than it is to make them care about it. And if you think comedy is easy to write, try it.

Jane Yolen gets me where I laugh and care. She's written innumerable short stories in genre, as well as novels, and children's books (and try to do that without killing yourself or the children). She has a way with a legend and can usually be found in someone's "Best Of" anthology. Her recent SF novel from Ace Books, Cards of Grief, *was critically applauded and followed by two marvelous collections of short stories and verse,* Dragonfield *and* Merlin's Booke.

Her poem "The Storyteller" prefaces this anthology for very good reason: it's our theme, what this volume is all about. In the present story, as with most of her tales, Ms. Yolen's alchemy mixes magic with plain earth, and suddenly you find you have a whole new definition of sorcery.

※※

Meditation in a Whitethorn Tree

by Jane Yolen

I am a man much abused by women, a thing set spinning on the wheels of their ambitions. Three women betrayed me during my overlong and lonely life, though the betrayals were not what I thought at the time. And the only one I accused of treachery, my Niniane, nymph of the darkling woods, she was none of those three.

Niniane, woodsgirl, your sweet sorcery did not betray me but rather be-treed me, if an old man may be allowed a small joke. Yet if you had not, I would never have had the time to come to this self-knowledge. There was always too much else to do than to indulge my vanity. Running a kingdom takes many hours of hard work; running a king takes even longer. But time moves slowly within the trunk of a tree, as sluggish as winter sap or the blood in an old man's veins. I have had many years of this slow time to think about my past. I have no future but this whitethorn cask.

So I will rehearse the stories of the three, that the very wood may bear witness to my witlessness. It is no small irony that a man reknowned for his wisdom should, in fact, be the greatest fool in all Christendom.

1

Igraine

Who has not heard her story? When she is spoke of, it is as Gorlois' lovely wife, beguiled by the wicked machinations of a mage, the victim of a wizard's plot.

Victim! She was never such a gull. It was she tempted Uther, poor, dumb, besotted brute; tempted him—and used me.

I remember the very moment they met. Indeed how could I forget? He told me of it often enough thereafter, or at least what he remembered of it. What he remembered and what *was* were nowhere the same. Love lays a mist on memory. But wizards deal in such moments. We turn them into crystals and store them in the cabinet of the mind.

Igraine had been much talked of that year in the rooms where men gather and speak of harlots and happiness in a single breath. She was a beauty, no doubt of it: gold hair, green eyes. It was as if dark hair and dark eyes held no fascination for them, so limited were their collective imaginings. She was the season's darling and men—when they are driven to it—can spin romances as silken and fine as any village granny.

So word came of her to Uther long before he gazed upon her. He was tempted by the portraits his men drew in the air. He was, shall we say, prepared for his passion as meat, long in a marinade, is prepared for the heat.

The golden beauty and the thickened, middle-aged, battle-scarred king. Who would have guessed it? He had no manners, except with a sword. He could not dance without a horse beneath him. He was as blunt and as brutal as a mace. Who would have guessed it indeed.

But Igraine had. She was tired of the strong winds, the lofty folds of cliff, the narrow roadway, the stony beaches, the cold waves of Tintagel. She wearied of the duke's same stories, the repetition of faces, the rota of Cornish ways. Such familiarity wilts even the loveliest of flowers. Some women thrive on the strange, the brutal, the ob-

scene. She begged for a month at the court, but Gorlois
wanted her rooted only in Cornwall like some wild, beautiful hedge rose planted in a pot. Besides, he coveted king-
ship and made war upon the king.

I had all this from Igraine's serving woman who had
escaped to the east to beg a love philtre from me. Often I
exchanged magical gifts for gossip, which is the common
coin of magery.

The serving woman leaned over the stew I had cooked
for her, drinking in the smells of love, and turning to me
with eyes as narrow as needles. "But how can my lady
come to court when her husband is at war with Uther?"

I did not then hear the play on her words. I reserved all
such trickery to myself. Fool that I was, fool that I am. I
replied to her, *"What was is not necessarily what is."*
How we mages love obfuscation. Then I added, that she
take my meaning exactly. "Truces can be made in a day."

It was not a month later that Gorlois sued for peace and
was invited to Uther's castle for the Easter coronation
feast. Women have much more to do with war than warriors, believe me.

I thought Igraine would be happy just to see the new
faces at court, but she came dressed for seduction in a
gown that would have been daring even on a whore. Yet it
had an innocence, too, lent it by ribbons and lace.

Uther came to my chamber that same night, his face
flushed and angry.

"I want her," he said heavily, undoing the clasp at his
neck as he slumped into the great wooden chair by my
bedside. "I want Igraine." Uther was always direct; it was
his greatest virtue and his greatest fault. One always knew
where one stood with him. In a plowman that is a good
thing, in a king it is not.

"You have just signed a truce with her husband," I
pointed out. "After months of trouble from the west your
kingdom is now secure. He is your liege man; he has
sworn fealty. It is simply not good form to seduce his wife."

"I do not want to seduce her," Uther said bluntly. "I
want to take her and make her my own."

I spent another fruitless hour trying to counsel him, but he left with desire unchecked and I fell to sleep. Or at least I tried to sleep. Uther stormed back into my room less than an hour later, his face like a Cornish sky, troubled and dark.

He roared, "They have left me, gone secretly, without my leave."

"Who?" I asked, afraid I knew.

"Gorlois has stolen her from me."

"She was not yours to steal."

It did no good. He would be neither comforted nor controlled and we were back at war within the hour. Within days Uther had troops ravaging the ducal lands, but he had no great success of it, except for the good men slaughtered on both sides, which is the legacy of any war, whatever the cause. The duke had taken to his castle Terrabyl and left Igraine in the safer house, Tintagel, where she could be guarded easily by placing soldiers across the narrow ridge of land.

Uther became a raging bear. What work there was in the newly formed kingdom—taxes and truces and the ordinary seasonal rounds—were all left undone. Farmboys were yanked from the fields to serve in the army. Farm wives were conscripted to serve as cooks and camp followers. Plows were turned into swords. And I knew that unless I intervened decisively, there would be neither crops nor kingdom come the fall. So I suggested magic, albeit reluctantly, for the consequences of such magic are often hard to bear.

"Glamour," I said to the king when he had interrupted my sleep for the third time one night with reports of the ongoing war. "You need a bit of glamour to win this lady."

"I need more men, not magic," he said. "Gorlois is a fox but I . . . I am a dragon. I will swallow him alive and I *will* have her."

But I would not leave him alone. I played the same tune again and again that night until he was finally forced to dance to it. At last, if only to shut me up, he agreed. My plan was a simple one. With magic it is best not to be too complex. I would cast his features and mine as Gorlois and his faithful Jordanus. We would ride thus disguised past guards and gates and he would—I promised him—sleep that night with Igraine.

"But I want her to love *me*, not that simpering dukeling. *Me*, for myself." His coarse features twisted in a parody of passion.

And then I knew things were more treacherous than I had thought. I had hoped he would make a quick sweaty night of it, his face the duke's, his loins—that was another matter altogether. I could not counterfeit what I had not seen. But my master wanted more, and more my magic might not stand. If I turned him into Gorlois' twin for more than a night, well, that kind of glamour carried its own danger. He might never again wear the face of the king. And Britain needed *this* man, brutal and frank though he was. That was well writ in the stars, that he carry the kingdom for fifteen years yet. What would rule instead of him would be chaos, or so the firmament warned. I did not believe the prophesies of crystal balls or the fuzzy omens told by cards. But the skies over our green land did not lie.

"You shall have her," I said, my heart heavy with the promise. *One step at a time*, I chided myself. "So prepare yourself to ride, my lord. Unarmed."

"Unarmed?" Uther had not ridden unarmed since he was a babe.

"Cold steel will pierce the glamour. You must be unarmed that your face may carry another's features."

He nodded and left to get ready. And I? I leaned out of the window to look once more at the stars. I saw a kind of swirling passion writ there. And then without warning, a comet blazed across the sky. It meant a birth or a death. Or both. The stars do not lie, but they do not give up their secrets easily. I would have to think on that bright light. Praying for the birth. I went down the stairs to meet my king.

We rode through that night and the next and another to Tintagel, and in a forest near the headland where the castle

sat, we made a small fireless camp. It was there, under the
night sky, ablaze with information for those who could
read it, I cast the glamour that turned Uther into the
likeness of Gorlois and myself into Jordanus. Uther did not
believe anything had happened, so subtle are the traceries
of glamour, until he turned and saw my face.

"The likeness is uncanny—" he began. Then he stopped.
And laughed. The change had made him quicker with
words as well, just like Gorlois.

"We can remain but a night with these features im-
printed upon our own," I warned. "Or we risk becoming
that self, though but a shadow of the living man."

He nodded, plainly unhappy with it, but also understanding faster than ever Uther had in his own face.

And so we were swept into Tintagel, across the narrow
conjunction, under the banners of Cornwall, and no one
dared stop our march, for they believed us to be the duke
and his best friend riding homeward. So men read one
another, by the face and not the heart.

Igraine met us by the great gate, having been warned by
some minion or another. She was dressed more plainly
than in court, but that did not change her beauty. Indeed, it
only enhanced it. She dropped us a small courtesy, and
then opened her arms. Uther drove into them, his passion
the only thing not counterfeit.

I saw the surprise on Igraine's face, and then a kind of
strange transformation as she struggled to control her mouth.
I did not read it right at the time, thinking she was not as
much in love with her duke as he with her.

"My lord," she said, and she stared over his shoulder at
me.

I put my finger alongside my nose, a gesture Jordanus
used habitually to signal understanding or compliance or
consideration. Perhaps I was a beat too slow, my own
body still aware of its own rhythms, so different from the
form it now wore.

"My lord," Igraine said again, looking deeply into
Uther's eyes. "I have longed for your embrace." And
then she drew him swiftly into her bed chamber and
locked the door behind.

* * *

We left in the morning, the king and I, though I moved with more grace. In him the two forms were already warring. As we went out through the portcullis on our horses, I turned my head and saw his features shift suddenly, as if the glamour were readjusting itself. I felt a corresponding tremor in my own limbs.

"We must hurry, Uther," I whispered urgently, leaning over to slap at the horse's broad flank.

We leaped away and galloped down the path. I felt a burning in my breast, as if I had recently eaten of some tainted meat. And a strange lightheadedness. I knew what it meant: both Jordanus and Gorlois were dead, killed I supposed in the early morning fighting. If we wore their features for an hour more, we would *become* them. I did not wait for the forest this time. I turned our horses onto a small path and there, almost within sight of Tintagel and its guards, I spoke the words that would bring us back the familiarity of our own features.

As I watched Uther's face, it seemed to cloud for a moment, and then the rough-hewn, broken-nosed homely king looked out at me, his eyes cloudy with lack of sleep.

"Her husband is dead and so you must be alive in your own body and face to be her suitor now."

"Suitor?" His voice was more weary than puzzled.

"Do you not still want her?"

He shook his head. I understood. She had proved herself only a woman in bed, not an angel, not a fairy queen. Then I remembered the comet. A death. But something in me said that these small deaths, Gorlois and Jordanus, were not what the blaze portended. A birth!

"She bears a child," I said, suddenly sure of it. "Your child. Your *son*."

That caught him. "A son!" he said. For all his rutting, his women had only borne him girls. "Then I must marry her."

"So you shall," I said. "I will arrange it."

Thus it was that Igraine became a queen and a mother within short months of one another. And as I bore the child away, my part in that unholy bargain, though I had not known of it at the time, Igraine looked up at me and laughed.

Oh, the tale tellers and the tale bearers say she screamed at me, begging me to return the boy. But it was not that kind of scream at all. It was a cry of triumph, for she had gotten it all, her heart's one desire: a king, a kingdom, and a crown.

2

Morgaine

The second woman to betray me was but a child at the time. I thought I had a way with children. What magician does not? We are but a few fingers from every child's laughter. A coin behind one ear, a flower from the other, a card plucked out of the air with ease, and the child is ours.

So I charmed Morgaine on our first meeting, the day her mother and Uther were wed. She needed much charming, her father lately dead, her mother married to a stranger. The coin I took from behind her right ear was a copper I let her keep. The flower from the left was a speedwell the color of my eyes. The card was the Ace of Death. I should have been warned, for the Eastern cards, though difficult to read, rarely lie, but I was too enchanted by her childish wit.

She said, "Are you to be my uncle, then?"

"If you wish," I answered, "though I am no relation to the king."

"But I heard my mother say that your relationship to Uther was too close for her liking."

I had to laugh at that. "Then I shall be your uncle indeed," I said, as I handed her the card.

The day after the wedding she found me in my tower room. The door was shut though not locked, and any adult would have respected its meaning. But Morgaine, being but five or six years old at the time, was a curious child. A locked door was simply more the challenge. She fiddled with the latch and pushed the door open, then stood trembling in the doorway, smiling. I thought at the time she trembled with fear, but now I know it was with anticipation.

When I heard the noise, I looked up and smiled back at her. She was such a slight, spindly thing then, her plaited hair the color of an old penny, not quite brown and not quite copper. Her eyes were a muddy gold; the left had a spot of green in it, the right a spot of grey which gave her a somewhat daft look when she willed it. Many a man was to be taken offguard by that expression. She had a smudge on her nose and a gap between her upper front teeth. They say such a gap portends licentiousness, but who would ever think it of a child.

"Hello, Uncle," she said, even then her voice was low and cozening, with a husky quality that was much remarked on when she was a child.

"I am busy, Morgaine," I said, "I have no time to play with you today."

She looked at me carefully with those particolored eyes. Her face was deadly serious. I thought it a joke at the time. "Oh, I am not here to play, Uncle. I am here to learn."

Who was to guess she knew full well what she meant? I sighed and signaled her into the room, warning her that I would dismiss her if she troubled me but once.

She scrambled up onto a stool by my side and sat there so quietly for the rest of the day, it was as if no child at all were in the room. I know now how unnatural that was, but you see I had only known children in groups and she was like no child before or since.

She came often after that, sitting still as a stone on the stool by my side, watching me work in my laboratorium, asking no questions but sometimes imitating in a kind of passionate mime what I did with my hands and my mouth. She taught herself to read long before I realized it. Indeed, I thought she was still on her *alpha* and *bets*, her mother being a follower not of Jerome but of the White One. But the child had a mind of her own and was puzzling out my texts before I thought her aware of them. If she had asked questions, she would have known the truth of the magic—

and its consequences. But she cared more for the form of it than the heart, and therein lay the doom she brought upon us all.

And I—the gods help me—thought her endearing. Even when she was full grown, a woman in form (though, alas, inside she was still a vengeful child, I see that now), I remembered her as the child she had been, my silent companion, my secret sharer. I did not see the simulacrum she had become. I forgave her her little sins. No, even worse, I *excused* them. And she knew me for the foolish dotard that I was, a drooling grandpap.

It was nearly two years after her mother's marriage and her brother's birth that Morgaine's first bout with the demons showed forth. We were all at a feast celebrating some god or another. When one is a king by the sword, as Uther was it is always best to honor too many gods than too few.

Morgaine wore her plaits atop her head but otherwise showed no sign of womanhood. Unlike her mother, she was not an early blossom ripe and ready to fall into the first hand. It was Morgaine who elected herself to be Hebe to Uther's Zeus. She brought the great wooden goblet carved with entwined dragons to the table and set it before him.

Uther picked up the cup, smiled unconvincingly at Morgaine—whom he had never professed to love—drank two sips, and fell forward onto the table.

The hall grew deathly still, and the only sound was Morgaine's voice crying out *"Father"* in a high, sweet tone. Then she threw herself on top of him and wrapped her arms about him.

I should have known the falsity in her voice, which was a good octave above her normal tone. I should have noticed that she whispered as she held him. But I, like all the rest, mistook it for weeping, mistook her for a normal child. If I had read her lips, I would have known it for a deadly spell.

I ran to Uther, pulled him over on his back, pushed

Morgaine away, and opened his shirt. Putting my ear to
his chest, I heard the erratic beating of his heart. He
smelled of wine and something sweet, something deadly.
From my bosom I drew up a small golden flask containing
huantan, the universal medicine that only comes from the
East. I unstoppered it.

"Prise open his mouth," I roared.

Two men leaped to do my bidding.

I poured three drops into Uther's mouth, then closed his
mouth with mine in the kiss of life. Breath for breath I
gave him till he took it, swallowed, gasped, and moaned
beneath me. Then I drew back and he sat up slowly.

The men cheered. Igraine, who had been sitting by his
side the entire time stunned, her beautiful broad forehead
beaded with sweat, gave a faint smile. Morgaine had
disappeared.

"Who has done this?" Sir Ector said in a whisper more
deadly than a roar. He took up the cup and sniffed it once,
then held it over his head.

"Not Morgaine. Not my child," said the queen.

But we none of us believed it could be she. She was but
eight or nine at the time. And so it was that the wine
steward was hanged, for messages to him in Latin were
found signed and sealed with the ring of a Western duke.
That the steward could not read was never considered alibi
enough. One can always find a reader in a court as large as
Uther's.

Uther recovered but he was never again as strong as he
had been. His enemies began to overrun the corners of the
kingdom.

I knew that only the king himself might check their
advances, and so we propped him up in a horse litter,
filled with medicines that made his eyes glitter and his
tongue a bit loose. And, like Moses in the Hebrew books,
when we raised his arms, his army won. We returned him
to Londinium and another feast.

Again the child brought him his cup, but this time he
pushed it aside. Worried, I sniffed at it, but it was clean of

any poisonous spell. However, the battle had taken its toll and Uther left the feast.

"Let me go to my father in his room," Morgaine insisted. "I will sing to him and rub his temples until he falls asleep."

And we all praised her daughterly concern, forgetting that though he was a father, he was none of hers.

In the morning Uther could neither speak nor sign with his hands, and on his temples were ten dark marks. If we could have read them as easily as a village witch reads palms, could we not have had a confession there?

For three days and three nights Uther lay in his stupor, neither awake nor asleep, neither alive nor dead. The castle was darkened and the servants walked with shoes muffled in cloth. Only Morgaine played with her dolls and sang brightly in the halls. But she was still so much a child, we excused her.

On the fourth day, as I sat by his side, Uther gave a bit of sound, like a rabbit caught in a trap. I pressed my ear to his mouth and he whispered to me.

"Morgaine," he said.

I thought he wanted to summon her, to thank her for her concern, so I called her in. She stood by his bedfoot and smiled, the kind one gives in a sickroom for encouragement. I marveled that a child should instinctively know what to do. But when I dream of it now, knowing what I know, it reminds me of her mother's smile, triumphant and sly.

"Morgaine," he said, his voice almost full. He struggled to sit up in bed and pointed his finger at her.

"For *my Father*," she said. And smiled again.

Uther said nothing more, but fell back with a bright red foam on his lips.

When the men gathered and the priests and Igraine and her women, I told them that he had said more.

"He said that Arthur should rule after him. He said, 'On Arthur I bestow God's blessing and my own, and Arthur shall succeed to the throne of pain for forfeiting my blessing.' No one questioned it. No one wondered that

Uther on his deathbed should have been more articulate than ever in his life. And the only one who might have dared call me a liar was too young to be there to witness my small deceit. Yet it was no lie but rather Uther's dearest wish. I read it in his eyes as he died, as I had read it in the stars. The heir, however he is begat, is still the heir.

But the words Morgaine spoke as Uther lay there, his lips bright with foam and his eyes pleading with death for more time, haunt me to this day. I thought them strange when they were spoken, but I understand them now, now that I realize the depths of her betrayal.

She said, "I shall care for little Arthur, my lord, do not worry on that account. He shall be as you were, father and not father. I shall love him as more than a sister, though I am his sister but by half. I shall bind him to his kingdom forever."

And then she smiled, her mother's smile, a smile full of treachery and deceit, that I took only for childhood's end. But Uther, knowing that smile, died without being shriven.

3

Guinevere

The third who betrayed me was Arthur's own queen, though the betrayal was not what the storytellers believed.

She was never the beauty they sing of. Her hair was not gold but rather corn-colored. Her eyes were not green but gray. Her nose was too long and her mouth was too small and she had a dimple in her chin that it was later said, was a cleft for the devil to hide in. She was neither tall nor small but of medium height and her bosom was certainly not one to make men swoon. Yet she could be serious in one breath and merry the next, and her voice was ever sweet and low. She had a genius for friendship—the making and the breaking of it. And best of all, her hips were well set apart the better for child-bearing which is of course a great virtue in a queen.

She was the second daughter of a noble Roman who had fallen in love in the wild country of the Silures and went to live there against the caution of his family. Her sister, Gwenhwyach, was the first recommended to me when it was known I was on a search for our king. But Gwenhwyach, though infinitely more beautiful than her sister, was a silly wench given to fits of giggles and hiding her mouth behind her hand. Besides, she had the small hips of a well-bred Roman wife. A king needs an heir. So I looked at the second sister, Gwenhwyfar.

Unlike her older sister, who had the graces and the eliptical manner of her patrician father, Gwenhwyfar was always to the point.

"I would be a good wife to your king," she said to me. "I would bear him many sons and be a kind queen. My faithfulness to my lord and his land would never be questioned." She cocked her head to one side, a gesture I would come to know well, and laughed. "Besides," she said, "I can read and write in three languages—British, English, and Latin. I am learning Frank, slowly, because I may have need of it some day. I can play the Roman harp and sing passably, I never giggle, and"—she leaned towards me—"and I know the mathematics of wizardry."

Startled, I opened my eyes wide, which she took for a good sign. She could always read me better than I could read myself.

"I know," she said, laughing again, "that the very word *wizard* is itself mathematically pure. The W and the D are both in the fourth degree, the W fourth from the alphabet's end and the D fourth from its beginning. I and R stand in the ninth degree. Zed is the omega and A the alpha, and thus W-I-Z-A-R-D is a perfect word."

I had to laugh with her. "And what then is *Gwenhwyfar*?" I asked.

"Call me Gwenny," she said. "That is what my friends do."

As I said, a genius for friendship. And she was, besides Arthur, my one true friend. That is why it has taken me so long to believe that she betrayed me.

I recommended her without hesitation to the king. It was not that he was an unromantic sort, but kings must choose queens for their bloodlines and their holdings. Love can be found in any wench's bedroom. Breeding cannot.

Their wedding was one of proper pomp and all the dukes and barons left off quarreling and came. Morgaine, as the king's stepsister, was there as well, with her little dark-haired bastard. His mewling and puking nearly made a disaster of the day. But Gwenny shone. She even picked up the child and dandled it on her knee and only when it played with the pearls on her bodice did it leave off its cranky cries.

Arthur seemed different with Gwenny. *Guinevere* he called her, not being able to wrap his tongue around the wild Silurian name. He seemed not only content but, somehow, complete. When I looked at them together, I was filled with a kind of paternal pride, as if my choosing had made a circle where no circle had been before. Surely self-satisfaction is one of the larger sins, though it is not in any litany.

Month after month and month went by and Gwenny's belly did not swell. There is nothing less satisfying at a new court than a queen with a flat stomach. All the news of the day begins and ends there. It was spoke of more than the weather. Gossip filled the ears, wine the bladder, but nothing seemed to fill our Gwenhwyfar.

I begged a private audience with her.

"Gwenny," I said, for she ever insisted I call her that when we were alone, "your duty to the king and the kingdom is yet undone."

She placed her hands over her stomach and sighed. "It is not that he does not try," she said. "Sometimes five and six times a week. He groans and sweats and sounds like a stallion, but still my womb is tenantless."

I shook my head and handed her a small vial filled with a grey-green liquid the color of leaf mold. "Give him this to drink, but half, and you to take the rest."

She reached for it eagerly.

"Pour it out an hour before bed into two earthenware cups. Take it moments before he enters you," I said.

She looked down and blushed. Then she looked up again and stared deeply into my eyes. "I love him, you know. I did not expect that. I did not hope for that. Just to be treated well, as my father did my mother. Just to be valued and trusted. But I love him, for he is strong and gentle and kind and bright and the best of them all. Even if this were poison you bid me drink, I would drink it—for him. For Arthur.''

I covered her hand with mine, the hand that held the vial. "It is neither poison nor a sop, but a tisane of periwinkle," I said. "It is to make you both more . . . more eager, so that the seed might ride high inside of you and touch that part which makes a child.''

"We are already *eager*," she said, and laughed. "Sometimes night does not come soon enough.''

I stood, bowed, and left, sweat running down my back. Talking of such matters to her made me extremely ill at ease, though only the gods knew why.

They consumed a tun of the stuff, and still it did no good. A year went by and then a second, and even Sir Kay came to talk to me of it. He had a filthy mouth and a cesspool for a mind, and the things he suggested would not have been fit for a sow, much less a queen. So I ignored him and read some of the forbidden herbalries, where I learned nothing new, just marjoram for dropsy and brooklime for St. Anthony's fire and alderberry for boils. But as Gwenny had none of these or the hundred more, my reading was of little use. Either the queen was barren or the king had no seed worth spilling or there was a curse on them so deep I could not read it in the stars. It was time for stronger medicine.

And so I went to her on an early spring day when the king and many of his men were in the woods to the west. We sat by a mullioned window and the sun dusted her shoulders like a golden shawl.

"The birds have returned, Gwenny," I said. "They are making their little nests." Indeed we could hear them outside, and one, a finch, was building above the window. A piece of straw hung down.

"You are here to speak to me again of an heir," she said.

"Can I never surprise you, Gwenny?"

"Merlin, you are a book whose runes can be read by anyone who cares," she said. "And *I* care."

I knew I loved her then and could say what had to be said. "This time I shall surprise you, Gwenhwyfar."

She opened her grey eyes wide, and they were the color of the tidal river Tamar on an overcast day. "Using my Christian name? Are we not friends?"

"We are and we will be again, but you will not like what I have to say . . ." I faltered.

"Then say it quickly. It is best to be quick when the news is worst," she said. She reached out to hold my hand, which was trembling.

"The kingdom needs an heir. You *must* have a babe or the king will be forced to put you aside. And we both know how good you are for him and our land. So if Arthur cannot give you a child, you must discreetly find a man who can."

She pulled her hand away from mine in the roughest gesture I ever had of her. "Are you putting yourself forward as the candidate, then?" she asked.

This time it was I who was angry. "Gwenny, I am your friend. And Arthur's. I am old enough to have fathered you. And a mage cannot . . . must not . . ."

"It is true, then? You lose your magic if you are . . . no longer . . . perfect?" she asked, the words bitter in her mouth. "Tell me, mage, does the W fall off the beginning of *wizard*? Does the Zed wilt? Does the D . . ." and she gave a sign with her forefinger that I had seen only Sir Kay and his gross companions use, meaning a man's tool faltering. I had not known that ladies could know such things, much less use them.

"*Gwenhwyfar!*" I said, my voice a roar.

It sobered us both. She lowered her hands to her lap, folded them quietly and kept her eyes fastened on the interlaced fingers.

"I mean you must seek out the most perfect knight in the kingdom, whose body and heart are the equal of Arthur's."

"And whose loins are more than equal . . ." she whispered.

"And whose mouth will be silent with love for you," I said.

"You speak of Lancelot du Lac of course."

I nodded.

She looked up suddenly and laughed. "I always knew my Frankish would be useful for something, though I never learned how to say 'Will you bed me now, my knight.' "

I said nothing.

"Is it truly the only way, Merlin?" she asked, her voice cracking twice on the short question.

"I have thought many hours and days and weeks and months on it," I said. "I have used all the magic I have, what knowledge of the body, all the tricks and sorceries. You have drunk and eaten all the herbal remedies and to no avail."

"To no avail," she echoed.

"I could . . . could help you. . . ." I stuttered. Then I summoned up the courage to complete the thought. "I could put a glamour on Lancelot so that he looked like the king."

She shook her head. "I am no Igraine," she said, "to want to try and fool my heart. I either do it straight or do it not at all."

I breathed out very carefully and thought that she was, indeed, the truest, finest woman in the land.

"But I must do it at once. Today. Tonight. Tomorrow at the last. Else I will be able to do it never." She reached out and touched my hand. "But I do it because I love Arthur," she said. "And because I love you. Not because of Lancelot du Lac. Never because of him."

"I know," I answered. "I know."

What she did that night or the next or the next was not written down anywhere, not in her diary nor on her face. And I waited for word of it, and Lancelot began to sigh out loud, and the court was filled with the kind of gossip I had hoped would never start. But for all that, Gwenny's body did not change with the passing of the spring. And before I could speak to her again, Sir Kay and his company laid a trap. When it was sprung, the queen and her perfect knight lay in it.

"I do not believe it, Merlin," said Arthur. "I cannot believe it." His voice was an agony. I could not meet his eyes. "But they were found in bed."

"You said there was a sword between them."

"Any man can climb over steel lest he be a man of the fey. And any couple that lies with a sword between them, a man can bridge that gap with his own sword, be it ever so broad a blade." So he whipped himself, with words and with images. Image is but the beginning of imagination.

"Ask her," I said.

"I did," he replied.

"And what did she say?"

"Riddles. She spoke riddles. She said: 'If I sinned it was for the kingdom. If I did not it was for you. Either way I am condemned. Either way my life with you is forfeit. Trust me, dear heart.' And I did, and I do, but my heart is within my breast and the crown lies upon my head. I cannot keep her though I trust her. I cannot lie with her again though I love her. I cannot let her live though I die without her touch." He wept.

And I—I said nothing, for there was nothing left to say.

So Lancelot took her away, rescued her or stole her, depending upon your side of the fight. But it was I who planned it and who taught him his part. He was always just a sword in another man's hand.

She left him for a nunnery as soon as she could, for if she could not love Arthur she *could* love God. In her mind, I think, the two were one.

A note was delivered to me that I could not at that time understand. It said, "The sword was true, as I was, to my heart and not to my head. Forgive me."

I did not know what it was she wanted forgiven, at least not then. But I know now. Oh, Gwenny, you could not bring yourself to sleep with another man though the kingdom called for it, you who drew the sword and kept it there all the long night for Arthur's sake, so willing to die with your name shamed throughout the land so that Arthur might be able to put you aside with anger and without remorse. Did you not realize that as much as you loved him, he loved you? Did you not know that without you he dies?

Oh, Gwenhwyfar, if you had trusted me, instead of telling Sir Kay's gossipy wife that you planned to lie with Lancelot that night so that you could be trapped. Why did you not just tell me no, and I would have looked for yet another solution. There are babes that can be bought in this great kingdom of ours. You might have even adopted your stepsister's child.

Igraine betrayed me out of love of power. Morgaine out of power and revenge. You betrayed me for so much less—and so much more. Why is it, sweet Gwenny, I find that the harder to bear?

Three women, and I a thing set spinning on fortune's wheel, I who thought myself the spinner.

Yet wait. Something in these tales rings false. Did I know so much? Did I know so little? Could an old man's memories be as muddled as time?

Niniane, woodsgirl, speak to me again. What did I know, what did I live, what did you spin out for me over the long wooden years?''

Well, time and memory are all I have now. Let me consider these three once more. I will tell all the tales like beads on a chain, that some day I may know the truth of it. Some day.

Long after this volume was finished and mellowing on the publisher's shelf, Jane Yolen sent me "Winter Solstice, Camelot Station" by JOHN M. FORD, *and even called to herald its arrival. I told her the book was closed.*

"Read it anyway," Jane commanded. "It's brilliant."

I read it—and gave thanks to Saint Jane for jotting Mr. Ford's phone number on the manuscript, because the closed book was about to reopen. The way of an anthologist is not always sunlit, but he doesn't pass up a piece like this; not if he knows what's good for him. Neither will you.

John M. Ford's work has appeared in Amazing, Analog, Asimov's *and* Omni. *He's been anthologized in* Liavek II *and* III, Dragons of Light *and* Laughing Space, *as well as authoring several books for children. There's also a recent Star Trek novel,* How Much for Just the Planet? *Writers kill for titles like that. But, then, Mr. Ford's novel* The Dragon Waiting *won the 1984 World Fantasy Award, so he hardly needs resort to such extremity, and his present gem of an entry is what this volume is all about.*

The author writes that he "grew up in the American Industrial Midwest, very near a railroad yard and a long way from the Forest of Broceliande. Or perhaps not so far, depending on how you look at it."

Not so far, John. On a clear day, there's Camelot from your window.

Winter Solstice, Camelot Station

John M. Ford

Camelot is served
By a sixteen-track stub terminal done in High Gothick
Style,
The tracks covered by a single great barrel-vaulted glass
roof framed upon iron,
At once looking back to the Romans and ahead to the
Brunels.
Beneath its rotunda, just to the left of the ticket windows,
Is a mosaic floor depicting the Round Table
(Where all knights, regardless of their station of origin
Or class of accommodation, are equal),
And around it murals of knightly deed's in action
(Slaying dragons, righting wrongs, rescuing maidens tied
to the tracks).
It is the only terminal, other than Gare d'Avalon in Paris,
To be hung with original tapestries,
And its lavatories rival those at Great Gate of Kiev Central.
During a peak season such as this, some eighty trains a
day pass through,
Five times the frequency at the old Londinium Terminus,

Ten times the number the Druid towermen knew.
(The Official Court Christmas Card this year displays
A crisp black-and-white Charles Clegg photograph from
the King's own collection.
Showing a woad-blued hogger at the throttle of "Old
XCVII,"
The Fast Mail overnight to Eboracum. Those were the
days.)
The first of a line of wagons have arrived,
Spilling footmen and pages in Court livery,
And old thick Kay, stepping down from his Range Rover,
Tricked out in a bush coat from Swaine, Adeney, Brigg,
Leaning on his shooting stick as he marshalls his company,
Instructing the youngest how to behave in the station,
To help mature women that they may encounter,
Report pickpockets, gather up litter,
And of course no true Knight of the Table Round (even in
training)
Would do a station porter out of Christmas tips.
He checks his list of arrival times, then his watch
(A moon-phase Breguet, gift from Merlin):
The seneschal is a practical man, who knows trains do run
late,
And a stolid one, who sees no reason to be glad about it.
He dispatches pages to posts at the tracks,
Doling out pennies for platform tickets,
Then walks past the station buffet with a dyspeptic snort,
Goes into the bar, checks the time again, orders a pint.
The patrons half turn—it's the fella from Camelot, innit?
And Kay chuckles soft to himself, and the Court buys a
round.
He's barely halfway when a page tumbles in,
Seems the knights are arriving, on time after all,
So he tips the glass back (people stare as he guzzles),
Then plonks it down hard with five quid for the barman,
And strides for the doorway (half Falstaff, half Hotspur)
To summon his liveried army of lads.

*   *   *

Bors arrives behind steam, riding the cab of a heavy
Mikado.
He shakes the driver's hand, swings down from the footplate,
And is like a locomotive himself, his breath clouding
white,
Dark oil sheen on his black iron mail,
Sword on his hip swinging like siderods at speed.
He stamps back to the baggage car, slams mailed fist on
steel door
With a clang like jousters colliding.
The handler opens up and goes to rouse another knight.
Old Pellinore has been dozing with his back against a
crate,
A cubical chain-bound thing with FRAGILE tags and air
holes,
BEAST says the label, QUESTING, 1 the bill of lading.
The porters look doubtful but ease the thing down.
It grumbles. It shifts. Someone shouts, and they drop it.
It cracks like an egg. There is nothing within.
Elayne embraces Bors on the platform, a pelican on a
rock,
Silently they watch as Pelly shifts the splinters,
Supposing aloud that Gutman and Cairo have swindled
him.

A high-drivered engine in Northern Lines green
Draws in with a string of side-corridor coaches,
All honey-toned wood with stained glass on their windows.
Gareth steps down from a compartment, then Gaheris and
Agravaine,
All warmly tucked up in Orkney sweaters;
Gawaine comes after in Shetland tweed.
Their Gladstones and steamers are neatly arranged,
With never a worry—their Mum does the packing.
A redcap brings forth a curious bundle, a rude shape in red
paper—
The boys did that themselves, you see, and how *does* one
wrap a unicorn's head?
They bustle down the platform, past a chap all in green.

He hasn't the look of a trainman, but only Gawaine turns
to look at his eyes,
And sees written there *Sir, I shall speak with you later.*

Over on the first track, surrounded by reporters,
All glossy dark iron and brass-bound mystery,
The Direct-Orient Express, ferried in from Calais and
Points East.
Palomides appears. Smelling of patchouli and Russian
leather,
Dripping Soubranie ash on his astrakhan collar,
Worry darkening his dark face, though his damascene
armor shows no tarnish,
He pushes past the press like a broad-hulled icebreaker.
Flashbulbs pop. Heads turn. There's a woman in Chanel
black,
A glint of diamonds, liquid movements, liquid eyes.
The newshawks converge, but suddenly there appears
A sharp young man in a crisp blue suit
From the Compagnie Internationale des Wagons-Lits,
That elegant, comfortable, decorous, close-mouthed firm;
He's good at his job, and they get not so much as a
snapshot.
Tomorrow's editions will ask who she was, and whom
with. . .

Now here's a silver train, stainless steel, Vista-Domed,
White-lighted grails on the engine (running no extra sections)
The Logres Limited, extra fare, extra fine,
(Stops on signal at Carbonek to receive passengers only).
She glides to a Timken-borne halt (even her grease is
clean),
Galahad already on the steps, flashing that winning smile,
Breeze mussing his golden hair, but not his Armani tailoring,
Just the sort of man you'd want finding your chalice.
He signs an autograph, he strikes a pose.
Someone says, loudly, "Gal! Who serves the Grail?"
He looks—no one he knows—and there's a silence,
A space in which he shifts like sun on water;

Look quick and you may see a different knight,
A knight who knows that meanings can be lies,
That things are done not knowing why they're done,
That bearings fail, and stainless steel corrodes.
A whistle blows. Snow shifts on the glass shed roof. That knight is gone.
This one remaining tosses his briefcase to one of Kay's pages,
And, golden, silken, careless, exits left.

Behind the carsheds, on the business-car track, alongside the private varnish
Of dukes and smallholders, Persian potentates and Cathay princes
(James J. Hill is here, invited to bid on a tunnel through the Pennines),
Waits a sleek car in royal blue, ex-B&O, its trucks and fittings chromed,
A black-gloved hand gripping its silver platform rail;
Mordred and his car are both upholstered in blue velvet and black leather.
He prefers to fly, but the weather was against it.
His DC-9, with its video system and Quotron and waterbed, sits grounded at Gatwick.
The premature lines in his face are a map of a hostile country,
The redness in his eyes a reminder that hollyberries are poison.
He goes inside to put on a look acceptable for Christmas Court;
As he slams the door it rattles like strafing jets.

Outside the Station proper, in the snow,
On a through track that's used for milk and mail,
A wheezing saddle-tanker stops for breath;
A way-freight mixed, eight freight cars and caboose,
Two great ugly men on the back platform, talking with a third on the ballast.

One, the conductor, parcels out the last of the coffee;
They drink. A joke about grails. They laugh.
When it's gone, the trainman pretends to kick the big hobo off,
But the farewell hug spoils the act.
Now two men stand on the dirty snow,
The conductor waves a lantern and the train grinds on.
The ugly men start walking, the new arrival behind,
Singing "Wenceslas'" off-key till the other says stop.
There are two horses waiting for them. Rather plain horses,
Considering. The men mount up.
By the roundhouse they pause,
And look at the locos, the water, the sand, and the coal,
They look for a long time at the turntable,
Until the one who is King says "It all seemed so simple, once,"
And the best knight in the world says "It is. We make it hard."
They ride on, toward Camelot by the service road.

The sun is winter-low. Kay's caravan is rolling.
He may not run a railroad, but he runs a tight ship;
By the time they unload in the Camelot courtyard,
The wassail will be hot and the goose will be crackling,
Banners snapping from the towers, fir logs on the fire, drawbridge down,
And all that sackbut and psaltery stuff.
Blanchefleur is taking the children caroling tonight,
Percivale will lose to Merlin at chess,
The young knights will dally and the damsels dally back,
The old knights will play poker at a smaller Table Round.
And at the great glass station, motion goes on,
The extras, the milk trains, the varnish, the limiteds,
The *Pindar of Wakefield*, the *Lady of the Lake*,
The *Broceliande Local*, the *Fast Flying Briton*,
The nerves of the kingdom, the lines of exchange,
Running to schedule as the world ought,
Ticking like a hot-fired hand-stoked heart,

The metal expression of the breaking of boundaries,
The boilers that turn raw fire into power,
The driving rods that put the power to use,
The turning wheels that make all places equal,
The knowledge that the train may stop but the line goes on;
The train may stop
But the line goes on.

DR. RAYMOND H. THOMPSON *is Professor of English at Acadia University in Nova Scotia, where, among his other curricula, he teaches a course in the literature of fantasy. We became acquainted when he included* Firelord *as part of this class and invited me to read from my work and speak to his students. The germinal idea for this anthology was his to begin with, suggested over a long car ride from Kentville to Halifax in search of my lost luggage (Air Canada, please copy).*

From his long fascination with the Arthurian myths, Dr. Thompson has authored The Return from Avalon: A Study of the Arthurian Legend in Modern Fiction *(Greenwood Press, 1985) and is associate editor for* The Arthurian Encyclopedia, *(Garland Press, 1985). He writes frequently for* Avalon to Camelot, *a journal of Arthurian studies. Dr. Thompson is also the author of* Gordon R. Dickson: A Primary and Secondary Bibliography, *and has contributed articles to* Fantasy Review, Folklore, Atlantis *and* Forum for Modern Language Studies.

It's my personal opinion that the precise but overworn phrase "gentleman and scholar" might have been coined for Ray Thompson himself. His study, The Return from Avalon, *should be read by anyone seriously interested in this century's attempts to reconstruct the world and legends of Arthur.*

Afterword: Camelot Considered

Whether Arthur won the battle of Mount Badon (c. 500 A.D.), where the Britons beat the Saxons so badly that they turned back the tide of invasion for half a century, or whether he should be identified with Riothamus, the High King who led a British army into Gaul about the year 470, as has recently been argued by Geoffrey Ashe, remains shrouded in the mists of time despite the best efforts of historians. Yet this very scarcity of hard facts about Arthur has proved a boon to story-tellers. To them he is no shadowy figure struggling against the remorseless advance of barbarian tribesmen destined to transform much of Britain into England; rather he is a mighty emperor who not only vanquishes his enemies at home, but even sets out to conquer Europe. He is poised to capture Rome itself when recalled by news of rebellion back in Britain. His court is famed for splendid feasts and courteous manners, ennobling love and dark intrigue, the boldest warriors and fairest ladies who ever lived, or so the story-tellers maintain, and many a marvelous adventure they tell of Arthur's day.

These stories have been handed down through the centuries, each age and culture adding its own particular genius. To the remnants of the Britons, pushed back to the hills in the north and west, they recalled better days. Thus in *The Dream of Rhonabwy* a Welsh warrior has a vision in which he finds himself and his companions back in Arthur's time: "The emperor smiled wrily. 'Lord,' said Iddawg, 'at what art thou laughing?' 'Iddawg,' said Arthur, 'I am not laughing; but rather how sad I feel that men as mean as these keep this Island, after men as fine as those that kept it of yore.' " To the composers of French romance, who discovered Arthur in the twelfth century and spread his fame throughout Europe, he was no Dark Age chieftain but a dignified medieval monarch commanding the most renowned chivalry in the world. From his court knights rode in quest of adventure: to uphold justice, to serve their king, to win renown and, perchance, the love of a fair lady. And when the Grail beckoned, to save their souls. By the fourteenth century romances of King Arthur and his Knights of the Round Table had returned to England, capturing the imagination of those descended from their barbarian enemies.

As the Middle Ages waned, so did interest in Arthurian romance, and with isolated exceptions it was not rekindled until the nineteenth century, when Tennyson's *Idylls of the King* retold the timeless saga of mankind's doomed but heroic attempt to create a better world. Lured by the vision, other poets and dramatists created a romantic and often sentimental tribute to King Arthur. Since the Second World War, however, poetry, and drama have given way to fiction as the dominant literary form for treating Arthurian legend.

Yet while fiction in general and fantasy in particular have proven increasingly popular in recent years, one area that continues to suffer neglect has been the short story. John Erskine and T. G. Roberts each wrote a series in the 1940's, but otherwise only occasional stories have been published. *Invitation to Camelot* is thus doubly welcome: it is the first anthology of modern Arthurian fiction ever assembled, and it represents an important step forward for Arthurian legend in a genre that has long paid it too little attention.

The stories collected in this anthology interestingly reflect various recent trends in Arthurian fiction. Most of the authors are women, an indication of their growing numbers in the field of fantasy. They have encouraged greater interest in the women of Arthurian legend, which has led in turn to closer scrutiny of their behavior and motives than is traditional in medieval romance. In "Nimuë's Tale" by Madeleine E. Robins, Nimuë tells her own story; in Jane Yolen's "Meditation in a Whitethorn Tree," Merlin reflects upon three other women who deceived him (he never did understand women, for all his wisdom): Igraine, Morgaine, and Gwenhwyfar. Stories like these provide us with a keener awareness of women as individuals, possessing feelings and minds of their own. When men or, for that matter, other women forget this and treat them merely as pawns to be manipulated at will, they court disaster, as both Viviene and Merlin learn to their cost. Their fate offers a timely reminder of the need to respect others.

Modern fiction pays more attention to children than does medieval romance, but the three stories in which they appear are not trying to appeal to younger readers, as is usually the case. Instead they seek to explain the subsequent adult behavior of their central character. Parke Godwin's "Uallannach" and Chelsea Quinn Yarbo's "Night Mare" offer insights into the influences that warped the life of Modred. The former, which is narrated by Modred himself, deepens our understanding of the human consequences of the hard decisions and sacrifices that Arthur is forced to make in *Firelord* (1980), the first novel of Godwin's Arthurian triptych. The latter reveals the bitterness spawned by constant rejection and discrimination, together with the heavy price that must inevitably be paid, not only by the victim, but by all of society, innocent and guilty alike. In "Their Son" Morgan Llywelyn generates suspense by concealing the identity of her hero until the very end, at which point the significance of his actions falls into place. Like "Nimuë's Tale" and "Meditation in a Whitethorn Tree," these three stories bid us give closer heed to our actions. In the heat of passion lovers take too little account of the children they may conceive, and when they compound their error with parental neglect, they breed heartache for all concerned.

Yet while recent trends in Arthurian fiction are evident, venerable traditions such as the quest and love, one or other of which—sometimes both—remain prominent in all the stories of the anthology. In earliest legend Arthur and his warriors venture in search of marvelous treasures, and one of these tales, preserved in the ancient Welsh poem *Preideu Annwfyn*, forms the basis of Susan Shwartz's "Seven from Caer Sidi." Here Arthur seeks the immortality promised those who possess the Cauldron of Tyrnoc, not for himself but for those devoted followers who serve him with their lives. He comes to realize, however, that the only true immortality for humanity lies in song and legend celebrating heroic deeds. In Sharan Newman's "Palace by Moonlight" a bard sets out to discover the truth about Arthur and his court, so that he can compose a saga worthy of their memory. The truth he finds, however, is that humanity needs its dreams of a better world if it is to cope with the harsh realities of this one. And none need it more than bards.

Although the earliest Arthurian tales were heroic in mood, the emergence of the romance form and the convention of courtly love in the twelfth century elevated love to a central position in the legend. Tristan and Isolde, perhaps the most famous lovers in western literature, were attracted into the orbit of Arthurian legend, and the ambition of Modred was replaced by the love of Lancelot and Guinevere as the principle reason for the fall of the Round Table. Lancelot proved his devotion to the queen in many a trial. None of these proved more uncomfortable, however, than the passionate overtures of the many damsels who yearned for his embrace. The unrequited love of Elaine of Astolat for Lancelot is one of the best-known examples, but in "Two Bits of Embroidery" Phyllis Ann Karr counterpoints it with a love of her own invention, that of Tilda the scullery maid for Kay the seneschal. In the Middle Ages Kay's pride and bitter tongue contrast with the humility and courtesy of Lancelot, but in her novel *The Idylls of the Queen* (1982) Karr prefers the painful honesty of the former to the self-centered, and ultimately self-indulgent, duplicity of the latter. This story helps us to understand why.

Gregory Frost and Tanith Lee also tell love stories, but neither involves traditional characters. Nevertheless, the ability of Arthurian legal to accommodate new material has always been important to its survival. When the court gathers to celebrate Pentecost or some other important occasion, then are tales told of perilous adventures and marvels wondrous to hear. Such might be Frost's "The Vow That Binds" or Lee's "The Minstrel's Tale," which blend magic, passion, and revenge, the key elements in so many love stories set in Arthur's court.

All the stories in the anthology are heroic fantasies except one: Elizabeth Scarborough's "The Camelot Connection." Where heroic fantasy measures human achievements against high odds to reveal the potential of the human spirit, an ironic fantasy like "The Camelot Connection" measures these same achievements against the even higher expectations of the characters or audience to reveal a comical gap. Works in which the ironic vision dominates occupy a venerable position in Arthurian legend, for they range from Chretien de Troyes's *Lancelot* in the twelfth century to Thomas Berger's *Arthur Rex* in the twentieth. In Scarborough's comic tale a romantic young woman and a pop psychiatrist travel back in time to occupy jointly the body of a revived Merlin in an Arthurian world based upon T. H. White's *The Once and Future King* (1958). Things turn out very differently from what we and they expect, and the result is some affectionate humor at the expense of both medieval romance and modern psychoanalysis.

Finally there is John Ford's poem "Winter Solstice, Camelot Station," which ingeniously envisions Arthur's court in an age of railways. The bold anachronism reveals insights into both worlds, particularly the former; and as Arthur and his knights steam in from all directions, we are treated to a wealth of literary allusion, reminding us that "The train may stop / But the line goes on."

Irony plays a prominent role in the poem, as it does in all of the stories in the anthology. When Llywelyn's hero fulfills his destiny after years struggling against it, he not only redresses an old wrong committed by his mother but also discovers his own true potential. Despite his reputation for harshness towards others, Kay's rejection of the scullery maid's gift proves a kinder act than Lancelot's acceptance of Elaine's in Karr's story. For all his apparent cynicism it is love—"uallannach"—that fuels the potent hatred and despair of Godwin's Modred, as he himself finally acknowledges. The truth discovered by Newman's minstrel turns out to be his own vision of Arthur and his court, just as the immortality sought by Shwartz's Arthur proves to have been his all along. Yet while their quests are unnecessary from one point of view, from another they provide the tales without which the legend cannot survive. Frost's forest dweller is deceived by the raven into killing the one he loves, and this despite his suspicions of the treacherous bird. Robins' Nimuë realizes that the love of Viviene, the Lady of the Lake, is but a deception employed to make others, including herself, easier to manipulate; while Viviene, for her part, finds to her cost that the child she set to spy upon Merlin's secrets has done so to deadly effect. In Yarbro's story the Wish Horse grants the illegitimate Modred's request "to be Artus' son, to be his heir and to be remembered as long as he is remembered," but this is destined to be fulfilled in a way the scornful child does not anticipate. Lee's minstrel learns just how deceiving appearances can be when he stays the night with an old shepherd and his beautiful young wife. And in Yolen's story Merlin has ample time in the prison of his whitethorn tree to ponder just how badly he was misled by the women he sought to fit into his own plans.

These stories share an appreciation not just of the ironic potential of the Arthurian legend, however, but also of the vital importance of dreams to humanity. When our dreams are denied us as children, we can grow bitter and resentful, as do Modred in the stories by Godwin and Yarbro, and Llywelyn's protagonist before he gains experience of life.

When the dream is placed briefly within our grasp only to be snatched away, we may sink into a fatal despair as do Karr's Elaine and Yolen's Gwenhwyfar. From this despair we may turn to revenge as do Godwin's Modred, Frost's Lant, and Lee's shepherd; or we may be saved, either by the help of others as was Karr's Tilda, or by our own hard-won wisdom as was Robins' Nimuë and Shwartz's Arthur.

The dream sought by these characters is of a world guided by love and trust, courage, compassion, and common sense. These qualities allow them the freedom to develop their potential and grow into complete human beings. They are also, as Scarborough's Cecily and Newman's Miniffer discover to their delight, the very qualities that make up the Arthurian dream. They are what guide Gawain in his encounter with the Green Knight in the fourteenth-century English poem *Sir Gawain and the Green Knight;* they are what inspire Arthur to establish the Round Table in Sir Thomas Malory's fifteenth-century prose romance *Le Morte d'Arthur;* they are what raise many-towered Camelot in Tennyson's *Idylls of the King*. They are, after all, the vision of a better world that beckons to us amidst the troubles and disappointments of our own. And the brightness of that vision is not merely by contrast with the darkness that so often seems to threaten. It is also a tribute to the yearning that we all share, and to that imagination and talent of authors like those collected here.